This information is limited due to the nature and sources of the book. Nicky Brennan was born in the Irish Republic, and came to England to work initially on the buildings, which is the source of the subject matter for this book. The author later became a scientist and worked under the general umbrella of the NHS. For a long time, the author had an interest in the progress of the Irish people in Britain and what problems they encounter that inhibit such progress. It was from information garnered in this quest that the material for this book was sourced.

Nicky Brennan

MURDER IN THE CITY

How London Was Built

AUSTIN MACAULEY PUBLISHERS™

LONDON • CAMBRIDGE • NEW YORK • SHARJAH

ISBN 9781398406308 (Paperback)
ISBN 9781398406315 (ePub e-book)

www.austinmacauley.com

First Published 2023
Austin Macauley Publishers Ltd®
1 Canada Square
Canary Wharf
London
E14 5AA

Chapter 1

John Cormac O'Mahony was making a piss along the side of a portacabin, though he was near to the site toilets, having a piss in the open air enhanced his contemplations and as his contemplations were always about himself or his affairs, his contemplations were at this moment very pleasant, so the most was to be made of them.

He was on the third job, that he had on the go simultaneously; alright, it was hardly a prestigious job; it was five men putting in the sewer pipes and preparing the foundations for the site offices that were being erected for a large site on London Wall in the city of London and doing some general clearing up, but it was the third job he had on the go at the one time and might even make money. It all helped to establish him as a proper 'subbie' or subcontractor proper, not just some 'old dog subbie' who picked men up from the side of the street and went about cadging for work here and there, like some tinker.

He was making progress towards being one of the main men, one of the right boys or coming very near to it. He had learned the lesson early on that this was the way to do things. When he had first come over to England, he had gone out working 'bare' or as you could say without contacts. This was due to uncertainty about these contacts due to events that had occurred previously in Ireland and a sense of defiance on his part, which manifested itself as wishing to prove he could 'rough it' if necessary and didn't need to rely on any contacts if he didn't have to, due to the same events in Ireland.

It hadn't gone so well, he remembered the foreman on the only job he had been kept on, for any length of time roaring at him, "ye're like a hen scratching there ye little bollix ye," when he was working with the shovel and "ye'ed not break the tip of yer own shite, ye little bastard ye" when he was working with the jackhammer. After about three months and four different jobs, he decided the point was proven and he decided to invoke his contacts.

His father was John D O'Mahony, an auctioneer and publican, who also had a couple of farms of land which were worked for him by a fellow that owed him money; he was a man of affairs and who his father was not connected to or 'in with' in some manner or another, was not worth being in with. The family also operated in England, his father's brother Frankie, commonly called 'tot' (a tot of whiskey) was a subbie and well connected like his father; he was a hard man and knew what was what, like when he summed up life in London for the Irish, "ye're either the boss or the bollix": truer words were never uttered.

He placed himself under the patronage of his uncle 'tot', who started him as a storeman with a mate of his; the idea was that from this position, he could learn how the game was ran and how things operated. He was in a good position to see how things operated from all sides and especially from the boss's side, how things were controlled. From the first days he was advised to follow up the site general foremen, for it was they that had the overall view of the jobs and from them, he would be able to learn the nuts and bolts of managing a job.

Things were ran right from the start, he got uncle 'tot' to introduce him to the site management, showing that he was on the inside track from the get-go. This had the immediate beneficial effect of throwing all blame for shortcomings in the stores on the head of the old fuck who was working with him, this was fortunate, because as John Cormac even had to admit himself, he wasn't a startling success as a storeman. He learned from the general foremen, from 'tot' himself and indeed from others 'tot' introduced him to.

The important thing was control, not knowing about construction from the ground up or from any other direction for that matter, was neither here nor there. You got the men to do the work, that was their business, and was that not why they were called workmen; then you controlled the men, as 'tot' said "ye're the boss or the bollix", it was as simple as all that. The principal issue was control, the boss had to be the boss and had to have absolute say. The first necessity would be a hard and though foreman and charge hand's, well able and willing to fight if necessary. Next, you had to have some handle on at least a portion of the men, you had to know something about them, something they had done or some shortcoming of theirs.

He also gained invaluable insights on how jobs were run and successfully completed. From the start it wasn't really the right price that got the job, rather the considerations that went with that price and most importantly, who the considerations were from. There was no such thing as a bad or a good job really;

if properly handled it could always be made right; eventually, all mistakes were excusable with a backhander, indeed if the right people were taken care of, even up to the level of changed specifications or plans.

How to play the game was the issue, not success or failure for that matter at the actual building. It did not look like that from the outside, but it served the very good purpose of restricting entry to the right few, with the right contacts and ties: the right boys. He started off subbing on that job, nearly as much for practice as for profit. He got two oldish farts from the pub onto the site as dogsbody laborers; they were leased to the firm, a practice called 'day work'.

He got thirty pounds a day for them and paid them twenty, that gave him twenty a day in profit on a false tax exemption certificate, meaning no tax. The snag was he only got paid every six weeks, so he just gave them a sub for the first six weeks, fifty or sixty pounds, it was enough for them and he'd keep himself safe; at the six-week stage when he got paid, he would square up with them or nearly so, a few tenners less would do them no harm.

Then the old farts started complaining about the sub, he gave them seventy a week, a bare fifty short. It still didn't satisfy them, one old dog in particular was on about his family, he threw him a tenner more, still no good. At the six-week stage, when he got the payment, he decided to get rid of them, it would save him money and having to listen to their shite.

The one with the supposed family started to fight, he thought he'd manage him due to his age but he proved tougher than he looked and John Cormac had ended up on his back. Matters, however, were in hand, with 'tot's' coaching he had given the general foreman a backhander; for one, to prolong the work; for two, to watch his back, he made short work out the old bastard.

Much later on, the same old piece of dung tried to attack him on the main site he had going now, his foreman there Hughie Mac Bearta really made shite out of him. He had tried but failed to find out where he lived, but the piece of filth had been clever enough to give a false address but his time would come. He had got uncle 'tot' to spread the word to the right boys, so he'd be got at some stage or at least he'd have trouble getting work and as for the supposed family, well, uncle 'tot' said it.

"Anyone daft enough to breed with a man who did that to a subbie deserves starvation."

Things were different from that time on out, the lessons he had learned from the general foremen and uncle 'tot' and his mates were taken seriously and enacted. He knew now that he had to have a handle on men, they had to fear him somehow, he had to know something about them, about their past, their habits, what they had done, he had to have a foreman they were afraid of; at five foot five he found it hard to intimidate men despite the high heeled cowboy boots he habitually wore, but he knew it was a necessity to find some other way.

Being a subbie had many advantages, even at home, it certainly changed peoples' attitude to you. He had had the unfortunate habit of wetting himself until after the age of ten and sometimes, it would happen at school and for this, he acquired the nickname 'pissboy' and got picked on and this continued into secondary school.

One of the worst offenders was one John O'Dowd, many was the taunt and indeed the odd kick he had received from John O'Dowd. The last time he was at home he went into Maughans pub, one of his father's competitors, just to check out how they were doing. Who was in there and came up talking to him as though they were only the best of mates, only John O'Dowd. He took this initially as John O'Dowd was a big strong man but the conversation veered more and more onto England and what was happening in England, especially on the buildings in England and he gigged that O Dowd was angling for a start with him; finally he came out with it.

"If a man went to England tomorrow, would he be able to get a start with someone local, some one that would allow him a bit of rope, to get into the way things are done, in an easy manner like."

"I must go and have a pissboy and think about it," he replied, his mouth open, which with its natural twist to the side gave him a dry and sneering aspect, he considered it his best feature.

"A what?," went O'Dowd.

"A pissboy," he repeated.

"Heh," went O'Dowd looking completely confused, did he so easily forget.

John Cormac went to the toilet and when he returned there was a look of comprehension in O'Dowd's eyes.

"As you know I'm not enquiring on my behalf, I have a good farm from which I make my living." This was true but had momentarily slipped John Cormac's memory, he continued, "I, m enquiring on behalf of my neighbours because I'm always one to help and support my neighbours, in any way that I can and have good relations with my neighbours and not hold grudges, especially not from school days, as that would be ridiculous."

"Oh, I know, the same as me but with one difference, I back them that back me" and then the whopper, the stroke of genius, "oh yes and that's the other difference, I can actually help them."

In times gone by he would surely have got a belt for this but all O'Dowd did was stand there, going red his mouth opening and closing and emitting no sound. It was poetic justice, just who was the pissboy now, being a subbie counted everywhere. The second job was a somewhat better attempt. He got a fellow he knew from at home, who was on the run from the law for grievous bodily harm to run the job and he also had a handle on two of the four men on the job as he knew of their dodgy pasts.

There was never any fear of any interference from the authorities from such men, no matter how you dealt with them. He did, however, pay most of the money promised and the foreman skimmed a bit. The problem was that the foreman knew very little about the work and one of the other men had to constantly correct him and this gave him ideas above his station; firstly, he objected to the few pounds that he gave the foreman and this had to be accepted, as his knowledge was necessary to get the job done.

However, as time went by, he started giving orders and openly contradicting the foreman and even the boss John Cormac himself and this could not be accepted, so as the job drew near a close and they thought that they could get along without him, they tried to sack him. He protested that it was only due to him that the job got done at all, to which John Cormac countered that it was only due to him that he got any work there at all. It got heated.

"How did a bollix like John Cormac O'Mahony get any work when neither he, nor any of the men he put in charge knew anything about the work near or far?"

"I'm the boss and I'm telling you to go and that it," said John Cormac and pushed him, he levelled John Cormac.

The foreman dived in, however, despite his reputation as a hard man and an advantage in size he was losing, as quick as all that John Cormac now well up to the game reminded one of the dodgy pair of the wife he had put into hospital and asked him if he wanted the whole site and the police to know about it. He sided with the foreman and they got the smartarse who was daft enough to defy the boss off site and thought him a bit of a lesson as well.

His wages remained in John Cormac's pocket and furthermore, the foreman's bonus of three weeks was withheld, as he should have been able to deal with the man. The job still didn't make money as they had got rid of the wanker too early and they had to rely on one of 'tot's' men to get the job finished. This did allow John Cormac to withhold the wages for the last week from all the men on the grounds they didn't know their job and after seeing what happened to the other man and the knowledge John Cormac had about some of them, there was no ructions this time, only some grumbling and bullshit. This cut his losses to insignificance.

He who holds the reins drives the ass or asses where he wants, not where the ass or asses want to go. At this time he noticed the site agent lurking around behind one of the containers and nodding him over.

"John, me old matey, them men of yours ain't getting enough work done."

"What improvement would you suggest?" asked John Cormac.

"There needs to be some oiling of the wheels."

"How much?"

"K."

"For five men for five weeks, half k and when I get paid," responded John Cormac as these were the going rates.

"Ton now and a half k afterwards."

"OK," said John Cormac and handed over a hundred pounds, it was alright, he was fairly new and he always cut the hundred off the men for being late or something. John Cormac was well able to play the game.

He resumed his observation of the men and his pleasant ruminations. A lot of it was in the blood. The real trump in the whole affair was good old aunt Myra, the oldest of his father's family, it was she who provided the money.

Aunt Myra had come over to England to care for her widowed aunt, John Cormac's great aunt, who lived in a big house in Kennington and who had married a man who worked in the civil service, since before the time of Irish independence and thus, could afford a good house. Aunt Myra inherited the house when her aunt died and most shrewdly had married the hardest Irishman around, fighting Jack Mulcahy, who was a walking pelter (gangerhand) with Mac Alpines.

They let rooms and with fighting Jack the rent was always paid. They got another house and done the same thing and so on. Today, she had seven and over forty Irish tenants; her son collected the rent and if he wasn't as hard as his father, he was a long-term member of a boxing club and thus, had the right contacts to sort out any rent arrears. Fighting Jack was found dead by the side of the road, some said he cracked his skull when he fell over with too much drink and some said he met his match and some said things caught up with him.

The family opted strongly for the first option, there would be no beating of fighting Jack. This also suited the police who really didn't like to trouble themselves too much over a dead paddy. His aunt after a life spent judging people by their worth or possible worth towards her, figured that her nephew had what it took to make it big, so she financed him.

The plan was simplicity itself; he'd get as big of an operation going as he could and he pull as much money as possible from the jobs, this would be easily enough accomplished by hitting them when the jobs were half way through, exactly when a subcontractor would be very difficult and expensive to replace, for as much money as possible, the excuse would probably be trouble on another job.

He'd also run up as much credit as possible with suppliers, again if they failed to supply him during the middle of the job, he could say he couldn't get the job done; therefore, he'd not get paid and couldn't pay them, so they would have to accommodate him, these supplies could then be sold to his mates; and thirdly he would go sick and the men would be forced to exist on a sub, as he would be unfit to get to the bank, if they left then they could never expect to be paid and lastly he borrow as much as possible from the banks and firms and then he'd bankrupt the lot, the amount of loot should be in the millions.

Aunt Myra would get her money back with major profits and he would be made up. There were indeed happy and above all, greatly prosperous times ahead. Three jobs, though there was only two men on the second job, snagging the groundworks mainly the pavements around a new estate, but it should last a few months and there were the prospects of getting more men on that job, but it did expand his empire and his name and contacts were increasing by the day.

The main job was a different kettle of fish, this was the one that would make him, it was his entrée into the big time. It was within easy walking distance of this job and also in the city of London. It was in St Swithuns Lane off Lombard street. This was the job his main interest was vested in and it was in many ways the fruit of his labour.

He had a proper foreman on that job, the other jobs were too small for a foreman and a creeping Jesus and a handle of some sort on a number of the men there: thus, it was under proper control. He'd stroll up there at his ease later on and take a look. John Cormac O'Mahony, the subbie, the boss man, the big boy.

He began to think of a hard type nickname for himself, to increase his profile like many of the notable men around, 'tot' O'Mahony, 'jop' Flannery, 'the bull' Ryan, 'elephant' John, 'boy' O'Malley, it was the signature of a hardman. J con John Con was the best he could come up with and that didn't really work, ah well it wasn't the end of the world. A few years down the road, he'd go home with his loot or as he should say his reward and all would be fine and dandy.

He might attempt auctioneering, like his father, his father would arrange for him to be qualified and he could set himself up in a neighbouring town, well not too near, all things considered. He has a fine house and cars and somehow a fine piece of a woman, though his record on women was poor, still a big house and cars it would surely count; or it should count, unfortunately that was not always the case.

There was that fuck up on the third job, with that woman that was involved with a young idiot that he had working for him on that job. He brought her to the old navies dive of a pub the gang drank in. This even rose the eyebrows of the wife beater that he had retained from the job before.

She was a fine long-legged piece, just the type that'd be great for breeding, you'd be likely to get fine lumps of sons out of her. The young fellow was tall and good looking but not long over and as green as grass, he'd not have brought her in here otherwise. Desire rose in John Cormac. He knew that she wasn't available but he was the boss, wasn't he; the young bollix worked for him, didn't he and he was sort of aligned with this pub, he brought his men in and he got the odd cheque cashed and bits of credit and a fair few free drinks. Where else would he get the chance of getting his hands on such a woman.

Shrewdly, he didn't make a direct approach but waited until the man beside them went to the toilet, then he approached the young man in a furtive like manner, looking about him and asking the young man if he was alone. Without waiting for an answer, he set about giving him a bit of confidential sort of advice, employer and boss to wanting employee.

"Well, me boy, is there anybody around. No, right. I'll just take this opportunity to give you a piece of advice on the quiet like as your employer and the employer of all these men here," pointing to the other four men sitting at the bar. "Now me boy, your work rate is hardly outstanding and if you want to hang on to your job, you'll need to buck up a bit."

"It's at least as good as anyone else's," the cheeky young bastard responded, it was, but that didn't excuse cheek.

"I'm trying to give you a hand, you cheeky little bastard you," John Cormac said up to him.

"Right, what exactly is the problem."

This stymifyied John Cormac, but quickly he said, "well you know, mustn't you."

"I'm not the most experienced."

"Correct, therefore you must make up with it through speed."

"Er, em, right."

John Cormac was pleased with his quick response. Then he noticed the girl as though for the first time.

"Oh, er, have you company? It's just that I'm his boss and the boss of all these men here and I wanted to give him some quiet advice. I didn't mean to interrupt."

The girl looked completely unimpressed.

"I'm the boss of all these men here," repeated John Cormac.

The girl made some sound like uh, oh. At this stage John Cormac seemed to see someone signal him from the other side of the room, first he pointed to himself, then the young fellow and said the wife beater wanted to see him, then he gave the nod to the wife beater to hang on to the young fellow and allow him a chance with the girl.

"You're a nice piece of stuff," went on John Cormac turning on the charm, "I could go for a bird like you myself." The girl starred at him in shock.

"Like that lad alright but what has he got, sure he hasn't got a pot to piss in, while I'm the boss of all here and more. What do you say of us two making a go at it?"

"Jesus, I must have a fucking piss," she said running out to the toilets, the only escape route she could think of.

The vision of such a bird having a piss, somewhat unbalanced John Cormac and he became excited. Though he dimly realised the signs were negative, his excitement overcame this insight. The entrance doors to the toilets were hidden behind a wall, which was this pub's only attempt at sophistication and John Cormac went behind this wall, to await the girl's emergence from the toilet.

When she emerged John Cormac engaged her, "what do you say, surely a man is worth a shot, if that penniless bollix is."

"Fuck you, do you even have a pair of balls?" she replied looking down at him and getting heated at this behaviour.

At this, dirty talk reason departed completely from John Cormac, "I do and I bet they are bigger than your ones, let's find out," he said grabbing her hand and pulling it into his crutch and in turn, groping her in the same area.

She screeched, pulled her hand away and belted him in the mouth, driving him into the main part of the pub and then she kicked him in the balls getting him perfect; leaving John Cormac kneeling on the ground, trying to massage his wounded parts, making a screeching like sound and retching. The young fellow was already suspicious, as the ruse the wife beater had used to distract him was to invite him to partake in a darts match, and seeing that there was no such thing as a darts board in the pub.

Now he coped what was up, he rushed at John Cormac and was barely intercepted in time by the wife beater. With some effort the wife beater and the rest of the men threw them out of the pub. He saved the young bollixes wages but had to turn once again to uncle 'tot' for a man to finish the job, as the young fellow was the best worker that he had.

Not to worry, thought John Cormac upon reflection, in time to come when she would be dragging three snivelling kids behind her in the rain, he would pass her out in his merc and splash her and she'd think, I could be in that car and like everybody else that belittled John Cormac O'Mahony, she'd be sorry. He had just come on a bit too strong, he figured. From that on out things went far smoother, until now he stood at the summit of three jobs.

The main job was really a first-class proper subcontract on a commercial building. Though his thoughts were very pleasant in the main, intelligently he let no hint of this pleasure to emerge upon his features, rather his expression ranged from one of concern, to amazement, to bewilderment, on further to despair and finally, to an expression of affront and injury. The one lesson he knew better than any other was never to let the men know that you're pleased.

John Cormac O'Mahony was too clever for any mistake of that sort. He went up to a little office belonging to the main contracting firm but not yet in use by them at this stage of the job; here they let him store a few plans in a filing cabinet and use a desk and chair. There was no need for this, but it suited his image to be seen by the men, pursuing plans in 'his office', there was no doubt about it, John Cormac O'Mahony was up to every trick in the trade.

After a time and when he made sure that all the men had spotted him and growing weary with looking at the plans, which in the main he didn't understand, not of course that that mattered, were they not for the workmen to understand

and not necessarily for the boss to trouble himself with, he closed the door and put his feet up on to the desk, which was his usual position at a desk.

His thoughts returned again to the St Swithuns Lane job, it was his prize job, everything had come together there and it should be the making of him as a subbie.

Chapter 2

He thought about how he got the job. Through uncle 'tot' and at this stage, his own efforts he had made the contact of Paddy O'Riordan, who was a director of Amez construction and his brother-in-law, Mick 'boy' O'Malley, head of one of the biggest groundworks and foundation structures companies in London. Through them he had got this properly established job and a proper foreman and other key personnel.

This was the St Swithuns Lane job, which consisted of doing the ground works and putting in the ground beams for a prestigious commercial building. 'Boy' O'Malley had come up trumps on the double or indeed triple, he had got him the job and a proper foreman, Hughie Mac Bearta and as importantly as any, a 'creeping Jesus' Martin Mac Donogh.

This job was a bit below Hughie Mac Bearta, who usually ran 'boy' O'Malley's biggest jobs and had the status of being 'boy's' main trouble shooter, he had the reputation of being able to handle anything, but it was rumoured that Hughie had an argument on a job with a man which degenerated into a fight and the man was getting the better of Hughie. This would mean an unaffordable loss of reputation for Hughie, so apparently Hughie got hold of a nail bar and leathered the man with it, leaving him brain damaged and causing such a stir that he was no longer able to work for 'boy' O'Malley and had to lie low for a time.

John Cormac would happily give him sanctuary, if he ran this, his top job, well. Conceivably as valuable as Mac Bearta, he had also got him a creeping Jesus, Martin Mac Donogh. He was a hound of a man, lean and worn with drink and bad living, he was still alive with greed, for money, for drink, for power, almost writhing with the vain ambition of making back what he should have made years ago, he was like a dog trying to catch his own tail.

He was more or less beyond work but his vain ambitions and his hatred and envy of the men that could still do it, led him to a willingness to do anything to maintain his income and in turn drink supply. He was certainly willing to be John

Cormac's man on the inside, always watching the boys, always willing indeed anxious to report their faults and failings, both on and off the job, to the boss. The only problem was that he was over anxious to please and exaggerated or even invented faults. It was not a big problem, for the harder the hand on the men, the better.

His favourite method of control was to get them in the pub and get them talking; one particular method was to get talking to them and tell them stories about their workmates, what bad boy's they were and what they had got up to, with the slant that they were great crack and characters and thus, encourage them to compete as hard characters and as the drink went in and the sense and caution went out, what was hidden came forth and thus, Martin had his handle on them.

He also encouraged any craving for drink that they had, thus helping to tie them to subbie, they'd be wary of doing without the drink money, even if by moving they'd be better off in the longer run, which was a virtual certainty when they were leaving John Cormac's firm. In short, you gained control in the pub and if part of his 'work duties' was to go to the pub; well, he could hardly be blamed for drinking, could he.

The fact that he had also served jail time for assault on his wife and had broken his young son's arm was made known to John Cormac by 'boy' O'Malley, which gave John Cormac a proper grip on him. He never came out straight to Martin with what he knew, 'boy' O'Malley tutored him on that, he just came out with remarks like, "them are awful bastards that beat their wives and especially their children, what do you think Martin," "the world's worst," Martin would reply, but the message had got through loud and clear.

To control the controller, that was the way, you were above the fray yourself but still in control, apart and safe yet controlling all. Gerry Cawley was another man he had a line on. He'd worked for him on a job in the past and had been hired initially due to the info that John Cormac had on him, again the golden rule, control. A man in his late thirties, he was a right fighting man was Ger or at least, he had strong ambitions in that direction; the problem was, he wasn't that good and time and again he had to resort to using a weapon, usually a bottle and the result was that he was wanted in both Ireland and England for bottling cops and he had to be really careful what pub he went in to.

This reputation was what had led John Cormac to hire him. He was under excellent control but wasn't the best of workers; even comments from John Cormac that he wished he was as "lively with the shovel as the bottle", did little to spur him on but the fact that he stayed showed John Cormac's command over him. Cawley's mate on the job was Pakie Mac Grath and John Cormac had also used him on another job.

He was a bit younger than Cawley and again, John Cormac had a line on him and indeed had hired him for that reason. It was reported that he scarred a man for life in Canning town and he also had to stay out of a lot of pubs. No great worker but again completely controllable, "you'd make a better gouge with a bottle than with that shovel," was John Cormac's comment to him and the fact again that he stayed after that showed the level of John Cormac's control.

Pete Mac Namee was another hard man in his mid-thirties; it was reputed that he had kicked a man in the head in Ireland and the man never fully recovered from it; certainly, he liked to see violence and any violence visibly excited him. He had worked for John Cormac on the last job and being in need of men, he had kept him. His mate was Jimmy Mac Goldrick, again he worked with John Cormac on the last job.

He was supposed to be in some trouble in Ireland and to have run from it but it looked unlikely, as he was young and as green as grass, little more than twenty. He was a nervous and shy, even a backward sort, but he was big and strong and a good worker. He might be malleable enough that you could get him to give someone a beating for you, but he seemed anything but aggressive.

The 'rat' Kilfeather was a strange article, in his late twenties; he looked just like a rat with buck teeth underneath a moustache, all beneath a large beaky nose. He was a smallish thin man and he was always looking around, ever on alert, just like a real rat. John Cormac didn't like him at all, but he was a good worker, especially handy at a multiplicity of different tasks, he could lay pipes or fix steel in reinforced concrete or make up wooden forms for concrete.

Mac Bearta had hired him on the recommendation of the creeping Jesus and insisted he was necessary to get the work done otherwise John Cormac would have got rid of him; instead, he ordered that he be given no quarter if any problem arose with him and got rid of as soon as it was feasible. Also, John Cormac had nothing on him, no handle, which he didn't like.

John William Mac Elvinney, the 'rat's' mate was a different prospect altogether, he was a right sort of man. He was a few years older that the 'rat', a bit over thirty, he was not much taller than John Cormac but was a well-built, well set up man. He always said, yes boss, right now boss with a nod of compliance to anything John Cormac told him to do and John Cormac liked that. John Cormac had hired him from the pub.

Mac Bearta pointed out that he wasn't the best worker but John Cormac could see other qualities to him. If he got hurt in some way, something fell on him for instance, then he'd get agitated, he'd get the temper up and he'd plough into the work manfully, frothing at the mouth even, unfortunately this didn't last very long, but it showed what was in him. John Cormac always considered he'd be a great man in a fight, perhaps some display could be arranged, against some old fart that John Cormac owed wages to for instance.

Having a few hard men at your beck and call was another necessity for the right subbie. He had no line on Mac Elvinney either, but he knew he was sound. The last pair were the best workers by far and necessary as far as getting the work done went, the problem was he had nothing on them and the creeping Jesus couldn't for all his wiles get anything on them either. They had been sent to him by 'boy' O'Malley and Mac Bearta rightly described them as good workers, so John Cormac employed them, despite having no handle on them.

The best of them was John Devine, he was a big strong man in his thirties and a great worker, he stuck into any job manfully, until it got done. He was married with a family and as steady as they come. His only vice was to take a few pints but only a few, he seemed to have no other weaknesses.

His mate Liam Mac Faul was over ten years younger, and an even bigger man and great worker, again when he started a job, he stuck to it with zest until it was done. However, he was innocent, as green as they came. He was still well fit to acquit himself at work, one day they were filling shutters or concrete forms with concrete with wheelbarrows from a truck, Devine and Mac Faul out preformed the other eight put together, despite Mac Bearta's roars and even threats of the boot.

The last member of the crew was Jimmy the bolowan (simpleton) O'Meara or at least it was thought O'Meara was his last name. He was nearing sixty with an idiot's smile always on his face; with his tongue protruding a bit between his lips, you didn't need to ask to estimate his intelligence. He was always telling some daft story and those experienced with him, expressed amazement which got him to leave you alone; if not, he'd pester you until you did or lost your cool with him, where upon he retreated, his threshold for understanding was at least the threat of violence.

John Cormac's reason for hiring him, which he did from the pub, were threefold; one, he went into pubs boasting that he was out for John Cormac O'Mahony, something not ever the creeping Jesus could be got to do; secondly, he was a well-known character and thirdly, John Cormac paid him only twenty five pounds a day, half of what he paid the creeping Jesus and Devine, the rest he paid forty pounds a day and Mac Bearta was on eighty pounds a day and a third extra bonus when the job was finished successfully.

If all went well, he stood to lose something in the region of fifteen grand, but he intended to lessen this loss by other means, he'd cut the wages perhaps for one or two, the 'rat' or MacGoldrick or maybe even Mac Faul, they were good workers especially Mac Faul, but it was who you could get away with cutting, not who deserved it, that you did actually cut.

He could charge obstruction, in which he'd claim that he was being held up, in some respect by the firm. The main way would be to get the site agent on side, then things like daywork where men were let to the firm by the subcontractor for a fee above their wages, dead men these were men that daywork was being charged for that didn't exist were in the offing and if he could get on to the level of changed plans or deliberate mistakes by the main contractor, then he would be made up.

The grand plan still remained and he'd be a winner by millions and until that time, good old aunt Myra would bear the heat. A proper gang properly controlled was in hand, all was progressing very sweetly indeed. He often wondered as he strolled down the road between jobs, if the people he passed would ever think that he was a man with tens of men in his employment.

Being that it was the city of London, the home of self-esteem and self-interest, even John Cormac realised that they would only see an Irish navvy as a necessary blight on the street scene, like a dustbin; aye maybe but would they ever realise further that this Irish navy would soon be dealing in millions, sums of money even they were unlikely to see. Things still weren't perfect, he had no handle on Mac Goldrick, the 'rat', Devine or Mac Faul and he would have liked to have had. He had no handle on Mac Elvinney either but that was OK, he was sound, nor on Jimmy O'Meara, but he was just a bolowan, so it didn't matter in his case.

In general, all was in order, the job was well up to spec with all the awkward bits handled and he had to admit the 'rat' was good at this and well up to speed and credit for this fell mainly to Devine and Mac Faul. He'd go along with the way things were, even if he would have liked more control and anyways things could always change when the pressure of work was off. He would try to get a machine on the job for himself and some muck away to expand, he'd do anything he could to build up, towards the great hit.

About two more years and all should be his and this goal he would keep constantly in mind. The key was Mac Bearta, he would be able to control the bigger jobs to come and had experience taking care of any problems that arose. Things could hardly be better.

That great man Paddy O'Riordan had done what he was going to do and was still top of his game. He was on a realm above John Cormac, but 'boy' O'Malley was available and was a great asset and mentor. Though John Cormac had no interest in sport, he always did try to participate in the subbies Monday morning golf game.

The crack was always mighty, "I hope them fucks of mine are getting up a good sweat because I reckon, I'll lose this round of golf to O'Driscoll"; this would give rise to a powerful round of laughing and the next one would try to better that, "I'll have leave them pack of bollixes that work for me on a sub for a month, if I don't beat O Flaherty" and an even greater round of laughing.

It was great to have a game of golf and a drink afterwards, while the men were sweating, it was the company of winners and they knew it. It was also where many deals were made. John Cormac attended regularly, pairing as much as he could with 'boy' O'Malley.

He was one of the few members who could lose to 'boy' without pretending and 'boy' liked winning, especially if he could win it fairly, which was a bit of a novelty for him. He could handle drink well and could remain wary and alert for longer than others; if necessary, by losing or dumping drink or pretending to keep up, yet not drink as much as others, but he was abler for drink than many, this was one genuine advantage he had over others, not for nothing was he a publican's son.

It was on an occasion like this that the breakthrough deal was made. He was playing with 'boy' and they came to the ninth; 'boy' was slightly ahead of John Cormac forty-eight to forty-nine and 'boy' suggested a move on to the nineteenth hole. John Cormac handed over the ton, they had bet even thought they were only half way round, if he knew when to do people, he also knew when to get done and be glad of it.

21

"ye' re a fair talent at the golf, 'boy', I can never beat you, no matter what I do."

"Aye, I have," 'boy' never refused a compliment no matter how ill deserved, no more than he refused money no matter how ill earned. Then into the session about 12 o'clock which could go on until 12 that night or later; John Cormac never did make a Tuesday morning but was always better off for it. This was where you learned things about work, about life about everything.

"There's two ways things work between the men and the boss on a building site, they screw you or you screw them. And if you are the one paying the money, then it better be you that screws them," just how true was that.

"Get a feel for the greedy bastard, you'll see the glow in his eyes when he see's money. That's the man you approach if you want the contract altered or day work that isn't done, signed for or whatever is extra curriculum, because he'll take the bung. You notice it in a man that works for you, then you street him."

"Think the worst of any man you're paying money to, then you're on the right track," true pearls of wisdom.

The conversation developed over time, eventually getting around to John Cormac's job especially his problems with control. To start with 'boy' was uncommitted but over time, began to see, possibilities in the little dog subbie that was always brown nosing him. If one was to look at things from the outside, John Cormac could appear to be a competitor or to be more correct, a potential competitor to 'boy', but things were not like that in reality.

John Cormac was on the inside track, he was one of the boys, he was from the right background, he had the right contacts, he could therefore be trusted to do the right thing, to act correctly in any or at least most, circumstances. It was at these sessions that the breakthrough deal that was going to make John Cormac was made. The week before 'boy' was wondering how you would keep a man and get rid of him at the same time.

As the day wore on and the drink went in, it became clear what the problem was. Hughie Mac Bearta was 'boy's' top foreman and general trouble shooter, but there was a burst up with some man and Hughie had to rely on the nail bar and the man got badly hurt.

John Cormac's well appreciated comment, "so the bollix hit a foreman, did he, what did he expect would happen to him?" showing he had the correct mindset, impressed 'boy' and showed he saw the problem from 'boy's' angle, thus could be of help. 'Boy' just couldn't hang on to Mac Bearta but Mac Bearta was one smart man, as well as a great foreman, he could work his way out of any amount of tangles. The worst of it was 'boy' could move him from site to site but as he worked for the same main contractors, who used the same subcontractors and agencies, then word would spread and this was only looking for trouble.

He needed some place where Mac Bearta could be safely stored, so to speak, then safely retrieved, when all the fuss had died down. He had looked, to some degree, at the little dog subbie that was licking up to him, before with poor interest, he just hadn't got the outfit to suit Mac Bearta but the well-placed comment when he explained the problem to him, piqued his interest; he was also one of the right boys, from the right background and what work he had, was outside 'boy's' area of operations.

Helping him get work, good work, for a contractor with whom 'boy' wasn't welcome, removed further the prospect of raising competition against himself. If 'boy' couldn't access the work, then it was better that an ally had it. When discussions got detailed, John Cormac was quick to assure 'boy' that there would never be any possibility of trespass onto 'boy's' work; 'boy' knew 'never' was a very long time, but it was still reassuring to hear.

The fact that John Cormac was not a genuine player in the field, could just make him ideal, who'd be looking for anybody in a place that they did not know existed. Giving him a serious leg up, kept work from 'boy' real competitors and gave him an ideal hiding place for Mac Bearta and Mac Bearta would remain under 'boy's' influence and be eminently retrievable at any time and for any period, to take care of emergencies for the short term or later for good, when of course the heat had died down.

John Cormac was elected. Following up these conversations, 'boy' himself had brought matters up, there was a site on St Swithuns Lane in the city of London where a ground works job was going; it was ground beams and pipe work and backfill coming off piles and going up to the subbasement floor in a sizable commercial building. It was not a big job and one that Mac Bearta would handle with his eyes closed.

In all, it would take about ten men working fairly constant for about six months, mainly on their own but sharing the site in the beginning with a piling crew and with concrete form workers at the end. In addition to that, he'd probably get men onto that site on daywork, for months afterwards doing bit and pieces, thus giving him a regular source of revenue. That great man Paddy O'Riordan had the shout there and he could ordain where the job would go.

'Boy' O'Malley had a word with him and John Cormac was in the picture. The deal was worked out in the golf club bar and it was simple. Mac Bearta the foreman was provided by 'boy' and he later included the creeping Jesus. John Cormac would provide most of the men but 'boy' would send any likely prospect to him. He already employed Mac Goldrick and Mac Namee, MacGrath and Cawley he had used on another job and he picked up Mac Elvinney and the 'bolowan' from the pub.

'Boy' had then sent him Devine and Mac Faul on the recommendation of Mac Bearta and Mac Bearta had hired the 'rat' on Martin mac Donogh's recommendation. It all came together perfect. It was at a county association dinner the final deal was agreed. That great man Paddy O'Riordan was there. He was dressed up in a pinstriped three-piece suit, he looked important. He was a big man and bald, he had a powerful jaw and a low forehead and eyes that turned down at the edges, giving him the appearance of a tube train coming out of a tunnel and this was a sort of visual reflection of the power he had.

He gave a hint during the night that John Cormac was on for the job. The whole thing was sealed later on that night. Paddy was having a piss on the side of the street outside the club and John Cormac joined him. It was a little awkward as Paddy had so much drink on him, that he forgot to take his cock out of his trousers and was pissing down the inside of his trousers leg, but he was a man of such importance that John Cormac did not feel fit to mention it and anyways, what did he have a wife for.

The job was agreed in such confidential and intimate circumstances that it could be relied upon. He would get about one hundred and sixty thousand, about fifteen short of the total price when all wages, insurance, tax, plant hire and materials were considered. He'd cut that one way or another. Meanwhile John Cormac O'Mahony was established as the ground working subcontractor on a commercial site in the city of London for up to a year.

Another good effect was that uncle 'tot' had been showing impatience with him of late.

"How many other jobs will I have to send men to you, so you can finish them?"

This coup silenced uncle 'tot' and when John Cormac managed to get one of uncle 'tot's' machines on the job, they could not be greater friends. Things were going 'a one' and he was managing it all. The main job was well ran by Mac Bearta, who knew well what to do and if he was anyways absent, John Devine could run things, at least for a while and Martin Mac Donogh had a tight hand on the boys.

The template was laid down and it was working perfect. There was only one member of the site management around full time as yet and that was the site agent, he was a tall balding heavyset Englishmen, aged about forty, called Neville Jenkins. He was generally very full of himself and authoritative but according to Mac Bearta, he was thick and didn't understand the work properly and Martin Mac Donogh sided with that opinion, but he usually did side with Mac Bearta's opinions.

John Cormac welcomed this opinion, it meant there was a stronger chance of getting him to co-operate with his 'cost cutting plans' and Mac Bearta was considering this problem for now. Even if he didn't get squared up, good old aunt Myra knew the game well enough to cover him until the big kill came in. It was a win-win situation.

John Cormac sat back for a time wondering if he should upgrade his car, he had a ford Cortina and he wondered if he should get a merc like 'boy', it looked a lot better. He decided to get a license first; he had failed his test twice and he decided he'd buy one straight from an Indian he knew who sold them, no more mucking around, there was no time for that.

All very pleasant thoughts, these were great times, no doubt about it. He rousted himself and decided it was time to visit the main site. He would stroll down there at his ease even with a bit of a swagger, a man of consequence in the town.

Chapter 3

He left the office, ready for one last disapproving glance around at the men he had there, before he went down to St Swithuns Lane to the site that would make him. As soon as he left the office, he heard and was a bit startled, by a sharp whistle, he ignored it, as no one would dare whistle at the subbie. He heard it again and looked about him to see who was whistling at who. He heard it again and looked in the direction of where it seemed to come from, as it was getting a bit annoying.

He was looking at the entrance to the site roughly where the whistle had come from and there under the scaffolding was none other than the creeping Jesus from the other site, the good site, it had been he who was whistling at John Cormac. Then he beckoned John Cormac over with one finger in a demeaning manner, akin to how John Cormac summoned other men. John Cormac was totally puzzled at this.

The creeping Jesus beckoned him over again with his finger, he also pointed to the ground to emphasise that he expected John Cormac to come over to him and even whistled at him again. Hold on thought John Cormac, did the creeping Jesus Martin Mac Donogh ever take over or what. He beckoned Martin over himself, in the same manner. Martin glared at him and beckoned him over again, emphasising the point by pointing forcibly at the ground before him.

The men came to the boss when the boss summoned them not the other ways around. It must be the case thought John Cormac, that Martin Mac Donogh was the boss now and that he himself was only the bollix. There was another round of beckoning and counter beckoning. Finally, John Cormac decided that Martin needed a lesson and though Martin was bigger than John Cormac, he was old and worn from rough living, therefore John Cormac decide to take his chances. He rushed over to Martin.

"Why in the name of fuck didn't you come when I signalled you," said Martin in a low urgent voice.

"What's up?" asked John Cormac, "I thought you had taken over."

"Big trouble, real big trouble," interrupted Martin, "why the fuck do you think I'm trying to alert you without drawing any attention to myself. Come on quick down to St Swithuns Lane."

"What's up?" asked John Cormac.

"There's a man dead on the site, now in the name of fuck will you get a move on."

A man dead, a man dead, oh holy fuck, John Cormac thought of the various savings he had made on safety, especially on scaffolding and shoring up trenches, did one of them collapse.

"Dead how?" stuttered John Cormac.

"There was a fight between the 'rat' Kilfeather and Mac Elvinney and a man has ended up dead; now in the name of the holy fuck will you get a move on, so we can go down there and try and sort something out," now roared Martin, all attempts at discretion abandoned in frustration, at the effort he was having to make, to get through to the boss.

A man dead, he was finished, finished, thought John Cormac, he'd be back working for that bastard of a foreman. He could see him kicking him up in the arse, "ye couldn't break the tip of yer own shite, what sort of subbie are ye now." There was no mercy on a fallen subbie, what the scum of workmen wished on other subbies, they'd take out on him.

No, it was even worse, aunt Myra and uncle 'tot' would never forgive the loss of money and they'd turn on him too, thought John Cormac now nearing blind panic; no, it was even worse again than that, he had only insurance for two men and he only paid tax for Mac Bearta and Devine, though of course he subtracted it for the rest. He'd get jail, jail, jail, there'd be huge bent balled headed English bastards shafting him every night. They'd have him by the knackers and—Martin Mac Donogh shook him back to the present, as they were at the exit.

"Pull yourself together to fuck and let's get down to St Swithuns Lane now," Martin shouted. He set off down London Wall and around the corner to Old Broad Street heading for St Swithuns Lane, with John Cormac following him like a lapdog.

His thoughts turned to the 'rat', 'that filthy rat, had he not warned them about him, him and his buck teeth, always on edge, always looking about himself, now how was he a right one; and what had they done, ignored, indeed contradicted him every time he had complained about him, had told them he didn't trust or like him and they had defended him and now look what happened?' thought John Cormac.

But his mind took another turn, was it ever a plot; could it be that Mac Bearta and Mac Donogh had conspired together to take the job from him. It was difficult to replace a sub-contractor in the middle of a job and expensive, it was the opportunity for another subbie to coin it but if the men doing the job could continue doing it, with one of the men taking over as subbie, then this would work out much cheaper for the firm.

All it would take was for one of the men to have a few pounds, which presumably at least Mac Bearta had and for him to cover the wages and other expenses for about six to as little as four weeks and they were in business. They were liable to get a very good payment schedule, as little as ten grand could cover it. He could see it all now, no doubt they see themselves as the key men who ran the job and should be entitled to the lion's share.

He'd be in jail and they'd be in the money. They'd be some laughing at him, at the subbies Monday morning golf match. The dog subbie that was capsized by his own men. Aunt Myra and uncle 'tot' would disown him. This was always the secret fear of the subbies, the men taking the job over; and he could normally rely on his fellow subbies for support but if he was in jail, well what support could he be given.

They would typecast him as loser and a wanker, an inept intruder to the subbies game, they'd have to do so to protect themselves, they'd have to make out there was something inferior and different about him' though John Cormac.

'It all made sense and it was a brilliant plan, him completely out of the picture and them in power and no hand was laid on him, there was no coercion, nothing the other subbies could hold against them. They kept the man, that they knew would cause a stir and when he did, they struck'.

They passed down Old Broad Street and on to Threadneedle Street and were now walking past the Guardian Royal Exchange, around which a hoarding was being erected in preparation for some form of refurbishment; there were some small alcoves inserted into the hoarding about the width of a sheet of plywood, where a person could stand into, to facilitate passage up and down the street at busy times of the day.

John Cormac now caught hold of Martin Mac Donogh and pushed him into one of these alcoves to settle with him.

"That filthy 'rat', I told you not to touch him, I told you time and again to get rid of him, but no, ye defied me and now look what has happened; well, I'll tell you something right now if I go down one way or another, I'll bring ye with me, I'll—"

Martin interrupted this flow by removing his grip from his jacket and pulling him fully into the alcove with him.

"A row started between the 'rat' Kilfeather and Mac Elvinney over the clear and obvious fact that he was constantly having to carry Mac Elvinney. Mac Elvinney started to shove, but the 'rat' though lighter shoved back harder, as the 'rat' would have muscles through work, which Mac Elvinney, of course, would have not. Mac Elvinney then struck him a couple of belts, the 'rat' said to stop but Mac Elvinney continued on, the 'rat' then fought back and clearly bettered him, putting him on his arse.

Mac Elvinney then got up and the 'rat' let him and he took a wood chisel out of his jacket, the 'rat' threw up his arms as though in surrender and shouted, no, no, but that bastard Mac Elvinney came on and stabbed him in the chest with the chisel and killed him. Now in the name of the holy fuck, we're in front of the stock exchange with an army of police no doubt near at hand, let's move on before we're arrested before we get to the bloody site at all," said Martin.

Just then a shadow covered them, a tall city policeman was standing in front of them.

"What's this then Paddy, forgot to take some water with it, eh."

"Yes, sir," said Martin touching the peak of his cap, "we'll move along now, sir," he moved on, more or less pulling a totally stunned John Cormac with him.

John Cormac was unfit to do anything else at this time, but follow Martin like an automaton, thought had simply deserted him. This lasted as they passed Bank Station and crossed over Lombard Street into St Swithuns Lane and the number of people walking along the street thinned out a bit. He grabbed Martin again.

"And. what was everyone else doing, where was Mac Bearta?" he asked.

"As I understand it, he was on some mission from you to a pub, to set up an arrangement for cashing cheques," replied Martin, this was true.

"Where was John Devine?"

"Down in the big trench with Mac Faul where they could see nothing."

This was right as they were in a hurry to finish that trench.

"Where were you Martin Mac Donogh?"

"I came on things late in the day."

"Where was everyone else?"

"Standing around enjoying the action; well young Mac Goldrick was shouting at them to stop and indeed I shouted at them to hold it, when I saw the chisel but as I say, I was late coming on the scene and I wasn't really tuned into what was happening," answered Martin.

John Cormac was stomached good and proper. To secure as much control as possible, he had hired men that he had some hold on and it had backfired, given the wrong circumstances, the wrong reaction took place, there was simply no decent or not enough decent men there to react responsibly and stop the fight.

Finally, he asked, in near total despair, "Where was the site agent?"

"Standing there, enjoying the action from start to finish," replied Martin and a spark of some sort appeared in the gloom.

"And why am I paying you more than, any other man, if you didn't handle things better," he asked Martin Mac Donogh.

Martin caught him and swung him bodily into the recessed doorway of a building they were passing, to get him off the street, "there is the site, where are the cops and the ambulance and all the rest? where are they? it's not half nor quarter enough what you pay me," replied Martin forcibly.

John Cormac had no answer to that. He entered the site, different now that from any other time he entered the site, not one glance sideways or otherwise was directed his way. There were more differences from other times, John Devine was sitting on a stack of sacks of cement, hands on his legs doing nothing just looking at the ground.

Liam Mac Faul was swinging a hammer at a wooden form for concrete again and again but never hitting it, just repeating this motion continuously; in contrast Ger Cawley and Pakie Mac Grath were in a paroxysm of hard work, they were putting up a form to pour a concrete beam into, work they normally didn't do. Ger Cawley was up and down in the trench like a sparrow hopping around eating seed, Pakie was cutting timber and getting props, indeed he was seen running, a sight never yet beheld on this or any other site.

Pete Mac Namee was over further and he was also furiously engaged in hard work, shovelling out a trench getting it ready to lay pipes in it, head down arse up all the way. Jimmy Mac Goldrick was carrying the same plank of timber over and back between Mac Grath, Mac Namee and Cawley continuously in a sort of circle again and again.

The 'bolowan' O'Meara was bouncing back and forth on widespread legs, a wide smile on his face and his tongue protruding saying, "I don't know what ye're all getting so excited about, sure didn't the likes of it often happen back in the fifties, sure don't I know, wasn't I there," time and again. There was no sign of the site agent.

Almost in the middle of the site there was a long thin mound under a blue tarpaulin that nobody was looking at but everybody was concentrating on. Barely fit to breath now, John Cormac followed Martin Mac Donogh over to the tarpaulin; John Cormac was hoping that somehow, things would not be as they said. But no, Martin Mac Donogh pulled back the tarpaulin and there was the fecking 'rat' with the two buck teeth stuck out of his head, just like any other dead 'rat' that John Cormac had ever seen.

Martin Mac Donogh covered him up quickly, muttering, "the fucking idiots." He then got planks and leaned against a low bank of earth near the body, so they were over the body but not touching it, he threw a sheet of ply on these planks and threw a few handfuls of earth over the tarpaulin saying, "no man on this site knows anything but myself, a body could easily be made out under that tarpaulin," shaking his head and slyly eyeing John Cormac who was in a blue funk.

'That was it, that was it, it was over, over, over and done with: he was no more. The asses that he had hired and granted the boon of employment to, had destroyed him. He was done, done, done, that chancer of a dog subbie or would they invent the title 'rat subbie' to describe him, as he was too much of a joke to describe as a dog subbie. The other subbies would laugh, the foreman would kick him up the arse, the English benders in jail would give it to him up the arse, every damn thing would be up his arse'.

Around him nothing changed, Mac Faul swung his hammer through the air never hitting anything. Mac Goldrick continued his revolutions carrying the same plank of wood around and around. Cawley, Mac Grath and Mac Namee continued their frenzied labours. No one looked at John Cormac or anyplace near him. The bolowan O'Meara continued the same mantra, "sure, I don't know what everybody is getting so excited about, sure didn't the likes of it often happen back in the fifties, sure don't I know wasn't I there."

John Cormac's mind was ablaze, 'would aunt Myra and uncle 'tot' go after his father for the money they gave him, they were more than capable of it, his father would disown him. He'd be in jail, where he'd be shagged by every bent bastard in the place, what other Irish that were there, would not stand up for a subbie. After that he'd be on the streets, he'd have to sleep rough, he'd be a tramp and he'd die along the side of the road. What about aids, surely, he'd get that in jail, that was his fate, he'd die of aids along the side of the street and everybody would think he was bent. All gone money, contacts, status, family and reputation, they wouldn't even take him home to bury him'.

Unseen at this time was the arrival of Mac Bearta back on site, where he was immediately briefed by Cawley and Mac Grath. John Cormac's mind was swinging back in an old direction, 'so Mac Bearta was a great man and could run any job and sort anything out, could he? Then how did he not spot this row brewing, such a good man or did he and deliberately turn a blind eye to it.

Just how could such a good man fail to see that something was up; and what of Martin Mac Donogh, was he not his man on the inside, was he not the man, who in his own words, could control everything, how come he spotted nothing, there was something up somewhere. The main facts were that he was dammed, dammed and dammed again and they were laughing. They would take over the job and he would go to jail and end up dying of aids on a street corner. There was some con on someplace, even if it was just opportunism taken up when a given situation occurred'.

Mac Bearta interrupted his thoughts, "this is a bad one," he said. "And where were you," asked John Cormac reflexively.

"Obeying your direct orders, you rang me this morning and told me to go to the 'Pig and Whistle' as soon as they opened at 11 o'clock, to make an arrangement with them to cash cheques for you, which is exactly what I did," Mac Bearta replied.

"And you didn't see anything brewing, no argument, nothing. I think my old friend 'boy' O'Malley was seriously exaggerating your attributes," came back John Cormac.

"I spotted nothing, it's true the two men didn't get on, but I didn't see anything different this morning, different than any other morning," answered Mac Bearta.

"And you," John Cormac said turning to Martin Mac Donogh, "you're supposed to be the creeping Jesus on this job with a handle on everything and a line on everyman, how is it you spotted nothing?"

Martin Mac Donogh looked about him anxiously, at the stating of his true position out loud, even before Mac Bearta, who knew well what his role was, as did all the rest of the men on site.

"No but it was pointed out that that fucker Mac Elvinney was not worth the money he was getting, only for it to be overruled and instead the 'rat', a fine worker, to be ran down," replied Martin angrily.

Then John Cormac had a flash of genius, "well boys, when this comes out, I'll make sure ye are known as the men who were in charge of the entire debacle and that I was not even on site, we'll see what happens to ye're reputations then, we'll see how many subbies will want to hire ye, seeing how ye've let this one down."

Martin and Mac Bearta looked at each other.

"This is getting us no place," said Mac Bearta.

"Well, what will get us anyplace," now roared John Cormac.

"We might just get out of this, let's think," replied Mac Bearta.

John Cormac mind now turned in another direction, 'was it really necessary for him to go to jail, could he not to some degree push the blame over on the boys, the irresponsible boys who let this happen in the first place and who should be blamed. He could say he wanted to be completely straight and pay tax and have everybody insured, but they objected to paying tax and being insured, because if they were insured it would point out to their presence working on site and then they'd have to pay tax.

And under the pressure of the contract and with it being a first contract of this type and all, John Cormac surrendered with protest to their wishes and with the intention of either replacing them with straight men that would pay tax and could be insured or forcing them somehow to pay tax, so he could then insure them. It might just work, it might at least reduce his sentence to a lengthy suspended sentence, certainly if he testified against them and what else did they deserve'.

Mac Bearta had been thinking, he finally said, "let's start at the beginning."

"With a knife, oh sorry no, a chisel," interrupted John Cormac.

"How many men are there on site and who are they," asked Mac Bearta.

"Just our own men and the site agent," Martin answered him.

"And you say the site agent just stood there and done nothing, enjoying the sight."

"Why would you not enjoy looking at a spectacle, when it's going on, it's hardly something you'd see every day," interrupted John Cormac.

"Your uncle 'tot's' driver isn't here?" he asked John Cormac.

"Unfortunately not, if he had been he might have done something about it, unlike the men that I grant employment to," retorted John Cormac.

"So, it's a closed circle and news has not got out yet, we might be fit to do something yet," he said.

"T'what," roared John Cormac now nearing the end of his teeter with Mac Bearta.

"OK first things first, does anyone know where the 'rat' lives, I know for instance that he isn't married."

Martin got very interested in what he was saying and a glint came in to his eyes, "he lives in a flophouse, short term rented rooms, no records, cash only, probably no right names, indeed I'd say a lot of the sort of people who'd live there wouldn't be too anxious that their real names would be known; the house is in Stonebridge and I'm pretty sure that Pete Mac Namee knows the address," replied Martin.

"Good any mention of family, particularly in this town?"

"No not here anyways, I think a mother in Ireland and some mention of younger sisters," replied Martin.

John Cormac was not listening, indeed he was once again concentrating solely on his own affairs, 'yes it could all work out, he might just be able to spare himself or at worst bring down the two traitors he had entrusted things to and whom he was sure had in some ways or another acted against him, if only by ignoring signs of trouble.

They probably thought, what have we got to lose and we might gain the firm and in a safe manner that means the other subbies won't oppose us, like they would if we used force, just let things play out and see what happens; well he'd scotch that idea anyways, so first things first, he'd ring the cops and that I'd be the first step in saving himself, he'd be the responsible one who alerted the authorities'.

"I suppose I'd better ring the cops," John Cormac said.

"No, don't," replied Mac Bearta.

"It'll look worse for us if I delay," answered John Cormac.

"No, we might get around this," came back Mac Bearta.

"How?" now roared John Cormac. "I'm calling the cops."

Both Mac Bearta and Martin Mac Donogh registered anxious looks from a number of the men, at this outburst and at least Mac Bearta almost smiled, for things were working out just as he had hoped.

"Give me twenty minutes and I think I'll get an answer," said Mac Bearta to him.

"How?" roared John Cormac in response.

"I've seen something like this before, give me a chance, what have you to lose in twenty minutes?" asked Mac Bearta.

John Cormac couldn't answer him. Pete Mac Namee was called over, he was a though looking man in his thirties with greying hair, he had a thin, though looking smile on his face and he glanced every side of him as he came over, he gave the impression of a man that was ready for anything. He was asked what he knew about the 'rat'.

He knew where he lived, it was a right dump, in the bad end of Stonebridge and that was bad. Rooms were let by the week for cash, little or no furniture, no records were kept, it was mainly drunkards or people just released from jail that stayed there, you came up with cash and there were no questions asked, in short it was a flophouse. He did know the 'rat' was looking for someplace else. He wasn't that long over here in England, just over a year and he didn't seem to have got his bearings right as yet.

Mac Namee didn't know him well, he was from Roscommon, but he wasn't sure exactly where. He had spoken of sisters including one doing her leaving cert, so he was likely to be the oldest of the family, he thought he was about twenty-seven. He also spoke of a mother, but he thought he mentioned that his father was dead. He had no knowledge of him being in any trouble, but he led a sort of loner's life; for instance, he had never seen him in company in the pub, indeed he had rarely seen him in the pub, so this could point to some sort of past.

Not wishing to be seen in public or keep company, would point to not desiring any attention and why was that? Mac Bearta then hit him with a key question.

"Do you know of anyone else on this site that is in any trouble?"

"No, well nothing serious anyways," replied Mac Namee in a light-hearted manner.

"Pete, my lad, the police will be conducting a murder enquiry here and they will be examining everyone, so if they are in any sort of bother it will come out.

It being a murder enquiry, there is even likely enquires to be made abroad, in the Irish republic for instance."

Mac Namee blanched and asked if people should make themselves scarce, this was not what Mac Bearta wanted to hear.

"You total bollix you, then you will become a suspect."

"Right," answered a now far from brave looking Pete Mac Namee, who then returned to his workmates.

Mac Bearta winked at Martin Mac Donogh who was co-oping on to the game. John Cormac said there was only ten minutes left, he wasn't co-oping on to the game at all. The frenetic work rate between Cawley, Mac Namee and Mac Grath had ceased and, an intense discussion was taking place down in the trench.

Mac Bearta went up to John Cormac, "we're thinking we might get away with this."

"How?" now squawked John Cormac.

"The 'rat' was living in very rough accommodation, where no account or record is kept of the people coming and going," said Mac Bearta.

"Most here are," answered John Cormac.

"Secondly, he seems to have no close mates or more importantly family living here, in all he seems a bit of a loner," said Mac Bearta.

"He was a weird one, alright," said John Cormac.

"You're speaking of the dead sir," said Martin Mac Donogh sternly, still a bit peeved at John Cormac for shouting out his true role even before Mac Bearta.

John Cormac failed to respond as he finally was getting interested, "you mean we could cover it up," he said.

"Thirdly, there were only our own people there, some of who, just do not want to see the police," went on Mac Bearta.

"What about the site agent," said John Cormac spotting the flaw in the reasoning.

"Exactly what about the site agent, where is he and why did he not ring the cops at once, might it not be because he should have taken action to stop the fight, instead of standing up looking at it, indeed revelling in it and taking pleasure in it as everyone on site can testify," replied Mac Bearta.

Hope arose in John Cormac's breast, "go on," he said to Mac Bearta.

"The rat lives an irregular undocumented life, in a flophouse, the rooms are rented weekly for cash, no questions asked, no records or accounts kept, people just come and go, he could just up and leave at any time and we do know he was looking for another place.

He had no close mates and no family here in London and he rarely went to the pub, so that covers the home, like he just moved, as he was planning and intending to. Here on this site, who is going to talk? The men, how many of them are dodgy or the site agent who should have stopped the fight, instead stood up enjoying the sight. Mac Elvinney is the only one unaccounted for and he'll hardly talk."

"The useless bastard, I always had a bad feeling about him," said John Cormac, that comment led to seriously raised eyebrows by Mac Bearta and Martin Mac Donogh. "Oh and that's right, there is still a body to get rid of," said John Cormac still showing some scepticism.

"We could bury it here," said Martin Mac Donogh. "Yes, but it would be far better elsewhere as this is the last place he can be tracked to but wait a minute, the site agent's uncle George Jenkins is a senior contracts manager with this firm Hoare and Collis, if we could get him on side, another site could be got," replied Mac Bearta.

"Wait now one frigging second, this firm has a site where piling is taking place just near here, up in Moorgate, it would be ideal if we could get access," added Martin Mac Donogh.

"That would be just the ticket, who's on that site," replied Mac Bearta.

"The demolition was finished over two weeks ago, so as far as I know or think is likely, just the piling crew," said Martin.

"It sounds more and more promising, getting more than one gang off site would be difficult, but one gang, safety or something," added Mac Bearta.

"And all the men will remain silent, of course," said John Cormac anxious to have some input in the proceedings if only as a critic.

"If handled properly, yes," responded Mac Bearta.

"Ye're fit to beat them all into line, ye're some man Mac Bearta."

"I don't intend to beat anybody into line, but there are other ways of doing it. A lot of these men are dodgy, they will remain silent and the other few will have to go along with them."

"They'll bully Devine, somehow I'd like to see that."

"Devine would be a tough one to bully, but you forget that he's married and has a family and family men don't like trouble."

"Mac Goldrick and Mac Faul."

"They're as green as grass and as weak as water, look at the two of them over there, sure they don't even know where they are."

John Cormac was becoming convinced, "Maybe me old mate, 'boy' O'Malley wasn't that far out about you after all," finished John Cormac, this was the nearest anybody had ever heard him come to complimenting any of the men working for him.

"And to finish the count, a bolowan is a bolowan so O'Meara's all right," said Martin Mac Donogh.

The plan was then formulated and went as follows, John Cormac was anxious to call the cops but thinking of the boys, Mac Bearta had acted to stay his hand, to allow them time to prepare themselves. They would be warned as it was a murder investigation, the investigation would be intense and through and every aspect of their lives, particularly their pasts, would be gone in detail, these investigations would probably spread to Ireland, so they had to prepare themselves.

The one thing they could not do was lie because if they were found out in a lie, they would be likely to become a suspect, they would think a lie in one thing; a lie in all things, this particularly, could go a long way because the true murderer had skedaddled.

If anyone was wanted for anything, well it was tough but that was the position everybody was in and they'd just have to put up with it. All that could be done was to alert them to what was coming and give them a bit of time to prepare themselves for it.

"How intense would the investigation be?" asked Jerry Cawley.

"As intense as they come, it is a murder investigation after all," answered Mac Bearta.

"And if somebody is wanted for anything else, they'll be nicked?" asked Pete Mac Namee.

"If it stops at that, it won't be too bad," answered Mac Bearta.

"What do you mean, they can hardly charge the wrong man with the murder," said Mac Namee, there was no answer.

"Well, they can't, can they?" asked young Mac Goldrick.

"Being guilty of one crime brings suspicion down on one," said Mac Bearta shaking his head, he continued, "I wasn't there, but I well er, I don't know how it was let get as far as it did, how come someone didn't intervene. Ya see it just doesn't look so good for anybody here. But I don't suppose there's anything we can do about it now."

"Hold on now, it's not good enough that innocent men be blamed," came in Pakie MacGrath.

"Oh, I don't suppose anyone will be convicted of murder straight up like but as accessories, I wish to hell someone had tried to break it up," replied Mac Bearta looking down at his feet despondently and shaking his head.

"No man here left a hand upon him," came in Pete Mac Namee, who was panicking now because years ago a young Pete had spent a month in Mountjoy prison in Dublin, which was an experience he had not enjoyed at all and never mentioned it and it was for this reason that he rarely himself partook in violence, but he did like it, particularly to see it.

He was the most enthusiastic of the onlookers during the fight with, spurring the 'rat' and Mac Elvinney on, indeed taunting Mac Elvinney and telling Martin Mac Donogh to fuck off when he made his belated and feeble attempt to intervene. He couldn't always restrain his nature, however and when he had got the better of a man, he had a longstanding grudge against in Ireland and had him down, he had kicked him in the head seven times and would have gone on to kill him, were it not for the actions of his own cousin, who was a guard, in pulling him off the man.

Later on, the same guard was instrumental in arranging for him to escape to England, when it became clear that his victim had suffered brain damage. His cousin the guard had used his position and the fact he had broken the fight up, with the local sergeant to claim the other man was the clear aggressor and sought the fight, which was indeed contrary to the facts and therefore made the case that to prosecute a case against Pete was useless.

Instead, the local sergeant promised the man's family that Pete Mac Namee would be 'ran' out of the country and would not return, they had to settle for this. Pete's father had to pay his wife's nephew, the guard a thousand pounds and the sergeant four thousand, this money Pete's father assured him was his entire inheritance.

Of late there was the matter of an old man in the pub that had borrowed money from him and them claimed to have forgotten about it, a ruse he had tried on others. Pete kicked him well and truly senseless down an alleyway and the last rumour Pete heard was that he was not going to recover, or at least fully recover. Would the police have evidence from the scene and could they match it to him.

"No, but I heard you led the chorus, cheering them on during the fight even stopping those that were trying to stop it, instead of putting out some hand to stop it yourself," replied Mac Bearta.

Martin Mac Donogh had briefed him well, Pete Mac Namee was left stuttering. "Oh and in case anybody isn't clear about the gravity of the situation, they can track you back to Ireland," added Mac Bearta for good measure.

"How would they do that?" asked Pakie Mac Grath.

Mac Bearta hesitated and Mac Donogh spoke up, "isn't Ireland and England both parts of the EEC," he had been prepped to speak up if Mac Bearta faltered.

"And did you break up the fight," ventured Pete Mac Namee incautiously, "and have you no authority here," alluding to the strong suspicion that Martin was a creeping Jesus.

"As you all know I came late upon the scene," this was not true he'd been the first to witness the dispute, but was shrewd enough to watch it from a hidden location unobserved, "and when I did try to intervene others intervened to stop me," said Martin with a pointed look and nod to Pete Mac Namee" and what am I but an ordinary workman," he continued to a series of sceptical looks.

"So, it seems that even when some attempt was made to stop the fight, people intervened to stop that attempt," said Mac Bearta scanning the crowd and shaking his head in a frustrated manner.

"I wonder how far away from the truth the idea of accessories really is," spoke up Martin getting riled at the looks he was getting for proclaiming himself an ordinary workman.

There was a chorus of protest at this. Mac Bearta silenced it by asking if they wanted to draw the attention of anyone outside the site onto the situation.

"Enough, enough ye have been warned, prepare yourselves. Its near two hours since it happened and we cannot delay ringing the police any longer," he said.

"Hang on," said Jerry Cawley. "Is there nothing can be done?"

"What do you mean? asked Mac Bearta. "Well, the body is here and is there not some way we can cover it up," went on Jerry.

"Doubt it very much, how would you do that?" responded Mac Bearta.

"Well Pete here, knew him well and there is no family here and he seemed to have few or no mates, it looks as though he was running from something," said Jerry.

"Definitely something dodgy," came in Pete Mac Namee.

"Look everybody loses if this goes public, the firm, the subbie, you if this goes public," went on Jerry Cawley.

"Well, I was in the pig and whistle at half ten this morning with any amount of witnesses and John Cormac O'Mahony was up on the London Wall site again with plenty of witnesses, everybody always knows where the subbie is when he's on site, so we have nothing to worry about," replied Mac Bearta.

"No, legally you may not but what about financially, this disruption will cost a lot of money," came back Jerry Cawley.

"It will just have to be borne," replied Mac Bearta.

"I have a problem," continued on Cawley. "I was arrested for drunken driving and this would be a second offence and I gave false name and I didn't attend court, so the consequences of a police investigation would not be light for me; on top of that, me and the missus aren't getting on so well and a spanner like this thrown into the works, could just fuck things up rightly for me."

Mac Bearta just shrugged and turned his hands outward in a helpless gesture.

Pakie Mac Grath broke into the conversation, "I have one question and one alone, how much effort do you really think the police will put into catching that bastard Mac Elvinney?"

Mac Donogh looked up and down and anyplace else but at Mac Grath. Mac Bearta could barely refrain from smiling, a good valid reason that would be likely to be acceptable to the men for a cover up had been brought up, which was if anything more than was hoped for. MacBearta didn't answer.

Pakie Mac Grath pressed his advantage, "well, Mac Bearta, what answer have you got to that?"

"Well, er, em, well," Mac Bearta seemed at a disadvantage.

"Well Mac Bearta well," Pakie pressed his advantage further.

"In all honesty, probably not a lot," answered Mac Bearta, looking down at his shoes.

"No," continued Mac Grath, "Does anybody here think the police will make any effort for a Paddy?"

"But surely the police have to try and get a murderer," spoke up Liam Mac Faul for the first time. A round of derision met this intercession.

"Try hard for a paddy, you're still wet behind the ears, me boy."

"Do ye know anything, me boy?"

"They'd barely arrest him if he walked in that door."

"So," continued Mac Grath, "we are all agreed or at least all of us that know anything, that no proper effort will be made to get that fucker Mac Elvinney," there was no disagreements. "So, it boils to this in the end of the day, we all get hammered and some of us possibly destroyed all in an aid of nothing," went on Mac Grath.

Mac Bearta just shuffled his feet and looked down at them, Martin Mac Donogh did the same. Finally he ventured in a watery manner, "I wish to feck somebody had intervened."

"We just thought it was an old scrap," said Jerry Cawley, "of course if we knew what we know now, we'd have intervened."

"An old scrap in Longford entails chisels, I thought it was only bottles," replied Mac Bearta alluding to Cawley's own shortcomings.

At this stage and at the mention of these shortcomings Cawley went red and sat down on a stack of plywood sheets that were in the secluded corner of the site, the conversation was taking place in. Cawley was not just bowing out, he did feel physically weak. He had always fancied himself as a hard man and when he was at school, he was though enough but afterwards, he began to lose ground, he ended up a bit below average height and not too well built, he simply didn't cut it any longer; this, he couldn't accept and it led to scrap after scrap.

When he began to lose as he often did, he usually resorted to the bottle and today, several men bore his marks including cops in both Ireland and England. However, of late his quest led him into more dangerous territory. He had always fancied a job as an enforcer and after a long quest for such employment, he was hired by an old dog subbie who had the name of being an even worse employer than John Cormac O'Mahony, who had got him and two others to go after a bloke that left him in the lurch, in that he had gone working for somebody else.

The man was married with a family and the idea was to invade his house and give him a good beating in front of his wife and family, thus showing, what it was to disrespect this subbie. They got into the house and as was agreed beforehand, Cawley would give the man a beating to show what he was made of and to dispel the badly concealed doubts of his companions.

Here things went wrong, even with two men holding him, he managed to kick Cawley away, then Cawley had produced a nailbar and hit the man a few times on the head with it before the men with him could stop him. This had the effect of blinding the man in one eye and leaving him with a permanent shake in one hand, thus ruining him as a workman. The man's wife had gone to the police and they were after him.

The dog subbie and his henchmen had to go to ground and he was truly done for. Therefore, Jerry Cawley had both the police and the dog subbie after him. If the police investigated this, then he was finished. Behind it all was the realisation that in reality, he was no hard man and that if he went to jail he was finished.

Pete Mac Namee then spoke up, "I'm not in all that different of a boat myself, I was in a scrap in the pub last month, something I tried hard to back out of. Indeed, one man there told me later on that he thought for a while that I was a coward due to the length that I went to, to avoid the scrap.

Well, the upshot of it was that he ended up in hospital, oh nothing too bad but the police were informed, so this could go downhill badly for me too, if the police were called. My marriage is not in the best shape either and this could well finish it, certainly I don't see her waiting around if I go to the nick for six months."

Both the six months and the wife were inventions, instead of six months, in fact, ten years was more likely as he had kicked an old age pensioner unconscious and he hadn't recovered, the invented wife a further measure of his desperation. Others were surprised at this first ever mention of a wife, despite the fact that they knew Pete for years but as Pete always kept his address quiet, they couldn't disprove it, Pete Mac Namee had not come down in the last shower of rain.

He then sought an ally and nodding to young Mac Goldrick, he whispered to him to speak up, for had he not told them that he was also in trouble in Ireland. Mac Goldrick had said this but mainly to appear tougher in the macho company he found himself in. There was some trouble but the extent of the trouble or even precisely what it was, he was unsure of.

The problem was caused by neighbours of his; there were three brothers called Carey that lived beside him at home. They were small men that thought themselves to be tough and often sought to prove it by getting into scraps, with mixed results, but they were viscous and if they got you down you were in trouble. In earlier years they were bullies, and as they were older than Jimmy they used to bully Jimmy, but Jimmy's father had got wind of it and put a stop to it.

Time passed and Jimmy grew into a big strong lad. He was in a pub in a neighbouring town he was preparing to go to a dance, something he had done only a very few times before. The leaving cert results had come out just before this and he was also thinking about these leaving cert results, he hadn't done so well or so badly, all subjects passed with high grades in four pass subjects and one honour.

It was not good enough to go to a university but perhaps, the civil service or some office job, maybe even the guards, he was big enough. In short, something white collar, at least his old primary school teacher thought that such would be advisable. He was trying his second pint which was different from the first, to see what it tasted like, when a voice reached him. "Jimmy Mac Goldrick, is that not you?" it was the three Carey brothers and they were all round him.

He was wary but not afraid of them at this stage, as at six foot he was at least six inches taller than the biggest of them. This wariness was soon allayed as they seemed very friendly, "well, if it isn't Jimmy Mac Goldrick, you've made a fine big man Jimmy," said one brother, he continued on, "look, it's our neighbour Jimmy Mac Goldrick."

"How are ye, Jimmy?" chimed in the other two brothers.

"Will ye have a pint, Jimmy?" someone said and a friendly conversation took place.

There was even a reference to the past, "We were bits of eejits ourselves in the past, but that was all childish stuff, isn't that so Jimmy."

"Sure."

"Of course, sure, ye'll have another pint."

Having had eight pints instead of the three he had planned on, he followed the Careys into the dance; comments like, "it's mighty to think Jimmy that you're out dancing, when it seems only like yesterday you were going to school," lulling any doubts about the company.

He did register some wariness from the people he passed on the way into the dance, but with the drink and the crack and the company, it simply didn't sink in. He went into the dance and was walking up the side of the hall behind the Careys, when someone tugged at his arm, it was a girl he knew from school.

"I never seen you in this place before," she said to him.

"Oh, I come here regularly enough," he replied, this was a lie, he had only been there once before; indeed, it had only had been since Christmas that he was let stay out after 12 o'clock at night.

They started chatting and Jimmy began harbouring ideas that she might just be interested in him and this intrigued him as he usually got no place with girls and he got heavily involved in the conversation. With the company and the drink, he didn't notice the ruckus that had broken out at the top of the hall, until it had grown into a major conflagration; in fact, it was his 'girlfriend' that had to point it out to him.

There were now screams and a great din coming from the centre of the fight; Jimmy tried to push forward to see what was going on, but could get nowhere near the centre of the action. He returned to the girl and told her he didn't know what was going on. It appeared to get worse, the two oldish bouncers who were known for letting combatants in a fight wear themselves out a bit, before they intervened were getting involved and the manager and the bar staff were moving in to support them, things looked serious.

Screams of his eye is gone erupted. The girl's sister then rushed up to the girl and Jimmy and told her to come home with her at once because things were going to hell there. Jimmy walked them to the exit and even offered to walk them home, but they refused as the girl's sister had a car. Jimmy went back into the hall, to find it was being cleared, as Jimmy walked out with the rest of the people the guards arrived, something quite out of the ordinary was definitely up.

The next day was Saturday and Jimmy spent the day thinking about what he was going to do with his leaving cert and doing some small chores about the house. If he did think about anything about the night before, it was about the girl and the surprising fact that she had time for him, generally girls hadn't much time for him.

However, things were a lot different the following morning. His mother shook him awake about 8 o'clock in the morning, which was surprising as she usually let him sleep until half nine of a Sunday morning, then he would get up and have to go to Mass. He soon found out that things were going to be very different this Sunday.

His mother looked worried and asked him what happened at the dance Friday night. His father was in the living with his hands on his hips looking angry.

"What the hell happened at the dance Friday night?" he shouted. "Young Michael Keirns, the son of the chief clerk of the county council John Jack Keirns is in hospital and it is feared he may lose an eye and his fifteen-year-old brother was ruptured in a fight, at the dance on Friday night, it's said that the Careys were responsible and also you."

"Who said this," asked Jimmy in a shocked and confused voice.

"Young Jim Hayes from across the road whose father works with me at the factory, told me he seen you going into the dance in company with the Careys."

"I met the Careys in a pub and I went into the dance with them," he began.

"Oh Jesus," interrupted his father, "I was hoping for a truck driving job with the council because you can't rely on the old factory and now, I'm fucked because John Jack Keirns has the over all say as to who is hired for the council."

"I never touched the Keirnses at the dance or anybody else, I parted company with the Careys inside the door," he now shouted at his father.

"Well, you seemed to be blamed for it, by all," now screeched his mother.

The story came out bit by bit over the day, the Careys were sore with John Jack Keirns over not being considered for council job and they started an argument with his son in a pub. This row was quickly broken up and a few days later, two brothers called Daly who were big hard men, who worked for Paddy John Murphy, an auctioneer and publican from a neighbouring town and who was the brother-in-law of John Jack Keirns, had given the Carey brothers a few slaps, just to remind them to behave themselves. This action was probably prompted by their reputation.

The Careys ever challenged by the world, hadn't been brave enough to respond and this loss of face could not be borne. So when they got a chance they responded, recruiting the only help they could, which was someone they could fool. As the day wore on, the seriousness of the situation became more apparent; for a start, they stopped him going to Mass which was the opposite of the usual.

Then the story took definite form, nobody claimed Jimmy had actually hit the Keirnses, rather that he had prevented others from intervening to stop the Careys. A number of people had specifically stated that the big fellow with the Careys had prevented them from intervening to stop the fight. It was only later when he was actually in England that he realised that these people were only using him as an excuse for not intervening.

Jimmy was not one, that was well up to the ways of the world. Repeatedly over the day he protested his innocence, naming the girl that was with him as a witness, but he didn't know her address or phone number, so he couldn't contact her. The local sergeant, who was known to the family, visited the house the next morning.

The change was obvious from the start, he was addressed as Mac Goldrick, not the usual Jimmy. His mother made the sergeant tea. Jimmy repeated his denials, naming his witness. The sergeant shook his head, he'd been seen entering the premises with the Careys and several people had said that he backed them up, preventing others from intervening. The Careys themselves had been in the morning sailing to England, they hadn't even gone to bed.

It was all too clear that they knew the damage they had caused. Jimmy was the one that was going to bear the brunt of the fallout. Eventually, after more questions and denials he was sent out of the room. He went to the bathroom window which was over the partially opened living room window and from where he could hear the gist of the conversation between the sergeant and his mother.

His mother protested that he had never acted like that before. The sergeant said that he doubted what had happened was that he had got roped in against his will, it was the sort of thing that did happen when drink and bad company mixed. Whatever did happen, the fact was that John Jack Keirns was a powerful and well-connected man and could, and pretty much undoubtedly would, cause trouble.

The best thing was for Jimmy to disappear for a while, to go to England; in the meantime, he would conduct a proper investigation and try and sort out what did and did not happen. Even Jimmy realised that running would make him look guilty and incidentally, take the heat off the sergeant. But there was nothing for it, he had three younger siblings and his father had a poorish unreliable job, so the family were vulnerable, if the sergeant said he had to go, then it was for the best that he had to go.

The best the family could do was look into the affair and see if there was anything they could do to clear his name. On Tuesday morning, he had found himself on the train to the boat, ostensibly running from the guards he had been considering joining a few days before.

About fifteen months later, he began working for John Cormac O'Mahony. The only thing of any value that his family found out was that the girl lived near the Keirnses and was probably known to them, so a possible approach to the Keirns might be made through her.

He spoke up, "Why should innocent people suffer for nothing, if the police would get Mac Elvinney it was one thing, but it seems that people are going to be destroyed for nothing and also, I'd like to say, I did shout at them to stop and more than once."

"It's an awful loss, big Mac Goldrick, that you didn't do a bit more than shout at them, ya must be six inches taller than that fucker Mac Elvinney," Mac Bearta answered him, despite knowing that for a greenhorn like Jimmy to assert himself was near enough unthinkable.

"I don't know what to do," said Mac Bearta uncertainly. Mac Grath spoke up again, "so it boils down to this, at least four of us and I say at least four," looking pointedly at the creeping Jesus, "four of us will get into serious shite for nothing at all. In my own case, I owe fines for drunken driving and a bit of a scrap I got into; it was nothing really, just a few belts and I tried to back out of it, as I've had enough hassle of any form in my life already but as bad luck would have it the cops came upon it and I ended up getting fined.

The worst of it is, however, that I'm doing a strong line with this quare one, in fact there is an informal engagement and the family is extremely straitlaced, the father for instance reads every Sunday in that catholic church up Highgate Hill, so if I end up in nick or even with a suspended sentence its goodbye to all of that. As ye know my time for such business is fast running out, I'm thirty-six."

This brought a few looks and indeed it was the addition of over three years.

"I might have let people think I was, a bit younger. Well in summary, its goodbye to all of that, wife, family etc, etc, it's a hell of a sacrifice for nothing. Catch Mac Elvinney, it's one thing but that simply will not happen and what of the people that are not in any trouble, will their houses not be searched, their families disrupted, will they get off free, without hassle."

This was a clear reference to John Devine, the only man that was likely to have the potency to halt a cover up.

"And again for what?"

John Devine looked at the ground in a state of misery and near total disillusionment, his mind was back in Ireland.

"The most important thing is that the work must be done, Jackie my lad," his grandfather said to him as he helped him up the hill, at half eleven that summers night, his breathing was noisy and heavy and he could barely speak.

"Work must be done, land must be farmed, houses must be built, tunnels must be dug, roads must be laid, you name it, some man must do it. They can plan what they like, they can talk about it, argue about it, fight about money, whatever else they get up to, but it is the man who does the work that is vital, without him all is nothing."

Earlier in the field where they had been saving hay, there had been a row between his father and grandfather, his father wanted to stop working at 7 o'clock but his grandfather insisted there was rain on the way and indeed, there was rain promised in the weather forecast. John's Grandfather insisted they finish putting the hay up into cocks where it would be safe from the rain or else it would be lost or of lesser quality when finally saved.

Young John, though only twelve, stayed with his grandfather and they got well into the field but at 11 o'clock, the dew descended making it too wet to put into cocks because it would rot. His grandfather was barely able to walk home. He had been a noted worker in his time, a ploughman and every autumn, he went to England picking spuds.

He built the twenty bog acres he inherited from his father into a farm of over a hundred acres of good land and reclaimed bog with every modern appliance and building necessary for running a modern developed farm, milking machine, tractor, all necessary machinery and buildings when he handed over the income of the farm to John's father at the age of seventy, a couple of years after John's birth.

John's father was an easier going man, he's done the work alright but didn't put any extra effort in, there was no over to England picking spuds for him. His grandfather entered his father's house and the row resumed.

"Ye lose the hay, then all is lost; ye're useless, if you had stayed even to 10 o'clock then we've have finished the field.

"This isn't the nineteen thirties old man, things aren't that desperate," his father answered.

"No, it isn't that desperate because you had everything handed to you on a plate, one of the finest farms in the parish. Well, I'll tell you right now that it's young Jackie that will inherit this place if God spares me until he's strong enough, at least he's showing every sign of being a worker and this farm was made through hard work and will be given to a hard worker, not a bloody dosser," roared his grandfather leaving the house and slamming the door.

It rained that night and for a full week afterwards and the hay that was left lying was of poor quality. There was a hard winter that year and the fodder barely stretched far enough. John's grandfather pointed out this fact to his father frequently. John's younger brother was born later that year. His grandfather died late the following year, at the age of eighty-three, getting John to virtually carry him out into the fields, to look at the cattle, three days before he died.

The words that his grandfather said stuck with him and became his mantra. He left school at sixteen, anxious to get to work. He virtually ran the farm and got work on neighbouring ones. But when it came down to it, he would have to wait at least until his brother grew up before he could take over the farm and he wasn't prepared to wait that long.

He went to England, where there was any amount of hard work to be done; get stuck in, get the work done, that was the important thing, the same old mantra. He married and by the time, 'boy' O'Malley, who he worked for sent him on a special project to John Cormac O'Mahony, he had three kids and a mortgage.

As he looked at the ground during that fraught conference, the vision he had in his mind was of his youngest child, a little girl. She was so delicate and so sweet to John's mind, despite his wife's assurances that she was a healthy vigorous child.

The contrast between her innocence and sweetness and vulnerability and this place, where he had to work, where a man could just be murdered and his workmates conspired together to cover it up utterly depressed him. Rough and ready for sure, the nature of the work entailed that but just allowing a murder to happen then covering it up, how come nobody had at least called him.

It wasn't even the murderer that was covering it up, nor his close friends, as far as he knew nobody was that close to Mac Elvinney, just the other men working on the site, what sort of situation was he in. The work has to be done, that's the important thing, nothing else mattered. This is where all the work got him, the company of a pack of criminals. How in hells name was he going to rear his children, especially his innocent little girl, in such an environment.

"Alright, alright, alright, I'll briefly see if anything can be arranged, if ye're all agreed that to cover this up is what should be done" said Mac Bearta his hands up in a placating manner.

"Are all agreed that that is what should be done."

"Yes," came back a strong response.

"Does anyone disagree?" went on Mac Bearta with a sideways glance at John Devine, who was still slumped in his own world, there was no response. Young Mac Faul didn't say anything either, he was truly frightened and completely confused by the entire event.

"All right, we'll give it a go, but where it'll go, I don't know," said Mac Bearta shaking his head. "OK, right," he said banging the scaffolding with a short length of scaffold pole as though for silence but which was a signal to John Cormac who was listening covertly from overhead to enter.

Chapter 4

"Enough, enough," shouted John Cormac entering the company, "they've had more than enough time to prepare themselves. I'm off to ring the police, it's long overdue that they were rang. If this goes any further, we'll have trouble explaining the delay."

"Ah ahem, hold on a second boss," stuttered Martin Mac Donogh.

"What now?" shouted John Cormac.

"Well, it's like this, the boys here were talking and it apparent that a lot of them will get into bother and have their lives disrupted seriously if the police are called. Also, in all fairness, there is little chance that the police will make any great effort to catch that bastard Mac Elvinney."

"Well, what do you want me to do about it?" shouted back John Cormac. "I've already given them time to prepare themselves, in fact too much time, if things are delayed any further we may all be in trouble."

"You'll lose money," came in Pakie Mac Grath.

"I've been losing money since the first day I hired you, what's different now," John Cormac answered him in the best subbielike manner.

Mac Bearta spoke up for the first time, "the point is, the boys will be badly affected if the police are called and as has been said, they will not make any right effort to catch the killer of a Paddy."

"What am I supposed to do about it; in the end of the day, how come no bastard could get an elbow in someplace to intervene in it and stop it," answered John Cormac.

"We've been thinking about that and we believe it could just be covered up."

"What?"

"Well, it's like this, the 'rat' was a loner and didn't keep any close company; possibly, indeed probably, there was a past and furthermore, he has no family in this country, so in other words he wouldn't be missed for at least a while. The place he lives in is just a flophouse, you know the sort, no records, people come and go without any notice, cash only, I doubt if he would be missed from there.

As well as that if we could get the remains to another site and dispose of them there; well, I think we could be safe. Further to that, if there was no early search and if he has no relatives or close mates, why should there be, it could just look like he moved from the place he was staying and from his job, we know he didn't like where he was staying, he even mentioned it to a few people."

"That's right and knowing the same place, I wouldn't blame him," came in Pete Mac Namee.

"And he wasn't over happy with the job either and if he mentioned this to others what would it look like other than he moved home and work; so by the time the family did start searching, the trail would be cold," finished up Mac Bearta.

"I'll just make one point if I may," started John Cormac quietly, "I expect sweat from the men that work for me not blood, no one murders someone on one of my jobs and gets away with it," finished John Cormac with a roar.

"Agreed boss," said Martin Mac Donogh, "but will he got and will the police make any effort to catch him."

"I hope you don't think we want the bastard to escape," came in Pete Mac Namee, "but the point again and again is, will he be got?"

John Cormac was silent.

"Alright, say I go along with ye, then am I supposed to believe that everyman will never to speak of this again, I doubt that somehow or another," said John Cormac.

There was more silence and John Cormac looked at his watch.

Then Martin Mac Donogh spoke up, "let the men themselves decide what to do and then, if a man does talk, he talks against all the boys and the agreement that they took part in. If he has any talking to do, then let him do it before hand, but after the decision on what to do has being reached, he is bound to silence and this will be enforced by all the boys, any way it's needed to be."

"I still don't like it; the thought of some piece of filth murdering someone on one of my jobs and getting away with, turns my stomach," replied John Cormac.

"It's turns everybody's stomach, boss but what is the balance of gain and loss, at least five men including myself badly affected by this. I'm separated from the missus and the terms aren't good and I'm behind with the agreed separation payments, so something like the police tramping through the house would give her the right excuse to go for a divorce and she's near enough as it is; as well as that I'm behind with the tax and insurance on the car and it's parked on the street, so overall the police could cause a lot of problems.

So to sum it up you'll be at least five men down for a while. What effect will that have on the job? Also given that this is the first job of this sort you've taken on, how does it affect your prospect of moving into such work fulltime?"

"It's hardly my damn fault that one bastard murdered another while I was on another job," roared John Cormac.

"Exactly my point, boss, so why should you lose out big time," replied Martin.

Mac Bearta turned out of sight of the men and winked at John Cormac, justification had just been provided for a cover up.

"Well in all fairness, why should I? If I had been here it wouldn't have happened," replied John Cormac.

The creeping Jesus breathed a profound sigh of relief, for he was afraid of a lot more than the car not being taxed coming against him. He had been separated from his wife, but she being a highly religious woman came back to him, with the deal that he never raises a hand to her or her children again; for a while this had held but bit by bit, he fell back into his old ways.

It cumulated one night, in him hitting his wife and when she tried to intervene, his eight-year-old daughter whose jaw he broke, realising he had hurt her, he tried to silence her screams by giving her a gobstopper but when she would not put it into her mouth, he lost his temper completely and tried to force it in and this had made the injury grotesque. At this stage his fifteen-year-old son whose arm he had broken years ago, lashed into him and somehow got him outside the door.

Today Martin Mac Donogh went to bed in his brother's garden shed, whilst his brother made strenuous efforts on behalf of his family and begrudged efforts on behalf of Martin to prevent Martin's wife from bringing charges against him. The sight of the police at her door would be an irresistible temptation to her to proceed with the prosecution of Martin. Five years or more in jail for a paddy that was convicted of child abuse was not an appealing prospect for Martin.

"I still don't like it," said John Cormac now playing a bit hard to get, "and there's also the question of the site agent."

"I wouldn't let that trouble me too much," said Martin. "He did nothing but stand there, looking at and enjoying the spectacle and the whole site is a witness to that fact."

"Plus, where is the police, surely it is his duty to call them," added Mac Bearta.

"He's one man but who cannot but look bad if this affair comes out," also added Pakie Mac Grath.

"And what the disposal of the body, it's hardly safe to leave it here, as this is the last place that he can be tracked to," said John Cormac.

"If we get the site agent on side, which considering his total lack of action, we should manage, then we should have a choice of sites and the van for transportation is here on this site," said Mac Bearta.

John Cormac still looked disconsolate and shook his head, he went on, "it still goes against the grain for this to be just covered up and a bastard murderer walk free."

"How would it not but go against the grain with a decent man like yourself, but what is the balance of cost and gain, there will be no murderer got and several men will be destroyed and yourself will be severely affected at best," came in Pakie Mac Grath.

Mac Bearta lowered his eyebrows as they had shot up involuntarily when John Cormac was entitled 'decent' and said.

"Right, what about this for an idea, every man has a vote either for calling the police or against calling the police; before that, he may say what he likes, make any comment, take any position but after the vote, there must be silence no matter which way the vote goes.

We all agreed to go with the majority and that decision is binding on every man here and after that, there is silence; beforehand, however, a man may say what he likes and vote any way he likes. Either we do that or lose the chance to do anything and endanger ourselves as well."

"Only those that were on the site," John Cormac reminded him.

"Well, that's true," replied Mac Bearta.

"Who hired Mac Elvinney, who supervised him, who'll lose the most money," came in Pakie Mac Grath bolder now.

"Right," said Mac Bearta quickly so the men couldn't contemplate Mac Grath statement. "Has any man anything to say or any suggestion to make?" silence.

"Again I say, has any man anything to say, anything to add or suggest, feel free to speak up now, speak your mind freely now."

There was no reply.

"I take it, therefore, that everyman agrees to go for a vote," Mac Bearta paused, "do we agree that each man has one equal vote and until the votes are counted each man can say what he likes, but when the votes are counted then what is decided, is decided and everyman is considered responsible for that decision and will abide by it and remain silent from that on out, does all agree."

There was a chorus of "yes."

"Any against," said Mac Bearta, "I repeat are there any against this idea," he said looking sideways at John Devine.

"Everybody is agreed," Pakie Mac Grath came in.

"No, everybody must get a fair chance to disagree if they want to," replied Mac Bearta.

"Of course," answered Pakie "but who's disagreeing?"

There was silence.

"Ye'd make a great politician, Hughie. Let's get on with the vote and less speech-making," said Jerry Cawley.

"No, I want to be totally fair to all men, everyman is going to be bound by this decision, so they must have a fair chance to give their opinion beforehand," answered Mac Bearta now looking directly at John Devine.

"Alright, alright," replied Cawley.

"Sure I don't know what ye're getting so excited about, sure didn't the likes of it often happen back in the fifties; don't I know, sure wasn't I there," said the 'bolowan' O'Meara.

The rules were simple, each man had a vote, if he thought the police should be called and the matter put into their hands then he voted 'for', if a man thought it should be covered up and that the police should not be called, then he voted 'against', it was as simple as all that. The vote then took place.

"Jerry Cawley."

"Against."

"Any comments?"

"We have no choice, otherwise we only lose out big time for absolutely nothing."

"Pakie Mac Grath."

"Against."

"Any comments?"

"The only thing that would be gained by anyone is, by the police, it'd give them a chance to hammer the paddies; and all of us would lose, even the most correct and law abiding would have their houses and families violated and their affairs minutely inspected with the aim of getting anything to prosecute them for."

"Martin Mac Donogh."

"Against."

"Any comments?"

"We have all to lose and nothing to gain for voting 'for'; in all reality, there isn't any choice at all."

"Pete Mac Namee."

"Against."

"Any comments?"

"Only to echo everyone else, there really is no choice in it."

"Jimmy Mac Goldrick."

"Er, well, er, well, against, I suppose."

"Any comments?"

"It's a loss nothing could be done about Mac Elvinney."

"'Tis indeed, but that's the way it is."

"There's nothing can be done it's as simple as all that."

"That's life in London for the paddies, my boy," were a selection of the comments that came back to him.

"Jimmy O Meara."

"Arra sure against, sure I don't know what everybody is getting so excited about, sure didn't the likes of it often happen back in the fifties, sure don't I know wasn't I there, ya'd thrown them into a shough in a site across the road or something and sure it'd be the—"

"Enough enough," shouted Mac Bearta.

"John Devine."

John Cormac and Mac Bearta held their breath, but there was no answer.

The vision of his grandfather was in front of him, "some man has to do the work, without him all is nothing"; this morphed with the vision of his daughter, she was so innocent, so sweet, so vulnerable and the way he had to support her, the knowledge of the type of men he had to work with to support her and as a foundation to all that the ethics of the Irish who ran the building trade, he had to work in.

"Ah, John," said Mac Bearta. "We need a vote and we know you don't like this."

"No one likes this," came back the chorus.

After a time he spoke, "who am I to go against everybody else," the vote was recorder as against.

Tentatively, Mac Bearta asked him, "Do you want to say anything?" He got no answer so he moved on.

"Young Mac Faul."

"Well, I don't know," he responded.

"Are you with your mates or not," said Martin Mac Donogh to put it up to him and get his mind straight.

"Well, it's just that I hate to think of some bastard getting away with murder."

There was a roar of a response to this, "for fuck sake ya don't think we want the bastard to get away with murder", "ya hardly think that this discussion is aimed at letting someone get away with murder", "ya thick young cunt, did ya hear anything that was said, if the police would get him and not the rest of us innocent men, we'd call them", "the police wouldn't even try to get him instead they'd follow us up for every little thing they could. Just how thick is that lad," "I'd hang the bastard if I got him," were some of the responses.

"Enough, enough," shouted Mac Bearta.

"No, it is not enough," shouted Cawley standing up and shaking his fist at Mac Faul. "Let's stamp right now on the idea that anybody wants that bastard Mac Elvinney to get away with murder; I myself would put up with the drunken driving charge and the wife's disapproval or even disappearance if I thought that the cops would catch that bastard Mac Elvinney and he would spend the rest of his life looking out through bars for what he did."

"The same here," Pete Mac Namee spoke up. "I'd happily do six months in the nick if I thought that bastard Mac Elvinney were to spend his life behind bars but it simply isn't going to happen and we'd get hammered to no purpose."

"The same as that," came in Pakie Mac Grath.

"Do you clearly understand that the purpose of the vote is to spare innocent men and not for the length of one second to let that murdering bastard go," roared Martin Mac Donogh at him, while he fronted him, the rest of the men gathered aggressively around him.

Indeed, it was likely that Mac Faul would be subject to more than verbal abuse if he hadn't been the biggest man on site at over six foot three and well-built with it; also the presence of John Devine mitigated against anything beyond the verbal.

"I know," he stuttered down at his accusers.

"Are you sure you know," shouted Martin up at him, "is it anything but crystal clear in your mind that nobody, nobody, nobody wants any murderer to escape, it simply not in the offing that he'd be caught and instead, innocent men would suffer."

"Yes," said Mac Faul nervously.

"You'll vote 'against', I take it," said Martin.

Mac Faul made some noise like "uh unh" and his vote was recorded as against.

There were still some mutterings about Mac Faul, "well stamp that anyways," "did he listen to no word we said all day."

"Enough, enough," shouted Mac Bearta.

"I know but it has to be beyond clear that no one wants any murderer to get away," said Pakie Mac Grath.

"Enough," now roared Mac Bearta.

"John Cormac O'Mahony,"

"For."

"Any comments?"

"I know you lads might think that I'm letting you down, but I just cannot stomach the thought of any bastard murdering anyone on one of my sites and there not be every possible effort to get him; and I do know that the police won't try," said John Cormac looking very despondent.

"One vote for and I will abstain as I oversaw the vote, to make the proceedings as fair and unbiased as possible," said Mac Bearta, this earned him a hard look from John Cormac.

"Subbie's vote," Martin Mac Donogh checked with John Cormac, thus was an allusion to the power of the subbie to overrule everybody else.

"No," said John Cormac, "I'll give in to ye."

"Right, time to count the votes," said Mac Bearta.

"Jerry Cawley, against; Pakie Mac Grath, against; Pete Mac Namee, against; Martin Mac Donogh, against; Jimmy Mac Goldrick, against; Jimmy O Meara, against; John Devine, against; Liam Mac Faul, against; John Cormac O'Mahony, for; that's eight votes against calling the police and one for calling the police. The decision, therefore, is not to call the police," said Mac Bearta.

"I have a question," asked Jimmy Mac Goldrick.

"You should have asked it beforehand but go on," answered Mac Bearta.

"What if we come across Mac Elvinney?"

"You let me know at once," spoke up John Cormac, "and I'll see to it that Mac Elvinney will never stab anyone ever again, because I know men that will cut the very hands off him, if I pay them and I will pay them to do it, despite what it costs."

"If I see him you won't need to I'll do the bastard there and then myself," said Jerry Cawley.

"Me too," chimed in Pete Mac Namee.

"Ya can count me in on that one as well," came in Martin Mac Donogh, "there was not one thing wrong with the 'rat' and he was a good worker."

"He could turn his hand to anything, steel fixing, shuttering, laying pipes anything," added Pakie Mac Grath.

"And killed then, by a useless bastard that wouldn't work to keep himself warm," further added Pete Mac Namee.

"Enough, enough, lets sort things out here," interrupted John Cormac fearful of his dislike of the 'rat' and liking of Mac Elvinney coming up in any way.

The plan for dealing with the site agent was simple, John Cormac and Mac Bearta would talk to the site agent and they would concentrate on his culpability, on why he did not intervene, what was he doing standing up watching the affair and enjoying it, they would especially stress that everyman said that he was openly taking pleasure out of the sight; thus, they would force him to co-operate with them, something that was vital for the success of the plan.

If the site agent did not co-operate, then two courses of action were envisaged, one was to ring the police and claim that the delay was due to the fact that they had assumed that the site agent would inform the authorities as would be expected of him; the second idea was to try to get rid of the body on the London Wall site, this was not favoured, as most men working on that site were not working for John Cormac so to get rid of the rat's body without being seen, would be difficult but even more difficult would be to find some place for the body that would not be worked on later, as work on that site was just starting.

In the meantime the men would form a sort of a box, in which the 'rat's; body would be placed to be transported, the top of the box would be open and a tarpaulin would be placed on top of the 'rat's' body and some steel bars and tools thrown on top of that as though the purpose of the box was to transport equipment, it should at least pass a casual inspection.

Cawley, Mac Namee and Mac Grath busied themselves with this task. John Devine was still immobile looking at the ground; Mac Goldrick resumed his pointless carrying of a plank of wood; Mac Faul just there shifting from foot to foot, clearly not knowing what to do; the bolowan O'Meara had resumed his bouncing back and forth from one foot to the other repeating, "sure, I don't know what ye're all getting so excited about, sure didn't the likes of it often happen back in the fifties, sure don't I know, wasn't I there."

Cawley, Mac Namee and Mac Grath were no carpenters and eventually they had to enlist Mac Goldrick to help them complete the task of 'coffin' making, this did at least stop the cycle of pointless wood carrying. The discussion between John Cormac and Mac Bearta was becoming protracted and taking a lot of time, it appeared that Mac Bearta was getting the better of the argument, in that he appeared to be taking the lead, this was a considerable relief to at least Martin Mac Donogh, who was fearing more and more that the boss was the weak link.

He couldn't very well maintain his status as an ordinary workman and interfere more, but he would dearly have liked to go into the meeting with the site agent, to see that it would go right, for in reality, all depended on another site being made available, the one up in Moorgate where the piling was taking place, would be ideal, but how they dealt with the site agent was vital, for only he could work this out for them.

Everybody now knew that the time lag was damaging, even reversing themselves and calling the police was now going to lead to suspicion being pointed in their direction. Finally after what seemed a long time, John Cormac and Mac Bearta were seen climbing the stairs to the site agents portacabin. They could see the site agent inside his head resting on one hand and shaking occasionally, his other hand combing through his thinning hair and his mouth opening and closing as he appeared to be talking to himself.

Chapter 5

John Cormac opened the portacabin door slightly, and as quietly as he could, then kicked it fully open as violently as he was able. He strode in and stood there looking at the site agent behind the desk with his mouth open, which with its natural twist gave him a scornful appearance, Mac Bearta also stood with his hands on his hips and a disdainful look on his face.

The site agent Neville Jenkins was a tall heavy set balding Englishman about forty, with a recessed chin which was quivering. He had tears in his red rimmed eyes suggesting that he was emotional and his mouth was opening and closing.

He spoke, "you fucking Irish, you murderous pack of cunts you, you have fucked me up rightly you have, my career is finished it is, I'm fucked, I am—"

John Cormac kicked his desk and sat down uninvited before the desk.

"What's this mister site agent that I hear from every man on site, that you stood there while this fight was going on, watching and enjoying it, indeed taking pleasure and revelling in it. Why is every man telling me this? I was on another site and my foreman was absent on business, is this really what happened," asked John Cormac.

"I just thought it was a ruck, I did," he answered.

"Why mister site agent, is fighting legal on site, is this acceptable behaviour, you tell me, you are the person with the highest authority on site, you are the person with legal power over all others," came back John Cormac.

At the mention of legal powers the site agent's face blanched a bit.

"What was I supposed to do," he replied.

"Stop the fight, that is what you were supposed to do," roared John Cormac now standing up and leaning on the desk over the site agent, "what bloody well else."

The site agents chin quivered ever more, "I could have been stabbed myself, I could, I could have been the one that was killed," he responded.

This gave John Cormac pause, but as he was primed to do in support of John Cormac, Mac Bearta intervened.

"Then why mister site agent did you not order the men to intervene and stop it as you have the authority to do."

"Indeed mister agent of the site, why didn't you who has supreme authority on site and can give orders to any man, including myself, me when I'm on site not order the men to break up the fight, certainly," here John Cormac kicked the desk again, "certainly" a further kick was given to the desk.

"Certainly when a chisel was produced, why did you not order intervention or even intervene yourself at that stage, instead of standing there getting a thrill out of the whole affair. Did you by any chance wank yourself off while you were at it, the boys all say you were revelling in it and openly taking pleasure in the whole affair; eh eh getting pleasure out of the Paddies whacking each other, ya English bastard ya, weren't you," emphasised John Cormac.

"The boys said it was that fact you were doing nothing but standing there enjoying the sight, that stayed their hand and put them off intervening themselves; you are their overall boss, aren't you? Naturally, they were taking their lead from you," came in Mac Bearta to add further emphasis on who they thought was ultimately responsible.

The quivering of the chin was increased further and no intelligible sound was now coming from the site agent.

"Certainly, you are likely to go down as an accessory to the entire event; at the very least, you will be disgraced and not even with uncle George's help will you hang on to your job and beyond that, you'll get no job beyond common labourer on any site," went on John Cormac referring to the open secret, that the agent's uncle George Jenkins a senior contracts manager with Hoare and Collis, had got the site agent this job.

"I'd hate to be a site agent in prison," he finished up sitting down and arrogantly putting his foot up on the desk. He took his foot down off the desk and stood up and once again kicked the desk, "why at the very least have you not called the police by now," roared John Cormac at the site agent.

The site agent eyes were watering at this stage.

"I was hoping, like, er well you know, er, like I was wondering, er, well, you know like," stuttered the site agent.

"Do you think I'm fucking physic, ya English bastard ya, what the fuck are you talking about?" shouted John Cormac at him.

"Well er, um, you know, well could there ever be any ways out of this, you know like, em, some deal we could come to," stuttered the site agent.

Mac Bearta had to use great effort to stop himself from smiling. Things were going even better than he expected. John Cormac sat down and looked at him, saying nothing and noticing the increase in the quivering of his chin.

"My way is to ring the police right now and do the correct thing, that's my way, all legal and above board," said John Cormac and he paused for a while, "but a number of the boys are afraid of incidental repercussions for them if the police get involved, nothing too serious, but interrupting their lives at a bad time, dodgy marriages and suchlike, so a possible way out of the problem has been figured out, but it can only work if there is great co-operation from you, mister site agent, do you uinderstand that."

"Yes, John mate," answered the site agent, the quivering of his chin stilled.

"I repeat that my way is to call the police. I will have you remember that I have nothing to answer for, I was on another site with any amount of witnesses present when this event occurred. Equally my foreman was not present and again, he has plenty of witnesses to say where he was, so the person I have in charge wasn't here either, needless to say if we were this would never have happened," said John Cormac.

"I know that well, John mate," the site agent responded.

"I wouldn't do it for you mister site agent, you could have stopped the fight long before things took the turn they did, indeed it was your duty to do so. However, the boys will be affected, two have divorce problems and another hasn't answered a drink driving charge, another lad has some family problems in Ireland and wants no further hassle to add to these problems. So, we have figured out an alternative way of dealing with the problem, but as I already have said your co-operation is vital," said John Cormac.

"You're co-operation is vital and some co-operation from your uncle George, do you understand that," came in Mac Bearta.

"I understand," he said.

"If you don't then I have nothing to lose by picking up the phone and ringing the police right now," said John Cormac.

"I'm sure we can come to some arrangement," replied the site agent.

"If uncle George does not understand the need for co-operation, then remember that when the shit hits the fan, questions cannot but be asked as to how you got your job and the answer to that question is well known, so will uncle George remain unscathed," said Mac Bearta.

The site agent blanched slightly at this, but answered, "I'm sure he'll see it that way."

"Also the money has to go up. I took this job at an extremely keen price, to show what I could do in the building line and not to cover up a murder for the sake of your reputation, mister site agent Jenkins; so, that deal is now void as far as I'm concerned. Do you understand that, mister site agent Jenkins," said John Cormac.

The quiver showed signs of returning to the site agents chin. "I'm sure we can do something, John mate," he replied uncertainly.

"I'm thinking of a lot more than just something, mister site agent. I was above on one of my other sites on London Wall when the creeping Jesus had to come to get me, to inform me that this murder had occurred on this site, while you just stood there and looked on getting a thrill and a high, mister site agent and now, I have the task of covering up the murder and letting the filthy murderer of a decent workingman, who could turn his hand to any task, go free. Something as you put it just will not do and if you don't understand that, then give me that fucking phone," shouted John Cormac.

"We, er, could see to five certainly, maybe ten," the site agent replied uncertainly.

"Give me the fucking phone," shouted John Cormac.

The site agent put out his hand to shield the phone, Mac Bearta went behind the desk and roughly pulled the site agent's chair away.

"Wait," the site agent gasped, "fifteen maybe twenty and day work later on, it's the best I can do."

"Then, mister site agent, we'll see how you fare out in jail, for you seemed to have missed the take home message here. I was not involved because I was elsewhere, you however were here and deliberately did not do your duty because you were getting a trill, no doubt sexual, out of the whole affair and by your example, you dissuaded the men from intervening to stop the fight either. Did you get an orgasm out of it, did you have a fucking hard on, you fucking English blackguard you," roared John Cormac at him; now was the crucial time to apply the maximum pressure on him.

"What have you in mind, John mate," said the site agent nervously.

"At least thirty-five more, wangle it what way you like; day work, dead men, deliberate mistakes on your part, changed plans, whatever and afterwards eight months daywork for five men," answered John Cormac.

The site agent returned to his earlier phase of ashen quivering and said, "there ain't no way's I could get that for you, John me old mate, not no matter what I tried."

"Well in the end of the day that's a good thing; for the sake of a few bob, I don't want something like this on my conscience, for the rest of my days," answered John Cormac standing up.

"Me neither," added Mac Bearta.

"Wait what about your men," the site agent almost shrieked.

"We'll just tell them truthfully that the site agent won't co-operate, when it comes down to it, their marital difficulties or whatever aren't of my making, I must tell them now," said John Cormac breezily moving towards the door.

"Wait, I can't do that but I'll try something better than twenty,"

"Let me give you another bid then, forty and daywork for eight men for twelve months; and if any of my men go to jail like you will, you are likely to meet them there, I wouldn't like to be in your shoes then, mister site agent."

"John mate, I couldn't."

"Then give me the phone please, we've delayed for long enough; oh and the excuse for the delay is that we expected you to ring the police, as was your duty and what would be expected of you but we had to finally resort to ringing the police ourselves, when we found out that you were trying to cover things up due to your behaviour during the fight and for your culpability in failing to get the fight broken up and to back this up, surely you must know that not one man here will support you for the length of one second," said John Cormac reaching for the phone, as Mac Bearta pulled the site agent back as he was trying to shield the phone again.

"You'll lose money too," he gasped at John Cormac; and John Cormac delayed answering.

"Oh maybe not," came in Mac Bearta, "you never know what deal uncle George may be willing to make to take the spotlight from himself when this all comes out."

John Cormac nodded to Mac Bearta, more and more he was realising just why 'boy' O'Malley wanted to hang on to Mac Bearta one way or another.

"Thirty and some of it may have to come from my own bank account and day work for four men for four months is the last thing I can offer," now almost shrieked the site agent.

John Cormac shook his head silently and put the phone to his ear and started to dial.

Mac Bearta spoke up, "boss, there is the men to consider."

"I don't want it, I don't like it, I don't have to put up with it, if that fucking English wanker made the first effort to do his job, we wouldn't be here; in the end of the day why spare him, he just does not deserve it," replied John Cormac.

"I fell the same myself, but the boys will pay, there will be at least two broken marriages," said Mac Bearta.

"Yes, John mate and how much heed will the police take of you anyways; you know what them is, all ex squaddies, ain't they; they hate the Irish, they do, them cunts, they'd never give you justice or fair play; they'd arrest any Irishman for anything, won't they," said the site agent.

It was a good point but Mac Bearta replied, "not us, we've got alibis."

They settled for thirty thousand on the contract and six months day work for five men after the contract finished also one thousand cash to Mac Bearta and four thousand cash to John Cormac from site agents personal accounts.

"I only get twenty-five thousand a year," moaned the site agent.

"Twenty-five thousand a year salary and twenty-five thousand a year bonus, not one penny of which you remotely deserve," shouted John Cormac at him; the knowledge of 'boy' O'Malley was beyond value. The further condition that was to be acted on at once was that another site which was near at hand and was suitable for the disposal of a body be found and made available.

The creeping Jesus was called in and repeated his recommendation of the Hoare and Collis site on Moorgate where piling was taking place and would, therefore, be ideal for the disposal of the rat's body.

The site agent was left to call his uncle George; John Cormac was going to stay and monitor the conversation, something that would never normally be contemplated but Mac Bearta signalled him to leave, figuring that he'd be most effective if allowed to talk privately, issues that were not fit to bear the light of day could be discussed openly and pressure from these quarters included in the discussions, thus expiating matters, something that was becoming more and more necessary.

Time passed ever more slowly; the site agent could be seen through the window standing up and gesticulating during his conversation with his uncle George, progress was not apparent. Finally, he reappeared and John Cormac said that he was going to ring the police immediately, as too much time was passing and they were endangering themselves. The site agent quickly interposed to say the deal was in progress and his uncle was working on it. They would try the site in Moorgate but the problem was to get a legitimate reason for getting the piling crew off the site, thus allowing the body to be disposed of unobserved.

"It's probably better all things considered to be unobserved," remarked Mac Bearta drily.

"This is only to save you, what the hell am I doing it for," shouted John Cormac at the site agent before everyone on site. "Don't worry, John, me old mate, everything is being taken care and you will be taken care of also," the site agent responded.

This answer in front of the men didn't suit John Cormac but before he could say anything, the site agent returned to the portacabin and was seen through the window in frantic discussions with his uncle George on the phone. Finally, over half an hour later when John Cormac was genuinely thinking his best option to save himself, late though it was, was to ring the police, the site agent reappeared with a smile on his face.

"I've arranged it for you, I have, it's a right pukka job, it is," he announced beaming at everyone.

"Thank fuck," "at long friggin last," "fucking finally," were some of the responses elicited from the anxious crew.

The plan was to bring the body to the site in Moorgate that had been pointed out as ideal from the start and dispose of it in one of the piling holes. The first problem was to clear the site. The site in Moorgate only had the piling crew and a couple of labourers from the contractors Hoare and Collis and the site management who only consisted of the resident engineer and the site agent present on it at this stage.

The clearance of the site personnel was accomplished by a random safety inspection; during the course of this inspection several faults would be found and the site personnel would be questioned as to how this state of affairs came about, it would be found necessary to give immediate instruction to these personnel to rectify the situation and this would have to take place on another Hoare and Collis site due to limited portacabin space on that site, this early in the job, so they would have to move to this other site so that the necessary instruction could take place.

The resident engineer would have to call on head office to collect further material relating to the safety inspection, this would not normally be a job given to a resident engineer but there was no one else available on site to do it so early in the job. The site agent would remain on site but out of sight.

There were a number of piles being dug and filled with concrete on this site by a firm called Concretation. One of these piles, luckily in a corner was ready for filling with concrete, this was clearly shown by the fact it had a round cage of reinforcing steel hanging from the tripod frame of the piling rig above the pile, this would be let down into the piling hole and the hole filled with concrete, completing the pile. There would be something else going into this hole, it would be the 'rat' final resting place.

The site agent then returned to the office, to get the final word from his uncle to go. Martin Mac Donogh led Cawley, Mac Grath and Mac Namee in getting everything ready for the 'rat's' last journey. The spread a tarpaulin over a temporary construct of scaffolding boards to shield their work from any possibility of spectators, people could come on site looking for work or just look in through curiosity or even from head office; though by the look of the way things worked, there was little danger of adverse consequences for this activity, from that particular quarter.

They put the 'rat' into his 'coffin' or box, and put two old tarpaulins on top of him and some old bars of reinforcing steel and a jackhammer and one or two air hoses on top of that. This would provide adequate cover, for the few yards of pavements they would have to cross, from the exit of this site to the van, to the entrance of the other site from the van. John Devine, Mac 36.

Faul and Mac Goldrick did nothing during this time and were all now standing up looking at the ground or the hoarding or anything but what was going on or each other. The bolowan O'Meara regaled them with a tale of something similar that happened years ago.

"'Twasn't it in '58 or '56' and sure didn't young Micking Mac Hugh get killed because the 'pig' O'Rahilly hit him on the head with a sledgehammer and sure, he said it was just bad aim because he had drink taken like, but some of the boys said like, it was because that young Mac Hugh had taken the 'pig's' woman off him and then we had to get rid of the body and sure the site was out in Thring.

We took the long way back through the country side and didn't we throw Micking's body into a farmer's shough along the side of the road, from the back of the pick-up truck that we were riding in the back of and sure then didn't the police come along and they got Micking and sure didn't they catch us like.

Sure, what could we say only that he must have fallen off by accident like and that we didn't notice because we had drink taken and the police just said the drink is the destruction of ye Irish and sure there was no more about it that all that and sure that how it 'twas them times, sure there was none of this big excitement about that sort of thing and sure the only thing that did happen was that the driver was fined four pounds seventeen and six for having bald tires and them times four pounds and seventeen and six was a lot."

"Shut up to fuck," roared Mac Bearta at him, silencing him.

They lifted the 'rat' up and Pete Mac Namee almost rose the box to his shoulder until a furious glance from Mac Bearta brought him back to himself. The creeping Jesus drove the van into place as near to the site entrance as he could get and the crew got ready for departure.

Mac Bearta spoke to John Devine and the other two non-participants, "ye lads can wait here and while I don't expect you to work, it might just be better if ye made some shapes like work, in case someone should look in from head office or suchlike."

"What use are they anyways," said Jerry Cawley.

"What?" said John Devine.

"Not you, John," replied Cawley hastily.

"We know you don't like this John," said Mac Bearta.

"No one likes this," came in Pete Mac Namee.

"Alright, let's get on with it," fearful of any dispute, argument or above all, further discussion breaking out.

They carried the box into the street and put it into the van, taking care not to hurry or to act in any manner that was in any way suggestive, of anything but the most regular and banal proceedings taking place. It took six to carry the box with ease, which did look a bit unusual but they put the box into the van and stood about talking with the doors open and the box partially in view, to do everything to emphasis the commonplace and casual nature of what they were about.

After a short time three of them, John Cormac the 'bolowan' and the creeping Jesus who was driving got in the front and the other four who were taking part got in the back and they set off for the short trip to Moorgate. The boys left on the site made no move to do any work. John Devine was looking at himself and was not impressed by what he has seen.

How come he had made no move to do anything and if he had made some move to stop this from happening would the other two have backed him up; true, they were green but they were big strong men and far stronger than the others, if they had stood by him then yes, in all probability he could have stopped it, why therefore had no attempt being made.

The simple fact was that, to save the clueless, spineless site agent; and that worthless little chancer of a subbie and that conniving crook Mac Bearta, a good man, able and a good worker if not the most sociable or friendly, was going to go into a piling hole as his last resting place; a family was bereaved, a mother without a son or knowledge of his death, mainly to save that little chiseller of a subbie, a man who if John Devine was any judge, was himself incapable of doing a day's work.

Three big strong men as useless as the pigeons that roosted on site, alright two of them were young and green but what about him. What was this anyways about work; 'some man has to do the work or else all is nothing', those were his grandfather's words. Where exactly did doing this work get you anyways, a man could be murdered on the same site and for one, no one would even call you, so you could do anything about it; for two, the body was going to be thrown into a piling hole by people not themselves involved in the murder.

Christ, was it not easy to get away with murder in this town, ya didn't have to trouble yourself with covering up the crime, it was done automatically for you; for three he had to go home to an innocent little girl and look her in the eye and know the only he could support her was by facilitating murder, because that was what he had done, he stood out of the ways of those who were actively covering it up and done nothing. What was all this vital hard work about anyways and what did it accomplish, but supporting useless criminals like John Cormac and even more so Mac Bearta.

John Cormac was naturally useless, not so Mac Bearta, he chose to be a criminal. 'Some man must do the work that is the vital thing', what a load of throttle and bullshit, how much more wrong could a man be. Liam Mac Faul was totally confused, why would the police do nothing, surely it was their country that the murder had happened in, why would they not go after the perpetrator; what would the police do to the other men on site, they had nothing to with the murder, surely they would not touch them, why were they so sure they would get into trouble, what the hell was really going on.

The site agent who was English seemed the most anxious of all to cover up the murder; wasn't someone with high authority and power a person of integrity, of high standards like the priest or the school master at home. What sort of place was this? What sort of life was this? What the hell was he going to do?

Mac Goldrick was just about out of rational thought; he went to a dance, he talked to a girl, he got blamed for something he didn't do, he came to England to work and hopefully, let things settle down at home and now, he was as near as dammit a participant in covering up a murder and it was not so long ago that he was considering becoming a policeman.

What was up, what was down, why was everybody so afraid to call the police, what did they do, why, how, what, for what reason, what now, how safe was he, what was up with everybody. He couldn't fathom it out, make any sense of it, logicalize it at all, the entire series of events were beyond him.

The creeping Jesus drove the van carefully up to Moorgate; say what you like about the creeping Jesus, but he could keep his cool. They reached their destination, which was a Hoare and Collis site along Moorgate, the exterior of which had been preserved showing that it had once been an African bank.

They drew up the van outside the site and got out; acting as casually as possible at all times. Martin Mac Donogh got out and stretched himself and let the others out of the back of the van, leaving the door open and the 'rat's' box in plain view. Mac Namee and Cawley lit up fags and stood around, in no hurry at all. John Cormac and Mac Bearta strolled over to the door into the site in a casual manner, John Cormac with his hands in his pockets, they moseyed on inside, people in no particular hurry to start work.

Inside they quickly located the correct piling hole, it was the only one with a round cage of reinforcing steel hung over it, showing it was ready for concrete to be poured into it. Nobody else could be seen on site; apparently the safety instruction was taking place with all Concretation's men constrained to attend it and the couple of laborers that worked for the firm were apparently also brought along for good measure; then again safety was very important.

It was known that the site agent was present but not visible, his role was two-fold; one to keep any unexpected visitors off site or at least away them from that corner and two, to inspect everything afterwards to ensure all was in order and that there was no sign that any strangers had been on the site; meanwhile, he kept out of sight to minimise his role in the entire affair. John Cormac saw that all was in order, so he went out to the boys to get them ready to finish the job.

Chapter 6

They hoisted the 'rat's' box out of the van; Cawley and Mac Grath to the front and Pete Mac Namee and John Cormac himself at the back. Martin went inside to check all was clear, that there were no hidden trips or anything else that could in any way impede progress. Mac Bearta supervised and the bolowan O'Meara bounced back and forth on his two legs as usual but at least, he was silent.

A loud prearranged argument took place between the men, who made sure only to look at each other during this dispute, to enhance the impression that this was the most commonplace ordinary event.

"I don't know why so many tools are needed for such a small job."

"It's because you never know what they are short of around here."

"Well, they must have some gear."

"You can't be sure and it's late when you find out they haven't got what you want," and so on.

The enthusiasm with which they partook of the argument, plus the fact that the box was heavy for four meant they didn't see the approach of the tall policeman until his shadow covered John Cormac.

"What's this then," he said possibly recognising John Cormac from earlier on beside the Guardian Royal Exchange.

John Cormac immediately let go of the box which tilted over and threatened to unbalance and spill its contents at totally the wrong moment, in totally the wrong company.

Mac Bearta made a grab for it but he was never going to be in time. Luckily, however, the policeman was in range and he got his hand under the box and stopped it tipping over, which would have meant the undoing of all. Mac Bearta relieved him at once, while getting a hand to John Cormac who was standing there with his eyes glazed over in a state of shock.

"Thank you, sir," he said to the policeman while he held up the box and somehow pulled John Cormac into the door of the site.

The bolowan O'Meara showing intelligence or appearing to show intelligence for probably the first time in his life stepped between John Cormac and the street, thus shielding him from the sight of the tall policeman.

"Steady on their Paddy, we don't want any spills, do we," said the policeman.

"No sir, we certain do not," replied Mac Bearta.

"Had a couple or more at lunchtime eh," asked the policeman.

Mac Bearta smiled sheepishly and replied, "'Fraid so sir," won't happen again."

"No never does with you Irish, does it," said the policeman and then he walked off, probably considering he had given an appropriate and timely caution, given the circumstances.

Not for the first time that day John Cormac was being homosexually raped by a number of large bald English thugs. The boys carried the 'rat' past him unseen; indeed, it took a severe shaking from the creeping Jesus to awaken him back to reality. The boys laid the box down by the tripod and they pulled the tarpaulin up over the legs of the tripod to shield what they were doing, from any possible viewer.

Mac Bearta went through the 'rat's' pockets principally for his house keys so that later on someone could go to the 'rat's' digs and prepare them to give the impression that the digs were wilfully abandoned by the 'rat'; he also took any money he found, which he said he was going to donate to charity and to get a couple of Masses said for the 'rat's' soul, and whether he was believed or not, no one was in the humour, given the surroundings and circumstances, to question him.

The preliminaries now completed, he stood up and said "we may as well get on with it."

They simply slid the 'rat's' body, with his two buck teeth sticking out of his mouth, just like any other dead rat they ever saw, down into the piling hole. That was all there was to it. They quickly wrapped up the tarpaulin and threw the few bits and pieces of steel and the tools back into it and withdrew under the scaffolding near the entrance.

The creeping Jesus got an old brush on site and brushed out the marks made by the box and some of their footprints, to remove any sign that they were here, given that the site was covered in boot prints this was probably going a bit far, but for Mac Bearta at least, too many precautions were better than too few.

John Cormac now recovered, sent Pete Mac Namee out to check that the policeman had gone, they weren't going to rush, in case, anyone noticed the very brief amount time they spent on the site. John Cormac now thought it necessary to say a few words over the 'rat's' resting place, he drew the men up and told them to take off their helmets or in some cases caps.

He started, "we're laying to rest here in this place our friend and workmate the r, eh em," he had forgotten the 'rat's' right name.

"James Patrick Kilfeather," whispered Mac Bearta to him.

"I know that," replied John Cormac indignantly, "our friend and workmate James Patrick Kilfeather. He deserved a lot better from all of us, but this is all we can do for him sadly and it isn't good enough. He was a great worker and a good man and should have a lot better ending than this, but a decision was taken."

At this point in the eulogy John Cormac shook his head regretfully, "which we agreed to stick to and which we have," again John Cormac shook his head regretfully and looked around at his companions clearly placing the onus on them, "for better or for worse. We must ask God almighty to take," at this stage, just as Mac Bearta was thinking that the prayer session was a bit too prolonged; The bolowan O'Meara spoke up, "and down with the rat into his hole."

Overcome with a sense of outrage and blasphemy at this comment and at the interruption of his eulogy, John Cormac ran at the bolowan and grabbed him by the throat and shoved him up against the hoarding in some form of an attempt to kill him. Mac Bearta quickly parted them and led the way out to the van, without even bothering to check with Mac Namee if the coast was clear and they all got into the van; Mac Bearta and John Cormac in the front with the creeping Jesus and the rest in the back, including the now silent bolowan.

The journey back began in silence, but the bolowan O'Meara was still a bit sore at the method of his silencing so he decided to show how experienced he was in such affairs.

He began, "Sure, I don't know what everybody is getting so worked up about, sure didn't I often see the likes of it back in the fifties, sure 'twasn't it in '54 or was it '53 and sure, didn't the bull lynch who was a total bollix get killed when a few of the boys threw lumps of concrete down on him, when he was down in a hole.

Sure, he used to batter the lads if they didn't give him some of their wages or if you were in his way he'd give you a clout or a kick in the bollix or anything and then sure didn't he get made the gangerman and the boys didn't like this,

76

because he'd go mad on them then altogether, so the threw lumps of concrete down on him when he was down in a big hole and sure, they killed him.

There was six of them at it and what did they do then, only they took him out of the hole and threw him into a big shough on a site down the road, that their mates were working on and tad, sure then what did they do, but didn't them all make a piss down on top of him below in the shough and—"

"Shut up," roared Mac Bearta at him, "I swear bolowan that you will go down in that hole on top of the 'rat' this day."

"James Patrick Kilfeather," John Cormac piously corrected him, "and it a great loss we didn't through the fecking bolowan down the hole when we were back there."

The bolowan now became silent. They arrived back at the St Swithuns Lane site to a smiling site agent anxious to know that all went well.

"All go well, John, me old matey."

"Yes, your bacon is safe," replied John Cormac.

The site agent rubbed his hands together, a wide smile now on his face, "that's a fucking relief, that is. I wos worried, I wos, that we were all fucked up rightly," and humming he turned and went up to his portacabin.

John Devine, Mac Goldrick and Mac Faul were standing there doing nothing, not even talking to each other.

"Best to get some work on and work to the usual time so as to leave no suspicions behind," Mac Bearta said to them, all rushed to get some shape of work on, except John Devine and wisely Mac Bearta left him alone.

In the end of the day the only man that really matters is the man that gets the work done, were stupider words ever uttered, the last man that mattered was the fool that got the work done, for he could just be murdered over nothing much at all and what happens, his so-called workmates conspire to cover up the murder and let the murderer go free automatically.

"Bad days work that, John," said Pakie Mac Grath standing beside John Devine for a moment and shaking his head, "if only a man had the cop on to have done his school work properly when he had the chance and got to do something proper in life, anything but this bloody shit."

John Devine didn't answer him, as he remembered the person that seemed most anxious to cover it up in the first place, he also noted Mac Grath was sweating and in John's experience this was a first, so maybe this strange unpleasant sensation of sweating would be some penalty on Mac Grath for his actions, for he was highly unlikely to suffer any other.

The bolowan O'Meara was doing a bit of sweeping up and repeating his old mantra, "sure, I don't know what everybody is getting so excited about; sure didn't the likes of it often happen back in the fifties, sure don't I know wasn't I there."

Mac Faul and Mac Goldrick were doing a bit of cleaning up, as it was the only work they were fit to do in their present state of mind. Pakie Mac Grath, Cawley and Mac Namee were toiling hard putting up a shutter for a concrete beam and for once, no effort was being spared.

John Cormac and Mac Bearta were deep in conversation.

"Get some of the boys to go into the 'rat's' place, first thing this evening and clean it out," said John Cormac.

"No, keep the witnesses to this event as far away as possible from anything to do with the 'rat', if someone from this site was recognised now or later on, going into the 'rat's' place and he was reported missing, it would immediately point to something untoward going on, especially as no one was ever around at the 'rat's' place before.

I'll get two boys to come down and clean it out and deliberately make it look as though he cleared out voluntarily, you know some old or broken stuff left, a rough tidy up of the room. I know two boys from Luton who'll come down this evening about ten when everyone is either in the pub or in bed and they'll clean it out properly.

I'll tell them that a lad I know has to make a quick exit from the country on account he decked some cops or suchlike, he's a mate of mine so I want his stuff gathered up carefully, especially anything like a passport and given to me, I suppose if they find money, they'll have to be let keep it but they can be relied upon to give up everything else, they have good heads on them and they'll do a good job but it will cost about three hundred pounds."

"Right, I'll get another five hundred from the site agent. What else do we need to do."

"There is to be no comment made even in private by anyone and this has to be emphasised to all, one way to go about that is to stress the fact that they are all now accessories to murder, now even if they played no part in the disposal of the body or anything else, they also did not inform the authorities which they should have."

"This could be a handle on them," said John Cormac smiling at the thought of having a handle on someone like John Devine, "but what about the pub, men will talk in drink."

"This is Wednesday so nobody is to go to the pub for a couple of nights, by then say Friday we should have made the 'Pig' part of our 'manor' as the English say, then we can control what is said or certainly what comes out of the pub; if someone blubs, we can cover it by saying that he's a fool that always going on like that or say that there's some attempt to bad mouth the subbie.

We'll get the landlord to co-operate and if someone does talk then it must be driven in to them, that they are cutting their own throats and everybody else's, the point to emphasise is that they are letting down the whole crew, rather than just the subbie, at any rate that's the best we can do. Therefore, from now on until we can trust men, the 'Pig' is the only place they can drink."

"And we decide how long until we can trust the men," John Cormac finished his thinking for him.

This turn of events would also help in their attempts to make the 'Pig' their pub, a definite number of drinkers every night would be very welcome to the governor of the 'Pig'. Things were beginning to look up.

"What if someone comes here asking for him," asked John Cormac.

"We haven't seen him for the last few days, as casual as all that. Then we'll ask them, if they have seen him because we're wondering if he's jacked and meanwhile, we're a man down. Keep as cool and non-committed as possible, further questions should be answered by short answers or even shrugs, don't know, didn't come in, that sort of thing, in the end of the day it's just a man who jacked and during this time your attention should return to the work as though you're anxious to get back to it, above all nothing unusual, don't avoid the questions but don't elaborate."

"What of Devine."

"Sympathise as much as possible with him. Emphasise as much as possible how you would have stopped it if you were here. Make out your sorry for ever having a good family man like him in that position."

They went over to John Devine who was leaning up against the scaffold doing nothing. John Cormac shook his head and looked very downcast and went on, "bad days work that, John, a bad day's work all told; if only I had been here it wouldn't have happened."

"You couldn't afford to let it happen even from the point of view of business," interjected Mac Bearta in response to the clearly sceptical look that John Devine was giving John Cormac.

"And more than that I want sweat not blood on my jobs. I want no truck with anything like that," replied John Cormac fervently. "I'm sorry in all truth, John for ever bringing a good family man like you on to this job here," went on John Cormac shaking his head, "what sort of thick bollixes are them other lads anyways to allow such a thing to happen, in front of their face, as soon as I can I'll street a few of them."

"Not too fast, you have to allow things to settle down first," replied Mac Bearta.

John Devine didn't reply.

"Any man going home to a family after seeing that, I must try and give you a shift or something, to try in some way to make it up to you, you see I feel very bad about the whole thing. I'll never know if I was just better to call the police," said John Cormac shaking his head.

"Well, the lads would be fucked and in all honesty, what were the police liable to do," said Mac Bearta when John Devine still gave no answer.

"Double fuck the lads, they'd be in a lot less trouble if only they had intervened. How in the name of the living fuck, did they not think things were serious, when a chisel was produced, just how thick are the fuckers anyways," went on John Cormac, "but I suppose you're right about the police, still it's not a thing I'm happy about at all."

More to get rid of him than anything else John Devine nodded as though in agreement. He still knew who would lose the most money if the police were called and he knew that and that alone was the salient fact, theatrically manipulated vote notwithstanding. The facts were simple, a man was murdered and due to the fact that it would cost the boss money, not one thing in hell was going to be done about it.

What exactly was a man's life worth; he again recalled his grandfather's motto; in the end of the day, the only man that counts is the man that does the work and if he's murdered he'll be thrown into a hole just like a rat, a real rat, as long as the boss and his so-called workmates think they can get away with it; in the end of the day the only man that counts is the man who does the work, was greater shite ever talked.

John Cormac and Mac Bearta moved away satisfied that they had things going the way they wanted. They went over to the two youngsters, Mac Faul and Mac Goldrick who were near each other; a mixture of soft soap and street cred and to a small degree apportioning blame was the formula that was thought most useful approach to use here.

"This London can be a tough place at times, but I tell you straight up that I never wanted anything like this to happen. Are ye completely sure that there was nothing that could be done to stop it," asked John Cormac.

"I was down in the big trench with John Devine the whole time, you can ask him if you doubt me," replied Mac Faul.

"I shouted at them to stop; I didn't think it'd go anyways as far as it did," answered Mac Goldrick.

"It's a great loss that you didn't do something more than shout young Mac Goldrick," said Mac Bearta.

"Well, you know well that a youngster interfering is not liked," answered Mac Goldrick.

"There's times when you heed that and times you do not," came back Mac Bearta.

"It's late now, isn't it," said John Cormac.

"If any of you come across Mac Elvinney let me know at once and I'll put a stop to his murderous ways. Now, there are a number of further things to be done, if anyone talks they will fuck everybody else up especially those that were on site at the time of the murder, myself or Mac Bearta here were not here. You have to be especially careful in drink, now there is a certain pub in Kilburn where I have control and if by chance someone slips up, then in all likelihood it can be covered up; there simply isn't any other pub that it's safe to go into for at least the time being.

We have to be guarded in all things, you'll have to stay on the job for a while to maintain the cover of normality, otherwise things will slip out and then, all will be finished. I would not like to be in jail with a load of other men that I caused to go to jail.

You might find this harsh but this is what we must do, remember you voted for it, I voted against, but I still bowed to your wishes, though as subbie I didn't have to and in all truth, I'm still very uncertain, that I did the right thing; but remember I didn't let you down, now it's your turn to return the favour and not let me down.

Always remember I was on another site when the murder happened. There'll be other things but that'll do for now."

The site agent appeared, beaming now and winked at John Cormac, "tough one that but we got over it, we did," he said rubbing his hands together, "but what is it they say, when the going gets tough, the tough gets going "

"There's a few hundred more that will have to be come up with to cover this up fully," said John Cormac.

"Fuck me, ain't this bill ever going to stop rising," protested the site agent.

"A few hundred did I say, I meant a thousand," said John Cormac, "and if there's any problem with that, well my conscience already troubling me about the whole affair, I could always say that you coerced me into it and in a moment of shock and weakness I gave in. I was provably on another site at the time it happened," replied John Cormac.

The site agent grew red in the face and appeared to swell and he muttered a few incoherent words and turned and marched back to his portacabin. Mac Bearta went over to the other men and informed them about the arrangement about the pub and the bar on using other pubs. Martin Mac Donogh proffered to try it that night, but Mac Bearta vetoed this, if Martin Mac Donogh didn't drink there during the week normally then he was not to start tonight, everything must be an ordinary, as was possible, in every way.

Martin would have to go on the dry for the next couple of nights, there was a bleak look on Martin's face as he acceded to this and staying dry was probably the highest price that Martin would have to pay. There was a slightly more muted but similar reaction from Cawley, Mac Namee and Mac Grath.

"Bastard this too," said Pete Mac Namee with a theatrical sigh.

"Yes letting a man get murdered in front of you can disrupt the old social life, 'tis a bastard surely," said Mac Bearta drily.

"I wonder what would your reaction be to the disruption of your social life, of a few years in jail," came in John Cormac to reinforce the point.

They didn't say anything to the bolowan O'Meara as it was considered unnecessary, as he was so unreliable and was constantly going around with some long tale or the other, he'd talk surely, but such was his reputation as a bolowan and so limited was his social round, for only a few pubs would serve him, that no one, that was likely to listen to him, would pass any heed of him.

Home time came after a long, long time. The boys were gathered together in the changing room and the opportunity was taken to give a final pep talk.

"Remember, no one utters anything to anyone, it's simple the die is cast," said Mac Bearta.

"And you cast it," came in John Cormac.

"You must not talk to anyone, not your mates, drinking buddies, wives, children, parents, the priest, not, no one or we're all fucked and rightly fucked at that and in all fairness if a man does talk, the others have a right to make him pay and pay dearly," went on Mac Bearta.

"That's easy I don't speak to the wife anyways," said Martin Mac Donogh, uttering the only few truthful words that he spoke that day.

"This is a slightly serious business," said John Cormac drily, "and once again if that piece of filth Mac Elvinney is seen, I'll put a definite stop to his murderous career."

With that they departed the site.

"Am I glad that that day is over," said Pete Mac Namee to John Devine; he didn't get any response, there was simply no response that John Devine could make.

Chapter 7

Liam Mac Faul got on the tube at bank station to go to North Acton where he rented a room or rather half a room with a mate of his from at home. A number of other workmen also got on the tube at this station and as time went on, it was obvious that something had riled them. Living now on eggshells and wary of everything Liam listened in and to his horror recognised what they were on about.

"What was all that safety bullshit on about, we should have red and white stripped plastic sheeting wrapped about the scaffolding nearest us."

"And we should have the red and white sheeting wrapped around the legs of the tripod; why the tripod is painted orange anyways as is all Concretation machinery; how is red and white sheeting going to make it more visible"

"Ya and ya need bollards around the piling rig; why there is nearly no one else on site but ourselves for one thing?"

"Ya and we had to go down the other side of Cheapside to hear it. What were they on about ' the facilities weren't right, what facilities are needed to hear a lecture especially a load of bullshit and what's different in Cheapside, anyways a portacabin is a portacabin."

"Ya would swear there was something going on."

Liam Mac Faul nearly fainted, but he found a hand on his arm it was Mac Grath. It appeared he was in the same carriage and had witnessed Mac Faul's reaction and felt compelled to intervene.

"Let's get off," he said to Liam and they got off at Oxford Circus station.

"What's up?" he asked Liam in a none too friendly manner.

"They were talking about their site and why they had to leave in the middle of the day; you know, the one the 'em, eh, err is on," said Liam.

"Shh, coincidence, that's all. Can you be relied on sonny, that's all I'm worried about," said Mac Grath in a menacing tone.

"Why should I be different than anyone else, any less reliable," replied Liam; he also straightened out to his full height which in close quarters showed that he had quite an advantage over Mac Grath.

This seemed to give Mac Grath some pause, "look son, you'll go to jail like everybody else if this gets out and you'll find it harder. I, at least, will probably know someone in there, I'm in England long enough but who will you know that are liable to be of any help to you. I'm just concerned about you, that's all," said Mac Grath.

"I won't talk it's just that I didn't think that things like that happened here," he replied.

This appeared to assuage Mac Grath.

"This can be one right though old town, at times," he said.

"I still don't know why nobody intervened, how things were let go until, well, you know," said Liam.

"Shh, we just didn't cop what was going on, in time to do anything. The important thing now is to keep the head and keep stumm. You get off in North Acton, don't you; I'll go that far with you, I'm just in Shepherds Bush," said Mac Grath.

Somehow the 'vibes' given off by Mac Grath were such that while standing beside him on the tube, Liam felt it best to stretch himself out to his full height and tense up his muscles to make himself as large and physically formidable as possible, despite the considerable advantage he had at any time over Mac Grath in that line and also, despite the fact that Mac Grath did nothing but whisper to him that he was only trying to help him; there was just something about Pakie Mac Grath that evening.

Cawley, Mac Namee and Martin Mac Donogh went home to a dry evening for a change; this was especially trying for Martin Mac Donogh who had to subsist on a bag of chips in silence and without any diversion, like a television in his brother's garden shed; his brother's wife had banned him from the house, except for use of the toilet, when the full extent of the damage he'd done to his daughter became known.

Neither Mac Goldrick or Mac Faul could eat or sleep that night. John Devine couldn't go home that night until he was sure his children would be in bed and he could not sleep that night either. In contrast to all this, John Cormac had a very good night; he went with Mac Bearta to the 'Pig' to finalise the deal with the governor.

Originally the deal was that John Cormac would pay wages there and 'hold court' there during the weekend, this would mean that men that wanted to see him over work or possibly, if fairly unlikely, seek work from him or they wanted to discuss something with him about work or whatever, they would come to the 'Pig' and this would increase the business of the pub. The governor could expect between ten and fifteen men one or two nights of the week and a few on other nights.

In return for this the governor would cash cheques for him and his men and give him some credit up to one thousand pounds and of course, a few free drinks. They would also look after him in the event of hassle, which in John Cormac's case and with his 'business model' was a fairly likely event.

The new deal was different, there would be up to twenty men guaranteed a couple of nights a week and almost certainly ten men every night and furthermore, these would be good drinkers; this was something that the 'Pig badly needed.

To secure these benefits, the price would change, cheques cashed as before; the tariff the pub charged would remain the same at eight percent, but John Cormac would get one per cent back; furthermore, John Cormac would get up to five thousand pounds credit, also the pub would back up John Cormac if there was any hassle but would also monitor the customers to see no one was bad mouthing John Cormac.

This would be easily tested by sending in the odd strangers with instructions to deliberately run down John Cormac and see if it was reported back, if not, then the pub was not keeping its part of the deal and in the case of really serious hassle, a distinct possibility given recent events though no one at the pub would know that, then the pub would provide a place of refuge for John Cormac; and on top of all that a few free drinks.

The sweetener was that John Cormac could pretty much guarantee this arrangement for a least a year; thus, it should be worth a lot to the governor. Initially this proposal was met with refusal even a degree of amusement at the effrontery of John Cormac for making such a proposal, but they pointed out that beside themselves there was five customers in the pub that night and one was clearly a scrounger and that there was plenty of other pubs in the local vicinity that were likely to be interested in their offer; after stewing on the idea for a while, the attitude changed.

The governor needed a supporter that could bring trade in and though dubious of John Cormac there was simply no one else offering. A deal was reached with two amendments from what John Cormac was looking for, there would be a three thousand limit on the credit he would get and that tariff to the pub for cashing cheques would be the same, eight per cent but they would raise the overall tariff to nine percent and give John Cormac the extra per cent back, so this was satisfactory.

This was no bad result and after a few free pints to celebrate the covenant, he headed for home in a highly satisfied mood. John Cormac lived in a flat in Colindale that belonged to the council and on which he paid council rent on. The tenancy had been held by family that had moved abroad and John Cormac took over the rent book and paid them a thousand pounds for it as 'key money'.

For thirty-five pounds a week he got a two-bedroom ground-floor flat with a garden and good shed, in which he could and did store materials. Good old aunt Myra had arranged the whole affair. He had just one call to receive before he went to bed, about the 'rat's' digs or hole as it appeared it should have been called.

It duly came, about10 o'clock that night two men acting on instructions from Mac Bearta had entered the douse where the 'rat' had rented a room, using his keys which Mac Bearta had given them after helping John Cormac transact the deal in the pub. They searched the room carefully and they quietly gathered up his belongings and packed them into two suitcases they had brought.

They left certain items, a torn shirt and a pair of very worn trousers and an obviously broken transistor and a cracked cup and a couple of other useless odd and ends, these were stacked in a corner, they made up the bed roughly and gave a rough and ready tidy to the room.

They found eight hundred pounds in an envelope taped under a drawer in the only chest of drawers in the room, they kept this as per arrangement, plus a few pounds they found in one of the drawers and on top of the chest of drawers, they found no bankbook or book for national insurance stamps that they were especially primed to look for, in fact they found very little correspondence or documentation of any sort only a passport and 'B and I' shipping line sailing schedule and the likes of a London A to Z and a blank writing pad; theses they gathered up and returned to Mac Bearta, whose mate, now lying low in Ireland, they were given to understand they belonged to.

Finally after a check that all looked totally normal, they left the keys inside the door of the room and the room unlocked and quietly left, the night was misty and cool and there were few people about, either when they came or left and no one that gave any sign of noticing them. It all portrayed a quick quiet departure, perhaps skipping a week's rent by a tenant that was known to be dissatisfied by the accommodation, absolutely nothing surprising or unexpected.

Any belongings the 'rat' had on site were already disposed of. All was in good order therefore. John Cormac went to bed and after a day as eventful as that one, he was going to have and indeed, did enjoy a good night's sleep.

The next day started off with an examination of every man to see if they had spoken of the events of the day before. This was followed by orders that it was just not to be spoken about on site and this order would be supervised by Mac Bearta, John Cormac and the site agent.

There was a labourer from the contracting firm Hoare and Collis due that day, the agent put him off, there was a machine driver from 'tot's' firm expected that day. John Cormac put him off, the men would get a day to practice keeping stumm, any breaches would be leaped on and the perpetrator severely reprimanded; it would be expected that then men in general would join in this castigation, it all would be good training for the future.

Mac Bearta, John Cormac and the site agent prowled the site, they hid behind machinery and piles of materials ready to leap out on any breaches of the silence. Liam Mac Faul badly wanted to have some word with John Devine about the events of the day before but Devine shushed him as soon he started to speak and changed the conversation to the work. He was just in time, Mac Bearta and John Cormac were on them, questioning about what they were whispering about.

John Devine replied they were talking about the work; nevertheless, they got a lecture.

"They had all the chances they could ask for to talk yesterday."

"There could be no talking not even a casual, aside about it now."

"If it got then we are all each and every one of us fucked."

"I'd hate to see a man with three kids go to jail."

"Me and Mac Bearta were provably elsewhere, so we had nothing to answer for only we went along with you lot."

"I voted for calling the police and Mac Bearta here didn't vote. So, if ye disagreed with what was done, ye should have spoken up and voted that way, in all fairness ye got your chance."

John Devine remained silent in response to all this only nodding grimly, Mac Faul did the same. The agent got Pete Mac Namee talking quietly to Mac Grath and leaped on them. Mac Bearta and John Cormac came to his assistance and Mac Namee and Mac Grath got a totally undeserved lambasting.

"So, ye have plans to get married, have ye; well, we'll put a hole in them plans; me and Mac Bearta were away yesterday when the murder occurred, it's you that were here that will go to jail and we'll see how much marrying ye'll do then, Mac Grath. I wish to hell that I just called the police, I had little to lose."

"We were actually just talking about the pipe work."

"Oh is that right and ye had to talk about that behind ye're hand in a low voice."

"The point is we need to practice being stumm or at least you do, it's you that will be going to jail," came in Mac Bearta in support of John Cormac.

"Why in hells name didn't I call the police, sure there's rakes of men coming from Ireland every day in search of work, there's no doubt that I could replace them with better in an hour. I might lose a pittance, but what of it, the right thing would be done," carried on John Cormac.

At lunch, the break was cancelled while a pep talk was given by subbie foreman and site agent. New rules were introduced or reinforced, there was to be no drinking at any other pub but the 'Pig' in Kilburn, men could quite simply not be trusted. All cheques were to be cashed in that pub.

Men were expected to attend this pub at least once or twice a weekend, so that to some degree their efforts at keeping stumm could be monitored. This was followed by the sure and certain assertion that all Paddies who went to jail were homosexually raped, the site agent claimed to have particular knowledge of this fact.

The entire effort especially with the pub was for their benefit and a particular burthen on the unfortunate John Cormac, upon whom the trouble of arranging it all had fallen and was getting sorrier by the minute for not ringing the police.

"If only I realised the trouble that I would have to go to, to save you pack of bollixes from yourselves and I myself totally in the clear," he lamented loudly.

By the end of the day if a man had to converse with another man, he walked a distance away from him and roared his message at him. It was simply easier to do it that way, than have listen to another lambasting and description of jail rape from the boss/es. The next day was a Friday and the company's labourer and 'tot's' driver were there, so more effort was needed to see there was no slips.

The man was kept as separate as possible from the other two men; all conversation were interrupted or at least monitored. This behaviour was continued to such an extent that Martin Mac Donogh had to interfere to ask John Cormac and Mac Bearta if they wanted to draw attention to their strange behaviour and thus, give rise to suspicions that something dubious was afoot.

'Tot's' driver was hopping from one foot to another to get going early, it being a Friday evening; this would normally never be allowed but on this occasion, there was no objections, work was not the object of this day. Everybody was supposed to attend the John Cormac's 'new' pub that night and to drink plenty so their ability to hold their tongues could be monitored.

"This is the first time in my life that I ever found going to the pub a burthen," said Martin Mac Donogh from Neasden to young Mac Faul from North Acton and young Mac Goldrick from Greenford with great truthfulness as they entered the 'safe' pub.

Mac Namee and Mac Bearta and a couple of men from one of John Cormac's other sites were there already. Pakie Mac Grath and Cawley from Wembley arrived soon afterwards. The subbie himself arrived soon afterwards and as befitted a man of affairs immediately went to closed session with the governor. John Devine was still missing. He lived in Willesden and was, therefore, pretty much the nearest to the pub.

A very common and mundane conversation took place but at a surprisingly loud volume. Why comments about the delays on the tube and the heaviness of the traffic needed to be so loudly proclaimed, certainly was a mystery to the governor. John Devine was asked for. But nobody knew anything about him or his intentions.

The lads from the other site could be a threat; so, John Cormac drew them to one side, overtly to enquire about the job that they were on as he himself didn't get there very often, though the men thought he was there too often. He also took this opportunity to extol the virtues of this new pub, cheques cashed one hundred percent of the time and 'we' have a bit of a say here.

Drink was being consumed at a far slower pace than normal. Mac Faul and Mac Goldrick were looking at the same pint for over an hour, so John Cormac had to relay a message to speed up the pace, this was an instruction that few in the company had ever needed before. Finally, John Devine arrived and John Cormac rushed over to buy him a drink.

John Devine had wrestled with his conscience for hours as to whether he would come here tonight or not. He knew that if he came, he would be their creature but he also knew, the time for defiance was over and that he should have defied them back at the site.

He was ashamed that he did not; oh alright, he had a family and some of the men he knew to be little short of dangerous, if not fully dangerous but he knew that this was only an excuse; if push came to shove, he was certainly able for any of them and if young Mac Faul would back him up, as he probably would have, they would not be fit for them or at least, all of them that would be likely to actively try to stop John from bringing in the authorities would not be fit for them, but he hesitated and vacillated and in the end of the day failed, the simple fact was that the a murderer was still running free due to his weakness.

Originally, he was not going to come but what was the point, the damage was done, was it going to be undone by him not going to this pub. The safer route at this stage was to go along with them, he thought and then he felt disgusted with himself for such equivocation. John Cormac came up to him at once and ordered a pint for him and started to talk quietly to him.

"You know John the further this goes on, the more that I regret not ringing the police. However valid the arguments that the men made for not ringing the police were, the fact is a murderer still went free and that quite simply isn't good enough; and now look at all the precautions we have to take and the risks we run of somebody opening their mouth."

John Devine just nodded in response to this.

"I should have overruled them, that's what I should have done and to hell with their troubles, there was none of that my doing or my responsibility, in the end of the day it's just that I'm too soft, that's the problem," went on John Cormac.

John Devine made no response to that.

"Not yourself now but I'll have to tighten things up considerably with that lot, more work and less time to go fighting," continued on John Cormac.

This also got no response and John Cormac was getting worried; John Devine would be a big loss, so John Cormac was afraid to put any pressure on him; all he could do was to try a mix of flattery and finding common ground with him, neither was responsible for the murder but they had to stick with the lads was the message he wanted to get across, stick with them, yes but be apart on moral grounds.

"If you knew about it of course it would be different" went on John Cormac, "I'll see to it you have a number with me as long as possible and if all fails here and who knows when you see what's going on, it might well, I'll see to it you have a job with 'boy' O'Malley but don't tell anyone else, for I won't do the same for them."

John Devine nodded appreciably and felt constrained to say, "I suppose it just one of these things that just happen."

Permanent work was not to be sneezed at in the building trade, especially to one with a family. This at least was the excuse that John Devine made to himself, that and it was too late to do anything now anyways but only time would tell if such excuses were adequate. John Cormac turned away, pleased now that he was making progress because John Devine was necessary to get the work done.

John Cormac went back to the governor and said, "there ye are now, well more than twice the crowd that you'd normally get even of a Friday night. Ya can see now that I'm a man of my word."

The governor nodded in agreement and indeed with the cheques he cashed and the drink and the other few bits and pieces like cigarettes, his revenue for that night would be around double what it normally was, it was just he wanted to get in with someone better than John Cormac.

"I was stuck for three hours on the central line last August in all that heat," more or less roared Martin Mac Donogh.

"That's nothing," shouted back Jerry Cawley, "I was stuck on the northern line for seven hours three years ago and several of the people pissed themselves, including most of the women."

There was a loud burst of laughter in response to this; nobody felt able to talk in a low or even normal voice. More beer was drank but the tenseness of the situation, mitigated against its effects, there was just too much adrenalin flowing for the alcohol to take the usual effect.

Mac Grath Cawley, Mac Namee and Martin Mac Donogh stayed in a group talking loudly in the centre of the bar, John Devine was off to one side, where Mac Bearta tried to draw conversation out of him out on several subjects, work, farming in Ireland, even football to little response.

Mac Faul and Mac Goldrick stood unspeaking at either end of the company like two bookends. It was a night of discomfort and awkwardness in a place that was supposed to provide relaxation and recreation. The governor, a man experienced with anything to do with pubs, sensed something was well different about that night but he just couldn't put his finger on what it was.

He was finding out like others that one way or another John Cormac O'Mahony gave poor value for money. It finally came to an end, the loud conversations about inanities and futile attempts to have the crack, running dry. Pakie Mac Grath's comment when he got outside at the end of the night, that he would end up a teetotaller, if things continued like this reflected the thinking of nearly every man there that night.

There was a series of silent and sober departures which further puzzled the governor, when or where did he last see such a total lack of atmosphere. John Cormac however was elated, he had rarely spent a more enjoyable night in the pub; upon consultation with Mac Bearta there was not a slip of a hint of a slip all night, things were simply looking better and better.

The way things were now looking, he was going to gain control of a pub; on top of all the extra money he would make, it was win-win all the ways. Saturday night came and if he was honest the governor would not have expected any of them back, given the strained and clearly unnatural atmosphere of the night before but they all came back with the exception of John Devine who claimed he always went out with the wife on a Saturday night and that it would look strange if he done anything different this Saturday night.

The very fact that he had to make this excuse to John Cormac on Saturday morning just showed the hold they were getting on him and it registered as a further mark of shame with him. Ultra-safe subjects only were discussed, the tube, the traffic, the weather were the principal topics of conversation. They came off to the landlord as loud and lifeless, was the only thing in your life the tube, something so exciting to you that you had to spend the whole night in the pub roaring about it.

Later in the night he even ventured to remark to John Cormac that they were too loud, an instruction was given to tone things down and the din subsided very quickly.

"And didn't I hand him the shovel and didn't he take the wrong end and pointed the handle not the blade at the ground," this resulted in a prolonged roar of laughter, as though it was quiet simply the best joke that ever was told.

The word the governor was beginning to think about was unnatural. Mac Goldrick and Mac Faul were again standing at either end of the company like two goal posts, saying nothing and partaking in no ways in the conversation, until the creeping Jesus Martin Mac Donogh hinted to them that they were expected to participate a bit more enthusiastically or otherwise things would look strange. Mac Goldrick made some attempt, Mac Faul couldn't.

Eventually, another strained unenjoyable night came to an end and despite the fact there was a fair amount of drink taken that night, even John Cormac bought a round, nobody got drunk or merry. Men left quickly and silently like they were leaving the shift, which in many ways was exactly what they were doing. Sunday morning came and the exact same state of affairs but a bit quieter, which was just as well as Sunday morning was the only time the 'Pig' got a good custom, there'd even be the odd Englishmen and a few women present.

The new customers were in a corner where they kept to themselves, again making inane conversation about virtually nothing. John Devine was not there, he went to mass with his wife and family on a Sunday morning. When they heard this excuse, several others began to give some thought to religion; in some cases, this was the first time, in a very long time, that their thoughts turned that direction, so enjoyable was their time in John Cormac's pub.

When 3 o'clock came they departed quietly and soberly, unlike so many other customers of the 'Pig', especially of a Sunday morning. The advantages to these new customers were that they were very well behaved and caused no trouble, nor did they linger and try to get more drink after time, like the 'Pig's' other customers, thought the governor but out from that he couldn't fathom them at all, they were like someone acting in a play or some such, it just was not right.

Young Mac Faul just couldn't make that drear company Sunday night, he just wasn't fit to stick it, he'd rather spend the night out in the rain in the park. On Monday morning, he told John Cormac that he had a bad head for drink and wouldn't be able to work right if he went out drinking Sunday night as well as Sunday morning; as John Cormac relied on him to get the work done, he had no alternative but to accept this; there was still a lecture, now whispered, about keeping stumm.

The same dreary charade took place that Sunday night, the men were dutiful and played their part, false crack and ultra-banal conversation all the ways; the landlord was still puzzled and to a degree wary and even disturbed, but the money was coming in and if he was to remain a pub governor, which was his life's ambition, then he had to accept this strange gang of customers and their clearly dodgy boss.

From John Cormac's point of view all went well, indeed very well, an entire weekend had passed and there were no slips, everybody or nearly everybody attended the pub that could be expected to attend and the pub was in his grasp; all in all, an excellent weekend. There was a little lingering wariness about John Devine, he would have to be treated with caution, an extra shift could easily be afforded to help assuage him.

Taken in full, however the results were first class and real hopes were springing up in John Cormac that he really would get away with the whole affair, something he really couldn't quite believe up until now.

He had followed the most advantageous way he could all during the incident, survival not profit was his initial ambition but now everything was evolving into a much more advantageous position in every respect; profit, ancillary benefits like the pub, above all control, excellent; just as long as nobody let the cat out of the bag.

Chapter 8

A new week began and as expected, a forcible reminder of the situation and what was expected from everybody, was made to all. A new week meant a more protracted period of consideration of the events of the week before, especially given the few sober nights spent in the pub.

Now back at the seat of the action, after the change in environment, when some contemplation could take place, what did men think. To start with however, contemplation was not facilitated, as a significantly higher pace was required to make up for the absence of two men.

Furthermore, the chance of saving some money by not allowing the men time to think or most certainly talk, in case that they endangered themselves was not lost on either John Cormac or Mac Bearta, so a yet greater pace still was sought for their own benefit. But thought was only delayed not stopped and like a stream that's dammed, the higher the water when the dam breaks, the bigger the shock.

Towards the middle of the week, men asked themselves, if that really did happen last week and when the fact impinged on them that it did, the jolt was greater. A man, a working man akin to themselves was murdered on this site and nothing had been done about it; they themselves had covered it up or at the very least done nothing to stop it being covered up, they were, each and every one of them accessories to murder, it was as simple and straightforward as all that.

Reality has its own schedule, but it is inexorable, with time it ever asserts itself. This it did to everyman and each man reacted differently. Jerry Cawley and Pete Mac Namee were coming to the perception that they were men to be reckoned with after all: that they were hard men, the murder of a man didn't faze them in any way and they were well fit to clean up the mess afterwards, they were the hard boys surely, they were up for anything.

John Devine was more and more disheartened as time went by, as the full reality of what had taken place sunk in. His mantra in life, 'the only man who counts is the man who does the work, without him all is nothing' was bust, was it the workers like the 'rat' that counted on this site.

His idea of himself was a reasonably good, decent workingman and family man, leading a pretty proper and correct life; but where was that idea now, that he was an accessory to murder. Would he let his little girl know that she was reared on the basis of an enterprise that facilitated murder, some day? Where in the name of hell was he going and where was he going to bring his family: to what sort of destination, morally, legally, financial etc.

Martin Mac Donogh had a rising feeling of pride at his own role in the entire affair, was he not the man at the centre of the storm and did he not handle things to perfection, maybe Mac Bearta has a place in the eventual clean-up of the mess, but he was the man on the scene when the shit had hit that proverbial fan and he had managed it with elan, the whole firm and the bosses and indeed many of the men would be destroyed only for him and him alone.

He was entitled to some decent award for such service which was beyond the call of duty; he wouldn't say anything just at the moment, he'd let things settle a bit, but then he would demand his rights, after all if it wasn't for him and him alone, how much would John Cormac have to give to anyone.

Hughie Mac Bearta was getting more and more full of himself. It had been one right tough one; in the end of the day, there was no doubt about that and he and he alone had handled it; he hadn't even been here when it had occurred but he came in, he assessed the situation, took the reins and steered the whole outfit to safety; the little dog subbie was going to pieces, the creeping Jesus hadn't a clue, only him and him alone, had the resources and mind, to rescue the situation from disaster.

A general fixers job for the likes of Paddy O Riordan should be suitable for him, he was now well fit for such a job. No more of the bloody sites or taking orders from some incompetent chancer of a dog subbie like John Cormac O'Mahony, taking orders from such an inadequate greedy little bollix was one of the most demeaning things he ever had to do.

There'd be more money and as for the work, well his hands were hardly clean now, were they. He didn't have the contacts personably but he knew enough to please those that had and that this was done by facilitating them in every way possible, he wasn't born into the club but he'd make his way there by other routes.

Jimmy Mac Goldrick was passing through a cascade of changing reactions, from shock and horror initially, to confusion and incredulity at what they were getting away with, to despair at his lot at having to work with such people, in such a place and under such conditions. Jimmy just couldn't get his head around the assertion that the police wouldn't investigate the murder properly but instead go after the men on the site, but everyone said this and even when he put a parallel enquiry to Irish people outside the site, he got the same response.

He had asked the question, if an Irishman was accused of raping a woman in a pub, he heard that the police wouldn't put any real effort in tracking down the rapist, instead they would hassle the other Irish customers in the pub and get what dirt they could on them; he was assured by more than one person that this was in fact correct.

The only conclusion he could come to was that he should go home as soon as possible and sort out the accusations against him and live there, where he could to some degree understand the system. He ventured an enquiry to Mac Bearta as to how soon he could move on.

The enquiry was met with incredulity, did he not know all the trouble and risk that they had taken on his behalf, had he not stood by while one man murdered another, all six feet of him in his prime and done nothing, how did he think the police would look upon that, did he not know that he'd be charged and convicted as an accessory and rightfully so, for what else was he? There'd be large English and black thugs raping him every night for years and if that didn't happen the boys would surely get him.

Mac Bearta himself was in the clear, he'd been elsewhere when the murder had occurred with plenty of witnesses; and as far as he was concerned they had already gone too far to cover up this mess and if they were going to desert, as thanks for the sacrifice of himself and John Cormac O'Mahony, then they were well entitled to throw the lot of them to the English police and claimed that they were coerced into co-operating.

In fact, if John Cormac O Mahony got wind of these notions, it was pretty much certain that that, that would be what he would do; did they not see how much against it he was in the first place, he even voted for calling the police. Mac Goldrick was back to square one, still very confused.

Liam Mac Faul never left a state of confusion and fear. He simply didn't know what to do or what not to do, what to say or what not to say. He lived in a state of great wariness at all times. He slept badly, he didn't trust anyone, not even the people in the house he lived in, nor John Devine. He done exercises to strengthen himself, even though he was a big strong man of twenty, in his prime. He bought books about boxing and practiced in his room and when, he could in the broken down shed in the back yard.

The other people in the house grew wary of him, why was he doing what he was doing and what was he working himself up to. He was jumpy when out and if anyone spoke to him, even a girl, he backed away from them muttering something that was usually unintelligible.

Early in the second week, John Cormac set up and gave a fearsome lecture to the crew with the help of the site agent. He couldn't believe it but it had come to his notice that some of them were thinking of deserting him, their saviour, after all he had done for them, though he himself was most provably in the clear. Had he not against all his interests and feelings made himself little better that an accessory to murder, something that they already were, for had they not stood around and cheered when one man murdered another and done nothing. And in thanks for him pulling them out of this pit of their own making, they were going to leave him their saviour in the lurch.

Well, he'd sort them out. He had any amount of proof where he was when the murder occurred and he'd simply claim that he stood to lose heavily if the details of the murder came out and that he was afraid of the men because of the bad reputations they nearly all had, so with the added shock of the event itself, he had acceded to their wishes, but that his conscience had come against him and he would turn them in. Of course, he would have to outline all the details of their bad reputations to the authorities, but so be it, he was not prepared to be made a fool of any longer.

"In the end of the day I even went as far as arranging a safe pub for ye to drink in, what in hell's name more could ye ask for."

As was becoming routine, this was capped by a bloodcurdling description of prison rape, which was the certain lot of all paddies, according to the site agent. Finally, all the men had their wages cut by a tenner a day as discipline; as John Cormac said, he was entitled to get something out of the situation as well as everybody else, especially considering the gross ingratitude they treated him with.

John Devine was given the assurance on the quiet that his wages would not be cut. There was open anger with Mac Goldrick at his stupidity for trying to leave.

"What bloody response exactly was he expecting, go to another site, go out and get drunk with the boys and blurt the whole thing out and ya thought, the boss would stand for it," said Martin Mac Donogh open-mouthedly, aghast at the entire episode of stupidity.

John Cormac was not that far from a state of ecstasy. He could manage anything, handle any situation, cope with any problem, sure he was a fecking dream; alright some of the details were sorted out by Mac Bearta and even the creeping Jesus, but it was he who was the overall manager and responsible for the mechanism that worked so well.

He took advice from the right people and he set things up properly, got the right foreman and creeping Jesus and when things went belly up in the most unexpected and serious manner, well things almost took care of themselves and the best thing of all, he was in the money big time and as a bonus he had a pub of his own as well or as good as.

John Cormac O'Mahony was proving himself a most able and a valid subbie. Enquires were made about the whereabouts of Mac Elvinney and the 'rat', by 'tot's' driver and the two laborers from the main contractors. They were met by vague uncertain statements, "don't know," "must have jacked I think," "they went someday last week, I think."

John Cormac, "they took their money and ran and left me in the lurch, ya have no idea where they are yerself."

"I don't."

"What no, well if you do happen to see them, tell them I 'd like to know why they left without giving me any warning."

"I didn't think they were mates, they were always arguing."

"Ah just raillery between mates, sure they used to drink together and everything."

With a bit of care anything could be taken care of. Hard work was the order of the day, which was lengthened by half an hour and would have been lengthened by an hour if the site agent hadn't vetoed it, he had sacrificed enough to cover up the crime, he wasn't going to sacrifice his social life as well.

Another week passed and this regime became de rigueur, plenty of hard work and as 'relaxation' a few regimented guarded nights in the pub making false crack and insipid conversation. There was no relaxation or relief even in a place like the pub, where such was to be expected.

John Devine was failing, it was clearly noticeable during the second week. John Cormac did actually come up with the extra shift for him as encouragement but it had no effect. Liam Mac Faul was becoming more and more jumpy, he had taken to jogging for a half an hour every morning before work, as well increasing the exercising he was at in his room, as a result of this his housemates were becoming ever more wary of him.

Going home one evening a drunk man pushed into him, either by accident or through belligerence with too much drink, he struck him as hard as he could knocking him out cold, he then ran home and avoided that route after that. He was rightly spooked, the only person that he could have talked to was John Devine but he was silent and struggling with demons of his own.

If he was a small or weak man, fear or trepidation would have been diagnosed in him by his housemates, but in a big strong young man clearly over six feet, his activities were considered dodgy at best, possibly even insane. He was without succour or relief and had no experience or even proper education to fall back on to comprehend what had happened, he simply couldn't get to grips with the situation.

Was murder not wrong, was it not a crime, why would the police not want to solve a crime, what was so different between the ways things did actually work and the ways they were supposed to work. He only wanted to work, now what was going on, what had he got himself into. A month passed since the incident and work, despite less men on the job was progressing well.

Cawley Mac Grath and Mac Namee were actually working hard and they were not amused, but there was nothing they could do about it. Mac Goldrick and Mac Faul were steaming manfully into the work, the goal being the finish of this job, so they could leave this accursed place as quickly as possible. John Devine was still failing, he was still giving a fairly good performance, but only to keep up with Mac Faul.

The bolowan O'Meara was lurching along complaining about the work and the fact he only got fifteen pounds a day, John Cormac gave him a good swift kick up in the arse in response to his complaint. Mac Bearta and more especially John Cormac were greatly pleased at the progress being made on the work.

When at the end of the month Cawley and Mac Namee ventured to complain about the pressure of work, Mac Bearta said he realised that they were under pressure, but that he just couldn't risk taking another man on, giving what had happened.

He went on, "look at it this way, it's better than being in jail especially for a Paddy," neither Cawley nor Mac Namee were over sure about that at this stage. When John Cormac heard about these ungrateful remarks, he ensured that the work rate was increased even further and delivered yet another lecture on gratitude and homosexual rape in prison.

He tried to cut the wages still further but even Mac Bearta could see that that was going too far. The false crack, insipid conversation and sober night drinking in the 'go to' pub of the moment further increased their misery. Towards the end of the month, certainly Mac Faul, Mac Goldrick and John Devine were beginning to doubt if they could hang on to their sanity.

Mac Faul for instance, now ran two miles every morning and did a half hour of exercise and at least an hour every evening. He was beginning to look like a prize fighter; the people of the house he lived in, were now greatly wary of him and took pains to avoid him. The fellow who shared the room with him left, though he couldn't really afford to, but Liam Mac Faul was getting too strange and he feared dangerous; the exercise, the jumpiness, the long periods of silence, it was just not right, not right by half.

The site agent came with nearly everything that he agreed to come up with. The pace at which the job was moving also meant that it looked increasingly likely that the job would finished earlier than expected and this would mean less outgoings from John Cormac and thus increased profit, it now looked likely that John Cormac could come out of the job with twenty thousand profit, instead of the up to twenty thousand loss that he was expecting; things could hardly be better.

There was now a great divide between the men who were each nearing despair in their own particular way and the bosses that were elated in accordance with how much they had to gain. Hovering in the middle but getting ever nearer the men was the creeping Jesus Martin Mac Donogh; originally he was prideful in how he had handled the situation, he was now coming to the realisation that his efforts would go unrewarded.

The one hint he had made to John Cormac was answered by the comment, that he would be a lot more willing to pay a bonus if he, the creeping Jesus, had done 'his duty' and had broken up the fight in the first place, wasn't he the one to boast that he could handle the men, well how come he failed so disastrously on that occasion. The man without who's efforts and quick thinking the whole edifice would have collapsed was now going to be hammered with the rest of the men, instead of being rewarded as he most richly deserved.

Yet another fibre of bitterness entered a bitter man's constitution. May turned to June and the same regime continued, plenty of hard work if anything increasing in pace, even 'tot's' driver who was only there occasionally was beginning to complain about the pressure of work; this was then regularly followed by a regimented evening in the pub where men were finding it ever harder to make merry or as should be said, pretend to make merry.

The landlord was getting ever more puzzled by this solemn, sober even sorrowful nights boozing. He simply didn't understand it, it was just not natural. John Cormac was getting ever more pleased with himself. He had control now of all the men, of the pub and of the site agent and that was key.

The best thing of all was that, over two months had passed by and not a word had leaked, not a jitter. John Cormac was now beginning to wonder if he had underrated himself, how many could manage such a thing? Maybe he had it in him to be a real big timer, a Paddy O'Riordan, a Murphy, would the situation he had handled or at least managed overall, not test even those sort of men. Could it ever be that he was a man of legend, a man that someday everybody in both London and Ireland would be talking about.

Mac Bearta was also increasingly feeling proud at how well things had gone, all his work, all his thinking; surely he was worthy of something more than John Cormac as an employer. The creeping Jesus was truly pissed off, when he finally did press his claim for something from John Cormac even the tenner that was cut from his wages earlier on, his answer was a threat from John Cormac to give him a kick up in the arse just like he gave the 'bolowan O'Meara'.

The same sorry regime continued on, hard work and no play for the pub was more a place of penance than relaxation. More than one man that had revelled in the row was now wishing he had broken up the fight instead. Cawley and Mac Namee felt they were harder men, which was important to them surely but the work and conditions were making them wish, they had found another way of proving this.

John Devine was continuing to fail; he was also drinking much more. He had always enjoyed three or so pints of a Monday evening, it sort of broke up the week, a few on a Friday night and out with the wife on Saturday night, maybe a couple a Sunday morning if he was doing nothing with the wife or family or about his house. This had been his usual habit for years, but now it had changed, he had seven of eight of a Monday night, another heavy session on Wednesday night, a heavier bout on a Friday and Saturday night in the 'new pub' and a Sunday night session had also being added to the normal routine.

His wife noticed and worried about it, but he claimed nothing was worrying him when she asked; the heavier drinking, he claimed was trying to 'get in' with the new crowd he was working for, a crowd he had once disdained and claimed he only tolerated to please 'boy' O'Malley, who had asked him to go to them as a favour. The silences, he said he was just thinking things over, what things; oh just things in general, these answer's in no way satisfied her, but she couldn't think of anything else to do.

Liam Mac Faul could now be easily mistaken for a prize fighter. The training he went in for, the moroseness as though he was always contemplating a future opponent, as well as his unfriendliness and avoidance of others, as though he was constantly mentally embattled, which of course he was but through fear not belligerence alienated others, even his workmates though no gilded saints themselves, left him alone.

He was also, now the best worker, a silent powerful automaton. Mac Goldrick was still at sea; he simply didn't know up from down. The only hope he had was that the job would soon end and he could leave England for good; he'd go home to Ireland and somehow, straighten out the mess with John Jack Keirns and his son. He had actually got witnesses to his innocence and when he thought over it, he couldn't believe that he was so stupid as to run in the first place, what else could he have expected to achieve but to draw suspicion on himself.

He planned and plotted how he would affect his return and establish his innocence; in his brighter moments he told himself it'd all work out and he might even try for the guards again; he certainly had experience of criminality, that he could never have had if he stayed in Ireland, did such things also happen in Ireland? It was an interesting question for a 'would be guard'.

The 'bolowan' O'Meara told the full story from the first night in every pub he went in to and he repeatedly it regularly, but no one believed it given the source. His old side kick the 'ferret' Mac Art did, however, have a moment of doubt as to the invalidity of the story, it was when the 'bolowan' actually bought him a pint and after calling for it to be put in a safe as a thing of unique value, the likes of which was never seen on this earth before, a pint actually bought for someone else by the 'bolowan'.

Jiminin O'Meara, the 'ferret' went on to think about it, buying a pint for someone else was not just Jimmy's style, not his style at all, why the 'ferret' knew him coming on forty years and in all that time, he never bought him or anyone else a pint or at least not that he could remember.

Could it ever be that something ever did happen, rumours of such things happening were often in circulation and he knew that some of the time, such things really did happen, but the more he thought about it, the more he came back to the source and you couldn't get a less reliable source than the 'bolowan' O'Meara, so eventually he dismissed it as nonsense.

As for Jimmy O'Meara himself, he was in first class mood, rarely better; in fact, they were laughing at the 'bolowan' little Jiminin O'Meara, well little Jiminin was still around, wasn't he and where was the 'rat', the 'rat' that knew everything and was a very smart man.

"Are you a bolowan for real as well as in name," "how many years are you on a building site anyways and you still don't know anything," "how come in the name of fuck is it that you don't know what a sheet a ply is," "just how thick exactly are you bolowan" and the rest, but where was this smart 'rat' now and where was little Jiminin the 'bolowan', who was it, that was sitting down enjoying a pint and who was not.

All these great men he knew over the years, that knew everything, well where were they now and where was little Jiminin the bolowan ?

Chapter 9

All things must finally come to an end, but the worse that that thing is the slower that end appears to come. The end of the job seemed to come very slowly indeed, even though it finished a month before it was scheduled to; it ended in late July not late August as was planned.

This generated a payoff of five grand for John Cormac and he could hardly be more pleased. Though he had to give a bonus of five grand extra to Mac Bearta for his work in taking care of things, he would still make a profit of over twenty grand, over forty grand more than he had expected. Truly he was a man to be reckoned with.

The site agent had as expected tried to stop John Cormac from getting more work with the firm, with the exception of the promised day work on that site. John Cormac in the site agent's office and in his presence lifted his phone and rang his uncle George and he then stated that he was a senior police officer and he wanted to assay the Moorgate site for a suspected body dump.

George Jenkins guessing from the accent that it wasn't the police, asked what the hell was going on. John Cormac explained to him that the agent, who was his protégée and nephew was trying to refuse him more work despite all he, John Cormac, had done for him; would not his nephew, certainly and possibly himself, be in jail this day, if it were not for his actions, it was scarcely believable, well he'd sort them out.

The upshot of it was that John Cormac ended up starting on a new job, despite another and more able and experienced subbie already being there; he was thrown off for lack of quality to his work, a first for this particular subbie though he had worked for this firm for over twelve years and John Cormac was the man selected to replace him. This added even more sugar to the dish, as there was quite simply nothing equal to keeping another fellow out, especially a better one.

For a start there was only place for three men on the new site, Mac Bearta and the creeping Jesus Martin Mac Donogh because he couldn't be let go as there was no replacement for him and John Devine as someone was needed that could do some work. Jerry Cawley and Pete Mc Namee and Pakie Mac Grath were to wait on that site doing some snagging and cleaning up, they would be joined by a man from the London Wall site as they were reducing the number of men on that site and there would be another man going on to that site soon as per agreement.

The 'bolowan' O'Meara, Liam Mac Faul and Jimmy Mac Goldrick, had nothing immediate to go to and were 'let go' but told to keep in touch and not to work for anyone else.

"What are we supposed to live on," asked Jimmy Mac Goldrick.

"There's free grub and accommodation in jail and a welcome there for those that are accessories to murder," answered John Cormac.

Nobody else would take on the 'bolowan' O'Meara so he could be picked up when needed. Liam Mac Faul asked John Devine what he could do and finally John Devine drew himself far enough out of his own morass of despair and self-condemnation to give Liam a valid excuse to go home.

He was to say that he had not being at home for eighteen months, this was not true he had been at home at Christmas and had been getting letters from at home enquiring as to why he wasn't coming home for a visit; of late, these letters had become somewhat frantic and his family claimed they were getting so worried that they would ask some or all of his three uncles that lived in Birmingham to come down and investigate; one uncle was a pub governor and another had a few muck away trucks.

When John Cormac resolutely refused him permission to go home, he told him this story. Fearing the intrusion of men of substance into his affairs, he reluctantly gave permission for a short break but added strong warnings about keeping stumm, it was no good him protesting that he had seen nothing; how was John Cormac who certainly wasn't there to know one way or another.

The fact was a man was murdered while he was on site and nothing was done about it; therefore, he too was an accessory to murder, there was also the fact that he'd bugger up the rest of the boys rightly if it came out and some of the would get him, no matter how big he was.

When Jimmy Mac Goldrick heard this idea he formulated his own plan based on this method, but only roughly based on this method, because if it was an exact copy, John Cormac would see through it. The idea in the back of his mind about joining the guards gave him an idea for twist in the method that Liam Mac Faul had used, that should cover the fact it was a copy of Liam's idea.

First he asked John Cormac if he could go home for a break.

"Er, excuse me or am I dreaming or did a man get murdered on this site while you, a big strong man, stood around enjoying it," went John Cormac in reply.

"I wasn't enjoying it," protested Jimmy.

"Well, why didn't you break up the fight and as for your claims that you shouted for them to stop; well, for one, how do I know what you did, as I certainly wasn't here and for two, it was hardly enough, now was it?" replied John Cormac.

Jimmy then stated that he had been receiving a lot of letters from at home, about when he was going to come home and this had reached such an extent that his uncle who was a guard stationed in a town near where John Cormac came from and at least knew of John Cormac father, was talking of going to see John Cormac's father and enquiring about his son's employee.

For more than one reason, this stumped John Cormac good and proper and won for Jimmy Mac Goldrick a reprieve for a short break and upon Jimmy's protestations that his family wouldn't like this, a break of two weeks. Bloodcurdling threats of jail and jail rape and how the boys would get him if he talked followed, but John Cormac had backed down and it didn't please him one little bit. When these men didn't appear the following Friday night in the pub, it displeased him more but for the moment, he was stumped.

Jimmy Mac Goldrick had long planned his return and what actions he would take so that he never returned to this place. He would first try to assess the situation at home, particularly with his own family, then he would try to settle things with the Keirns family.

If and more hopefully when he got that sorted out, then he still had a leaving cert to fall back on and he had he supposed some experience of the construction industry to fall back on, but only to be used if all else failed, he'd seen enough of construction; if all went well as he had thought before, maybe the guards, as it would be something to feel the collar of Mac Elvinney or better still of John Cormac, himself, for some reason or another, one thing was for certain, he would be apprehending a criminal.

The fictional uncle he said he had in the guards was actually based on a cousin of his mothers, whom he didn't know well enough to recognise by sight but who was to say if all went well, he might have a good reason to get to know him better. He plotted, he planned, he went back to the start and started planning again, this scenario, that scenario, what if things worked out this way or that ways, what he would do if things went wrong, then he went back to the start yet again and replanned it all from the start, one way, the other ways, the next ways, but he was not coming back to London, 'end of' as they said in England.

For over a week he plotted and planned and prepared before he finally set off for Ireland. The power that John Cormac still exerted over him was such that he didn't cancel the room, thought he thought his landlord a decent sort, he gave him two weeks rent and said, he'd be back; he was that spooked by the control that John Cormac exerted over him that he was afraid he might get wind of his permanent departure, even though as far as he knew John Cormac didn't know his landlord, reality was skewed from the normal for Jimmy Mac Goldrick, recent events made him uncertain of even reality itself.

The first point in his favour was that he was gone two years so passions must have cooled somewhat; the second point was that, he did have a witness and she or at least her family must be known to the Keirnses. Against that was the fact that John Jack Keirns was a powerful well-connected man; he didn't know if his father had applied for the council job but he certainly hadn't got it.

He would simply approach John Jack Keirns and have it out with him. How he would do this, what approach he would take, he had long planned and on the boat and the train over, he fine-tuned the plans, until he got it as good as it could be got. Realistically after it was sorted out, there would be rumours about, but they would fade out especially if he was seen in the vicinity and possibly talking to John Jack Keirns in public.

Once again, the principal thing was no more John Cormac O'Mahony. Maybe, he thought as the train neared the home he hadn't seen in so long or in what seemed so long a time, maybe there was some benefit in the whole affair, for at least now he knew what happened in the world and how things were ran and who got to run them, he understood the ways, the perils and the values of the world, better perhaps than he had ever wanted to, but maybe that would turn out to the good.

As he approached his home, he nearly broke down and had to turn back and walk up and down the road a few times to recover his composure, it was only now really that it was dawning on him, just how much of an effect the whole affair had on him. He had written a brief note to say he was calling home, just that, not how long or short his visit was to be, just that he was coming. His mother met him at the door.

"Well, Jimmy, how are you? I don't know if this is a good idea at all," she said.

"I've been gone near two years," going into the living room where his father was waiting, he just nodded at Jimmy.

"Well, I suppose a brief visit," his mother said looking at his father.

"Yes and no going out on the town or anyplace else, this affair is still being talked about," said his father.

Jimmy had prepared well for this and he answered.

"Yes and it never will, until it faced down, which is precisely what I intend to do."

"What the hell are you on about boy," said his father in a raised voice.

"Number one, I did nothing; number two, I never should have run; to do so only gave substance to the lies that I had anything got to do with the affair and there are witnesses that can testify to the fact that I did nothing, you know and number three, if it hasn't died down by this stage, then it's not going to, it will have to be killed off," he replied.

"Did you get the job with the council?" he asked his father.

"No."

"Did this have any effect."

"I doubt so, others were taken on after me, though the claimed there were no jobs available when I applied and that factory is getting very dodgy, we were on a three-day week in January and some have been let go of late."

"All the more reason that every effort should be made to stop this slander."

"Might you not make things worse," said his mother. "Mary, your sister, has done her leaving cert and is expecting good results, we're hoping she might be able to go to university and become a teacher, so we need every penny we can get."

"I should be able to give her some help if necessary," he said, he had a saved a bit over a thousand pounds and had brought it home with him, so he could afford about five hundred at a push.

"How much could you give us?" asked his father.

"Oh, near a grand if necessary."

"That won't go that far," answered his father.

"And there are two others in this house to consider," added his mother in a slightly elevated tone.

"All the more reason to get rid of this black cloud, which cannot be doing anyone in this family any good," answered Jimmy.

"What are you going to do," asked his father after some hesitation.

"There is only one thing to do, I'll go right around to John Jack Keirns and have it out with him. I'll make my case and state what witnesses I have and tell him what actually did happen and then let him put it to the test any ways he wants, anyway he likes, he can question my witnesses or he can even bring in the guards.

We see how many of these people who said I stopped people from intervening to break up the fight, will if necessary be prepared to swear to it in court, whatever he wants to do, but I'm just not prepared to live under this slander any longer. It was an atrocious mistake to leave like that in the first place, it gave substance to every one of these rumours," answered Jimmy.

"The sergeant thought it was a good idea," said his mother.

"The sergeant is more interested in an easy life and licking the arse of the likes of John Jack Keirns, which is probably how he got his job in the first place, than he is in investigating the event properly. I can just imagine him around at John Jack Keirns saying that he had cleared me out of the country as it would be difficult to make a case in court against me, which I presume it would be, given that I didn't actually do anything," answered Jimmy.

His parents didn't challenge, this showing that they were, at least to some degree, thinking the same thing.

"The point is boy that John Jack Keirns is a powerful man and he could have a widespread effect as he knows and can influence a lot of people. The old job in the factory is not a great one, but it's something to keep one going," said his father.

"That only adds more reason to put these lies to bed permanently," said Jimmy, "and what about Mary, say she does qualify as a teacher and wants to get a job locally, will there not always be this slur hovering over her. Can you imagine the children talking, did you hear what miss Mac Goldrick's brother did, if it's not gone by this stage it'll be there forever."

His parents looked at each other and said nothing, they seemed to be coming further around to his way of thinking.

"I still wonder if things are not better left the way they are, I mean things are quiet, it doesn't intrude day to day," said his mother.

"How quiet are things really mother if it still being talked about, even if it isn't being mentioned every day," answered Jimmy.

"I know but might this not only rise trouble," replied his mother.

"I'm slandered, you're all tarnished; it could have God knows what effect in the future, is that no trouble as it is," answered Jimmy.

"What precisely are you planning to do," asked his father.

"I am simply going to go to John Jack Keirns and state that I had nothing to do with the attack on his sons, I will then tell him what really happened. I will then name my witnesses, Maureen O'Driscoll and her sister Claire, that live in the near vicinity of the Keirnses and there was another mate of theirs there, Marie Lynch who I also think comes from out that direction.

All three should be able to testify that I was down the far end of the hall when the fight occurred and that even when I moved forward to see what was going on, I could get no place near the fight. If that doesn't satisfy him, I'll tell him to bring me to court where these things can be attested to under oath but one way or another, it's going to be sorted out," replied Jimmy.

I'm not convinced it'll be that easy," said his father, "for instance how are you going to explain running off to London."

"First of all, I should have never have ran. What I will say is that, I was planning to go anyways and that is why I was the dance, I was hoping to see some mates of mine, that I wouldn't see again for a while. I was only briefly outside the house that Saturday to go to the shops and I will say that I went that evening for the night sailing and never heard anything about the fight," answered Jimmy.

"Yes but the sergeant seen you here Monday morning," his mother interjected.

"True but I doubt very much that he told John Jack Keirns that he seen me or else he'd want to know why he didn't arrest me there and then; he'll just say he put pressure on the family to clear me out," answered Jimmy, he had thought it through carefully.

"Yes, but someone might have seen you about this house on Sunday or Monday, especially as talk about the fight went public," said his father.

"No from when the sergeant called on Monday morning you never let me out of the house, until I went to the station Tuesday evening in the back of the van and I see no neighbour at the station or on the train.

If by any chance I was spotted outside on Sunday and Keirns knows about it, I'll just say that I had to return as I hadn't brought my passport and people were expected to bring their passports with them for identification due to new security rules on the English side; this was due to some reaction to the Aughnacloy ambush in Northern Ireland and did actually happen at the time.

It sounds better to say that I went travelling on a Saturday evening in the middle of the weekend and arriving on a Sunday than travelling on a Tuesday and more importantly, how would I say that I hadn't heard about the fight, if I waited until Tuesday," answered Jimmy.

Jimmy had thought long and hard about the possibilities and the various stumbling blocks that could come up. His parents were still uncertain.

"What if it doesn't work. He could have an effect on your father's job, on anything" said his mother. "If things are allowed stand as they are, I'll be labelled as a thug who kicked the eye out of a lad's head and ruptured a fifteen-year-old boy, or at least assisted others to do it, for the rest of my days. I'm just not prepared to carry such a slander for the rest of my days and frankly, I'm surprised that you would expect me to," he answered.

"Yes, but that's not how things work in this country boy, people like John Jack Keirns have great power," replied his father heatedly.

"It shouldn't be that way," responded Jimmy.

"Yes, but that's the way's it is," his father replied.

"Well, he has done nothing so far," said Jimmy.

"Yes or at least nothing obvious. I didn't get the job with council but beyond that nothing happened, but that might not always be the case," his father replied.

The conversation continued thus, going back and forth over the same ground, but Jimmy was determined and eventually his parents gave in. They were not happy but could see the injustice of it all, so they acceded to his plan with misgivings. He would go over to John Jack Keirns house the following evening and with that sorted out, then some sort of a job here at home, but no more murders.

He slept well that night, the first time in a long time and late into the morning and got up and ate a good breakfast. He wandered down to the town for a while, where he met an old acquaintance or two but he refused to go for a drink with them, explaining his mission openly to them and stating this was one mission he needed as clear a head as possible for.

That afternoon he relaxed about the house, again going over the evening ahead and what to say if the conversation took a particular twist or turn. He figured the worst part to explain was the two-year delay in coming back to confront the charges; after some thought, he settled on claiming the delay was due to a sequence of events that occurred in London.

He finally settled on a plan that claimed he had trouble getting a place to stay and this caused disruption for some time, then trouble with getting good work, letters from his family simply didn't get to him and when they did get to him, he was slow in replying to them with everything else he had on; it was near Christmas before he was rightly aware of the accusations and he thought that they were just rumours and found it hard to take them seriously.

It wasn't until much later on, indeed it was coming up on the second Christmas when he was at reasonably last well settled in and had the time to go into these things, that he realised just how serious they were and as luck would have it, he was in the best paying work he ever had at the time, so he just put things off as so much time had already elapsed.

He then had a brainwave and said his family was reluctant for him to return, saying that it was better for him to let things settle down but only last night his mother had told him it was on the sergeant's recommendation, this might just serve to give one in the eye to the sergeant. He was at last satisfied that he was fully prepared, so he took a nap for an hour or so, then set off on his bicycle to see John Jack Keirns and sort the whole thing out.

He arrived at the Keirns residence about twenty minutes later, it was a fine double fronted two story house set in well-tended mature grounds; it portrayed a man of resource and status, which in an Irish context usually meant connections and influence or as it was commonly called 'the pull'. He tidied himself up and went up to the front door and rang the bell.

John Jack Keirns himself answered the door; he was a small narrowly built man with thinning hair that was dyed black and swept back from his forehead to cover the sparseness of the hair on the top of his head. He had severe features over a thin mouth, he wore a waistcoat even apparently indoors, he gave the impression of a proud and harsh man.

He began, "Mister Keirns, my name is Jimmy Mac Goldrick from Coolney and I have led to believe that I have blamed for an assault or assisting in an assault on your sons in the Mayqueen ballroom the August before last," went Jimmy.

"I know who you are," replied Keirns in a low hissing voice.

"I'm here to set matters straight. I never touched any of your sons, nor assisted any others in attacking them. I had not one thing to do with that fight, in fact I was not next nor near it," said Jimmy.

"No," hissed Keirns, "well, there are others that say different."

"I realise that only too well mister Keirns and I don't know why that is, but the facts are that I did not have anything, near or far got to do with an assault on anyone," replied Jimmy vehemently, "I was in company that night, who can testify that I had nothing to do with the fight and that in fact, I was not next or near it."

"Then why is it generally considered that you had," responded Keirns.

"I don't actually know why that is the case, but the facts are that I had nothing to do with the fight and I have got witnesses," came back Jimmy.

"Several people claim," started Keirns, but Jimmy interrupted him.

"Enough," shouted Jimmy as per his plan and to the obvious surprise and resentment of John Jack Keirns as seen by his startled expression and the reddened hue to his face, "we can shout you did, I didn't at each other all night, instead let you go to your sons right now and if any one of them says directly that I took part in the assault on them, then I will stand there, in this spot, while you call the guards and until they come and arrest me," carried on Jimmy, pointing vehemently at the ground beneath him.

"The older lad's memory of that night isn't great; he suffered memory loss and has great difficulty concentrating and the doctors consider it doubtful if he will improve; we thought that lad would make a barrister and now, it looks doubtful if he'll be able for the arts degree he had to fall back on.

The other lad still has flashbacks and panic attacks from the whole thing and I wouldn't want to put him under the pressure of questioning him," answered Keirns in a low fierce voice.

If Jimmy had been less focused on the subject of the fight, he would have had to wonder how someone who couldn't concentrate and had memory loss, was fit to attempt a university degree in the first place.

"I agree that it's a dammed disgrace," said Jimmy, "that's why I don't want to be blamed for it when I'm not guilty of doing anything that night."

"Anyways, it was never claimed that you took part directly in the assault but that you stopped others from intervening. It was said that you came in with the Careys and when they attacked my sons, that you backed them up and that you stopped others from intervening to save my sons; a number of people have said that," replied Keirns.

"That is a distinct lie. I have witnesses that know me well from at school, that can testify that I was nowhere near the fight that night," answered Jimmy vehemently.

"Well, what is your version of events then," asked Keirns with his arms folded and rocking back and forth on his feet, with a sceptical look on his face as he looked at Jimmy.

Jimmy was prepared, "as I was going away to England, I went out that night to see if I could meet friends I mightn't see in a while; first to Harrison's pub, with the plan to move on to the Mayqueen ballroom. while I was in Harrisons I met the Careys. Now, the Careys are near neighbours of mine. I live on the edge of Coloney village and the Careys live about five places out the road from me, towards Ballymore.

They own a bit of land and the father used to work for a cattle jobber, at least some of the time. They actually used to bully me when I was younger and at one stage, my father had to intervene to sort it out, but they didn't do anything to me in some time and they are near neighbours.

They came up to me that night and seemed friendly, usually they barely bother looking at me and we did end up drinking together and finally, going into the dance together. However, when I was just inside the hall a classmate of mine that lives near here, in Annaghmore I think, Maureen O'Driscoll started talking to me and we ended up getting into an in-depth conversation about the leaving cert that had just come out; how we got on; how other classmates got on; what we were planning on doing etc.

Her father drives a van for a pharmaceutical wholesaler's company or at least, I think he does. It was she, not me that noticed the commotion at the far end of the hall. I thought at first that it was only a bit of shoving and pushing, the likes of which often breaks out in dancehalls but over time, it became apparent that it was a major and unusual disturbance. I even tried to move forward to see what was afoot but couldn't get near where the action was taking place due to the crowd around the fight.

I went back to the girl and her sister, Claire, came up to her and advised her to leave, I went outside with them. There was another girl there with them and though she didn't come outside, she plainly seen me with the O'Driscoll sisters. She's called Marie Lynch and she lives near the O'Driscolls, I believe, though I'm not certain exactly where; she was two classes ahead of me at school and therefore would at least know me by sight.

That's three witnesses that can tell you what I was doing that night and I believe there are others around, but I can't get in touch with them on account of being away. When I tried to return to the hall. The people were being put out due to the fight. I didn't even get into the hall again," answered Jimmy.

"There are also witnesses that say different," said Keirns.

"Who are they, were they ever questioned properly, did they explain how they knew me, what they had to do with me in the past, that makes them so certain it was me," answered Jimmy.

"Why did you run then?" asked Keirns.

"I didn't, as I said I was planning to go to England and that is why I was at the dance, to try and see some mates that I wouldn't see again for a while. It was like this, the leaving cert results came out on the Tuesday before the dance, I didn't get good enough of results to get a scholarship to university and to be honest it was no surprise.

So, then the problem was what to do if I didn't get to university and I did expect that this would be the case, so I had been looking around to see what jobs were available, even before I done the leaving cert, but fairly intensively since and as you know there isn't or to be precise, since I've been away two years, wasn't anything about then. I certainly couldn't get anything, so as I had longed planned I was heading to England, not hanging around here, doing nothing and going no place and eventually, liable to end up worthless like plenty of them that are round. I had hoped to get a bit of money and a bit of work experience and come back when things had improved," answered Jimmy.

John Jack Keirns just stood there observing Jimmy with a hostile and sceptical look.

"It took you an awful long time to come back and plead innocence," he said.

"Yes, you could say that," admitted Jimmy; careful thought on the matter led him to begin his explanation by admitting the obvious and leading the conversation into a viable rationale for his actions, counter fastened by the sergeant's advice to his family, that he should stay away.

"I went to stay temporarily with mates of mine from school that were not well known to the family. I had been hoping to get about two weeks with them and in that time, get a proper place of my own and write to my family with the new address so that they could contact me.

Well, as I'm sure you heard tell of, it's common for people from England to greatly exaggerate what is in England and particularly to make fairly wild promises of what is available over there. Well, I ended up getting three nights on a floor and in that time I had to get a place of my own. This was far from satisfactory and I ended up having to move several times, until I got some place passable where I could settle down. To be quiet honest my expectations of what was available for the Irish, were well above what was really available.

It was, in fact, into November until I could give my family an address they could contact me at. It was the same with work, any sort of work was easy to get but something a bit decent was not that easy to come up with and this also occupied me. The first contact I had from my family in latish November was a note to demand to know how I was getting on and there was no mention made of the fight and I've since learned that they were worried by me not contacting them.

Things didn't work out perfectly even after that and as best I can remember it was after Christmas that I first got word of the accusations that had been made against me and to be honest, I thought it was a bit of a joke or some sort of windup, it seemed so farfetched, I was not able to take it seriously. Well, even after that and in to the new year, things did not settle down.

The room that I was in ended abruptly when some mate of the landlords wanted it, to give one example of what happens over there. The work and conditions and even the behaviour could be very dodgy," said Jimmy thinking wasn't that the gospel truth.

"It was well into the new year when I had a place of my own that was stable enough, that I could engage in reliable correspondence with my family and it was only then that I began to realise that these rumours were for real but with my concentration on work and money and the time that had elapsed and I suppose to some degree the distance, I failed to take them seriously or at least seriously enough.

Actually, it would have been only after last Christmas that it dawned on me properly how seriously the situation was and then it was only when my mother wrote to me saying that I was right to stay away over Christmas, when I had been expecting the opposite response; I mean anger at me staying away so long without making a visit.

First I didn't know what to do but began to realise that I was grossly wronged and would need to correct it. Then as luck would have it, I fell into good work and the temptation of this good work to achieve the aim of my move to England, which was to make money, caused me to delay further," wasn't that some lie about the actual job he did have, thought Jimmy.

"But it was not until last night in conversation with my parents, the full impact of the seriousness of the accusations struck me in the fullest sense. I was planning to come and see you, but in a few days, but with what I heard last night I knew that no further time could possibly elapse before this matter was straightened out. There was also something strange that came out last night.

I ended up upbraiding my parents fairly seriously for not making it clear much earlier on, just how serious the accusations against me were. For instance if they wrote me a letter, then mention of these slanders were made well down in the letters, not emphasised so to speak, this then led my mother to say that the sergeant said that I should be encouraged to stay away to let the whole thing die down and they took his advice and I simply don't know what to make of that," said Jimmy.

John Jack Keirns eyes narrowed during this explanation and were still focused on Jimmy, but for the first time he looked away briefly when mention of the sergeant's behaviour was made.

John Jack Keirns simply stood there looking at him, after a while he said, "of course, you've had plenty of time to invent an excuse."

"Mr Keirns, I have got witnesses as I mentioned, the O'Driscoll sisters and their mate Marie Lynch and they live near here and you can take your car right now and go and see them and I will go with you or stay here or whatever and that will be that checked out," answered Jimmy.

"The O'Driscoll girl went to England nursing, not long after you left I believe," said Keirns.

Of course, thought Jimmy to himself. Most of his classmates went to England and while this helped his case by making his behaviour more usual, it weakened as the O'Driscoll girl was not the to support his case.

"Yes, a lot of us left, but what of her sister Claire and the Lynch girl and even if there all gone they must come home sometimes, if you want to do the just thing and question them, then you can get in touch with them somehow," said Jimmy.

"Of course, it's not impossible that you met some of these people in England and arranged an alibi for yourself," said Keirns.

"Well I was in London the whole time and I don't know where they were or even if they were in England and I certainly don't know why several people would automatically lie for me; as well as that, when you are questioning them you can also ask what other people were in the vicinity and may have seen me and go and question them," answered Jimmy.

"Well then why do you suppose that other people have a different story to tell, why are people slandering you," asked Keirns.

"I can't say with certainty, mister Keirns but my best guess is that you're the chief clerk of the county council and a powerful man and that people who failed to step forward to stop the fight, might well be looking for an excuse to explain their failures and I'm an easy target, I'm not around and I made no secret of the fact that I was going to England so people knew I would be away, that's all I can come up with," answered Jimmy.

Keirns looked away from Jimmy and his face took on a contemplative look, not the hard glare that he had directed at Jimmy throughout.

"I suppose it's not impossible;" he said, at last thought Jimmy I'm getting through to him.

Keirns looked from side to side and not at Jimmy at all, finally he frowned, "you went to the boat on Saturday night for the night sailing is that right."

"Yes."

"But you were reported as been seen at your house on Sunday," said Keirns.

"Oh that," said Jimmy in an offhand manner, "I went up on the train for the night sailing, but when I got there they asked me for my passport, which I hadn't got as I didn't think I needed it.

I was told I would have to show a passport on the English side due to new security considerations that had just being put in place, due to the Aughnacloy ambush; I would imagine you would be able to look up the date of the ambush and check that out. I came back and got the passport and went that evening," said Jimmy.

Keirns nodded and looked pensive, "how did you get back that late at night," he asked.

"I didn't to be honest, we've no phone and all I could do was hang about the station all night and come down on train that morning; I was no length in the

120

house, just got the passport, a cup of tea and back to the station," answered Jimmy.

"The morning train to Ballamore on Sunday morning, is that correct," asked Keirns.

"Yes, I had to walk to the house and back. I had little time at home, I'm surprised anyone seen me," answered Jimmy.

Keirns glared at him more ferociously than he ever had before, "you filthy little liar, you're as guilty as sin itself," he said to Jimmy in more of a snarl than a normal voice, "there's no fucking train to Ballamore on Sunday morning. You're as guilty as sin and you nearly had me going there," he now roared, he came and swung his fist at Jimmy, hitting him in the mouth and though the blow had little effect.

Jimmy instinctively pushed him back, almost knocking him as Keirns was not a strong man, he only saved himself by grabbing on to the door handle; "and another thing," he gasped as he got set to launch another attack, "it was actually me that stopped you from being pursued, as I was unhappy with the evidence against you and here, I find out you're as guilty as sin."

"I'm not," stammered Jimmy, "why don't you ask the witnesses that I have named. The bit about the Sunday morning train was a lie but only that, it was just a reflexive response, as going up Saturday looked more natural," said Jimmy desperately.

"Reflexive," now almost screamed Keirns, "reflexive, the Aughnacloy ambush and I could date it, it was all a carefully worked out lie and there can be little doubt that the witnesses as you call them, were worked on the same way, you're as guilty as sin," and he tried to hit Jimmy again.

Jimmy fended him off and he fell on to the ground behind the door, without getting up he pushed the door closed, leaving Jimmy outside. Shocked and stunned at the sudden and disastrous turn events had taken. Jimmy didn't know what to do, he knocked on the door, but all he could hear was Keirns voice no doubt on the phone to the guards. He got on his bicycle and hit for home as fast as he could; along the way he berated himself for not realising what he was up against in the first place, it was a man who's motivation was vengeance not justice, he was looking for faults.

He was a small man in every way, who had big power, which without doubt he did not deserve, this made him potent and the assault on his sons lessened this and in a way he was a small man again and he did not like it. The stupidity of the elaborate lie about travelling Sunday now also struck him, how sure could anyone be that they seen him or not after two years, he had missed mass that Sunday, that if anything would be remembered, if he was seen about the house, it was only briefly and how certain could they be after this length of time.

Even if Keirns was out for vengeance as he clearly was, he would have to accept Jimmy's innocence if he could prove nothing against him. He had missed out doing this by the slightest and stupidest of slips. On the ride home he realised that he was too anxious, again the true effects of the events in St Swithuns lane and John Cormac's actions afterwards were only now becoming apparent. With that also came the realisation that it was back to that environment he was heading, at least for the time being, he simply had no place else to go.

He arrived home and didn't need to tell his parents how things had gone, for his face betrayed him. He gave them the most abbreviated account possible of what happened. His father quickly comprehended that the next event would be the arrival of the guards to arrest Jimmy for assault on John Jack Keirns in his own house. His parents and even his sister rushed about the place, getting his gear together and packing it up. If the guards got him, with the influence of John Jack Keirns and what he said about the sergeant to Keirns, they'd throw the book at him and after that, it would be doubtful if he would even be safe in jail.

Not fifteen minutes elapsed from the moment he entered the house until he had to leave again and barely half an hour since he left John Jack Keirns. It was too late to catch the train and they would have to make the one-hundred-and-twenty-mile journey to the boat in his father's rickety old ford escort van.

"Christ boy, if only you left well enough alone," was the only thing his father said to him on the four-hour journey up to the port.

He got the ticket and returned to the van for his gear and his father was still silent. He took out his money and counted out five hundred and proffered it to his father, it was all he could afford. His father refused it. He proffered it again and said it was in case his father lost his job.

His father told him there was a new union representative there that might be able to protect him. Finally, his father took two hundred and on further urging another hundred, as an emergency fall back.

Unbending a bit he spoke to Jimmy, "in truth, it's to some degree my own fault that this came about. I should have explained to you better, how this country works. John Jack Keirns is probably out for vengeance more than justice and someone like that can effect nearly anything or any institution that they want to."

"I'm still innocent, I never touched them boys nor supported anyone that touched them, does that not matter," said Jimmy despairingly.

"It's more a case of a wounded animal wanting to strike at something to gain satisfaction, than seeking justice," replied his father.

"And that's the sort of man who in many ways rules this country, its little wonder we all have to go to England or someplace," said Jimmy.

"You're getting a grasp of how things are running in this country as last boy, it's a great pity it wasn't sooner" said his father. "I don't know when you can come back but the Wynnes across the road have a phone, so we'll try and arrange an odd phone call, just to know how things work out. Beyond that I don't know, I just don't know," ended up his father.

Jimmy went for the boat that he had hoped never to see again. To some degree it could be said that Jimmy's mind evaded reality in the beginning, as he could not even formulate his thoughts into logical progression, his mind darted from one subject to another and came up in a mental haze that meant nothing. It was only when someone fell over him on the customary fight on the crossing over, that he returned to reality.

The realisation of the degree of mental stress he was in, really brought back to him the effect the entire affair had on him; maybe the guards were not such a good idea after all, if this was how though and resilient he was mentally and then he laughed to himself, for it was hardly as though they were still an option.

He went up on deck into the fresh air and his recovery continued and he pulled himself together somewhat. It was not the end of the world, he could get out of Greenford, get a job with someone else, initially in London as it was the only place he was familiar with but later on, out of town and then what about Australia and America a year or so down the road.

He was only twenty-one, it was not the end of life yet; yes, he had had a nasty break but then again, it did educate one as to what was out there and what really did happen in life. Calm down, he told himself, London was a big place and there were other employers than John Cormac O'Mahony and they could hardly be worse; in two years' time, he could go to America, doing his research better beforehand this time, a quick secret visit to his family before he went and maybe all would still work out.

When he thought about it he could go even further, how well would he have got on in Ireland anyways, without the 'pull' it was difficult to succeed, his life could only be like his fathers, a struggle with a poor job and always having difficulty making ends meet.

As for England, if anything he knew too much about England and for the moment he'd have to put up with it, but he'd be studying other options and he was certainly young enough to make the change to something better, which he pretty much felt had to exist; in the grand scheme of things maybe things working out the way they did, though difficult at this time, might be for the best.

He got on the train to London in a calmer and steadier mood, with some degree of hope for the future. Now, he was in a somewhat more contemplative mood, he began to wonder how did the likes of John Cormac O'Mahony get into the position he had, how did the likes of him have work or get to be in charge of anything.

He was wondering about this, as he sat across from two old Irishmen returning like from Ireland like him, both men's eyes wandered warily from side to side on a regular basis, a trait Jimmy had noticed in Irishmen before, especially when they were in a place they weren't used of.

Across the aisle two other old Irishmen were arguing about how you would tackle an ass and the argument got fervent, "thaa sure ya attach the chains to the hames not the collar, sure if ya ever tackled an as ya'd know that," "sure how many asses didn't I tackle in me time and ya attach the chains to the collar," "ya'ar an ass yerself if that's what ya think" and so on.

The two old men sitting across from Jimmy were obviously paying close attention to this and one remarked to the other, "them is right sort of men" and the other one agreed; finally, the argument got that heated that one man invited the other out on the platform at Crewe to settle the matter, with fists, the second one seemed prepared to go but the train moved off.

At first this seemed amusing to Jimmy but after a while he began to wonder, why was such a subject of such importance to them. As they were getting off in Euston one of the old men seemed to be struggling with his bags and Jimmy gave him a hand and remarked to him that he probably made this trip often, "every year for the last forty five I've been here," he answered, "thank ye for the help, boyo, I've shovelled too much shit and concrete in my time, so I have."

Jimmy continued the conversation as they walked out to the ticket booths, to attempt to explore while an old man at least in his sixties was ready to fight about tackling an ass, after forty-five years in England; he remarked to him that Thatcher, the prime minister, was no good for the working man, "and 'twhat 'id that got to do with, me boyo," he answered, despite forty-five years in England his mind was still back in Ireland.

Jimmy realised that this could in some ways, explain the toleration indeed the success of someone like John Cormac O'Mahony, if people's interest and even concentration was elsewhere, then they would be off their guard and ripe to be taken advantage of, if they were always considering a future elsewhere, living a life elsewhere, fantasising of a past elsewhere, then they would put up with rubbish in the present that should simply not be put up with, if real life was elsewhere for them then this one did not matter so much.

He was thinking so hard on this on the tube that he missed his stop, but he came to the supposition that what he was and the old man was were the banished. He was banished dramatically because a gombeen man was his enemy, but was not the old man similarly banished though no doubt in a less dramatic fashion than he was, but due no doubt to economic reasons, he was forced out of the country.

The Irish in England and elsewhere weren't adventurers or explorers, going out to conquer new places, to climb new mountains, to sail new oceans, though they often gave the impression that they were getting the cream, in whatever foreign land that they were in. Resentment, even denial of their lot, a longing for things to be otherwise, a feeling of being wronged, even of self-pity and the great danger of dwelling or wallowing in that self-pity, would serve to distract from a proper realistic concentration of the current events of their life, a necessity for any form of success in life.

Simply put, if people were concentrating on their business in a realistic manner, then John Cormac would not be tolerated. The conditions that placed one here, also seen to one's exploitation and indeed destruction, for after forty-five years shovelling shit, all you could do, was argue about tackling an ass.

He arrived out at the house in Greenford that he rented a room in, to find surprise at his early return and that John Cormac had sent a message via the creeping Jesus, that he had work for him and that he was to contact him at once; also no doubt he had also left the message that John Cormac was to be contacted once Jimmy returned, without of course Jimmy being told.

He asked the person the message had been left with, to hold off for a few days, as he had a few things to do. After only two hours of sleep he headed for Canning Town in east London, where he knew that there were flop houses where anybody could get a room anonymously and an Irish community where he could make some contacts and get work.

He intended to get some sort of room and get a job and evade John Cormac and start again; then in time someplace like Birmingham, then hopefully abroad. He went about some of the pubs that evening garnering what information he could, he got some few hints on work, but it wasn't much.

The next day he viewed several rooms and gained nothing but a shocking realisation of just how low the standards of accommodation for the Irish went; one 'room' was six feet by six feet, with a hole in the window, which was two by two inches and another similar sised one in in the roof which had a plastic paint can underneath it to catch the water that came in through the hole when it rained, it had no furniture or electricity and the toilet was in the back yard.

The next day he secured the minimum possible, even for one preparing to rough it, a room with a lock on the door, which some of the other ones hadn't, a mattress on the floor and a chair. The mattress smelled as though the previous owner was incontinent and he was told his three housemates were in the pub. It was poor and boded little of the good, but for a few weeks it could be borne until he got his feet under him, the principal thing was, there would be no back to John Cormac.

He moved from Greenford that evening, explaining to the landlord that he had not found John Cormac's employment good enough for him and wanted to change; the landlord who was a decent sort gave him the week he held in lieu back to him and wished him luck. He moved into the dump in Canning Town that Friday evening, he had returned to Ireland on the night sailing the previous Sunday night.

Work was the next thing to sort out, he didn't want to go working regularly for a subbie as he didn't know how far John Cormac's claws extended, so at least for the time being he would opt for casual work with a dog subbie; this would entail getting picked up at a certain point for a day's work for cash, this would make him harder to track, as there would be no need for him to give a right name and certainly no need to give an address.

The nearest major pick-up point was Tooting Broadway and he lined out there the following Monday at 6 o'clock to cadge for a day's work. The broken down the drunken, the drug addicted and the plain mad consisted of the majority of his fellow work seekers and a lot of those who sought to avail themselves of this workforce seemed little better.

The first 'employer' to solicit his services asked him if he was 'afraid of shite, plenty of shite,' he dismissed this one as too ludicrous to be considered, but over time found others to be little better, "ya look like a bollix, sure ya'd hardly be any good at a day's work," "right pick someone else," "well double fuck ya anyways" and off that prospective 'employer' went.

Finally he took a day's employment with an oldish man, as much for experience as for money and he spent the day clearing up on a site in the docklands, for which he received fifteen pounds and the breakfast; his employer barely spoke to him all day only to suggest that more could be done. He was beginning to realise that John Cormac was not such an anomaly as he had thought.

He met his three housemates that night, they were three rough drink worn Irishmen, ranging in age from the late thirties to the early fifties, two were civil enough but untalkative, nods and one word answers mainly; the third and oldest man barely acknowledged him, he was a particularly rough looking individual, with a rounded piece gone out of one ear, which Jimmy knew was the result of someone biting off that part of his ear in a fight, such injuries were not all that uncommon among the Irish.

The all cleared off to the pub early in the evening. He spent a few days with the oldish man until he ran out of work. The oldish man was in with someone in site or a firm's management and picked up pieces of work here and there and he then picked up men at a pickup points to do the work, the whole business was cash in hand, contacts and governed by backhanders.

The next man he worked with was a fat Donegal man who spent the whole day roaring and abusing the men and knew nothing because half of the work was correcting his mistakes, one day was enough with that man. He spent another day with a Connemara man who thought he could kick men up in the backside if they weren't going fast enough to please him, one day was also enough with that man.

He got a few more days with the oldish man, he had started with. He was getting more and more curious about how things were ran on the buildings and sought any opportunity to find out more about the subject because for one, he was going to spend more time on the buildings than he had planned and for two, knowledge is some defence, if things got sticky and he knew only too well that they could be very easily to do so.

The second week he was in a position directly above his employer, while he was talking to the site agent, as they were discussing the dealings that were taking place between them.

Jimmy's employer got forty pounds a day per man and was himself employed as a ganger for which he received about sixty pounds a day. He paid his men fifteen pounds a day and bought them a breakfast, which was a necessity, for the more drink worn of the men, to last the day. His costs for a man per day taking in to account, the costs of picking them up, would be about seventeen to eighteen pounds a day, so he would have about twenty-two pounds profit per day per man.

He gave a backhander of a tenner per man per day to the site agent, so he'd get about one hundred and twenty pounds a day when he had five men on site which was usual for him, also he had two dead men on site, one of whose wages went in full to the agent and the other to the employer, so for a usual six-day week, the oldish man had a profit nearing a thousand pounds.

The oldish man who was beyond much in the line of hard work and far from knowledgeable about the work in general, even Jimmy was able to correct him at times or running work, was getting a thousand pounds a week, or very near it because of basically his contacts and his contacts alone; this was his sole imput to the entire operation: his contacts.

His men were barely surviving, most of them were living semi rough, they were sharing rooms or sleeping on sofa's or in garages or sheds or even living rough on the streets, at least some of the time. Most were alcoholics or going there fast and the price of the drink and the most minimal of basics was all they wanted, the subbies breakfast their entire daily fare or often even weekly fare, as they would not eat at all on a Sunday to allow then to buy more drink.

Jimmy, meanwhile, gained the position of anchor-man, as far as the work went, this was easily achievable considering the physical state of most of his companions. He worked for another man that apparently didn't know how to read or write or do so only to a limited extent, but still managed to hire men and apparently run jobs.

This was Jimmy's work in August and thought he didn't drink now or smoke to the disgust of his housemates, indeed such was the degree of insult taken by the oldest one at this fact that Jimmy was thankfull for his six feet, he barely paid for his grub and rent which was cheap, during the month of August.

As soon as he could be sure that the accommodation was reasonably stable, he wrote home giving his new address and enquiring about what had happened since he left.

He was informed by a letter that arrived two days after he sent his, of the following facts; his father had been sacked but the shop steward had intervened and his father was rehired on a probation basis, having his wages cut from an already tight one hundred and seventeen pounds a week to ninety six pounds a week, even this would not have happened only the factory had secured a new contract and they were actually taking on people, but most of all they needed experienced workers like Jimmy's father.

The sergeant had visited and was vindictive and he wanted to speak to Jimmy on the phone, thus a phone call was arranged for the following Saturday week at 7 o'clock in the evening, to their neighbours the Wynnes. Jimmy would be expected to ring at that time, to hear what the sergeant had to say to him. Finally the letter informed him that John Jack Keirns was now going about openly saying that he knew for certain that Jimmy was guilty.

Jimmy duly rang the Wynnes number at the appointed time, from a nearby payphone. His mother answered and after a few perfunctory remarks like how he was getting on, she told him about his father saying things were very tight; she also told that his sister had got good enough results to go to university on a scholarship, which meant no cost for the tutorage or other costs directly relating to the education, but she would still need money for accommodation and keep, could Jimmy send some money?

Jimmy said yes; unspoken during this exchange but present, was the accusation that Jimmy was the one responsible for the lack of money in the first place. Then his mother said the sergeant wanted to speak to him. Despite the presence of Jimmy's mother and the fact they were in a neighbour's house, the sergeant didn't pull his punches.

"Ya fucking little bollix ya," roared the sergeant into the phone, "what the hell brought you back to Ireland after all the effort I went to save you and if ya did have to come back what in hell's name drove you to approach John Jack Keirns, at the very least without consulting me."

"Sergeant, I happen to be innocent of any assault on Keirnses sons or of supporting any assault on his sons and I don't want to be blamed for it," protested Jimmy.

"Listen to me my young shite, my information is as follows, that you physically stopped at least three people from intervening in the fight to save Keirns sons and put off other's by your example and I have at least five witnesses to this version of events. I have exactly no witnesses to the version of events that you put out, that you were up the other side of the hall at the time of the fight, so who do I believe," roared the sergeant.

"I intervened on your behalf because I figured you had been roped into it by the Careys and made a fool of, so I felt sorry for you, that and the fact that I went to school with and was friends with, your mother's family, led me at the jeopardy of my own position to cover for you and allow you to escape the law, which is the exact and diametric opposite to what I should be doing.

I didn't want some soft gopher going to jail, where in your case would be hard to survive, which is exactly what would happen to you with John Jack Keirns on your case."

"I am not responsible and I have witnesses that I was up the other side of the hall at the time of the assault. I intend to come back with these witnesses and a lawyer and prove in court that I didn't touch or support anyone in touching the Keirns boys," came back Jimmy heatedly.

"Ye stupid, stupid, stupid young fuck ya, are ye totally thick," roared the sergeant, "if ye come back ye'll be arrested and charged and convicted and jailed. I'll personally see to it, ye're jailed myself, if ye come back, ye little fuck ye," at this stage the sergeant was interrupted by Jimmy's mother, probably thinking the sergeant was going too far.

Jimmy could hear the sergeant's side of the argument as he still had hold of the phone, "what you're not bearing in mind missus is this fact, that I'm within two years of possible retirement, on a pension of over one hundred and fifty pounds a week and that I have a job that pays me four hundred a week, it took a long time to get here and I've put the whole lot on the line to save your stupid son and what thanks do I get for it, defiance and hostility. I could lose everything, in fact I might end up having to go to England for work myself at this age of my life, if I'm not careful."

Jimmy's mother spoke, "look what the sergeant says is right."

"So, I'm to live with this slur over me for the rest of my life; let me test this in court with John Jack Keirns and let's see if people are willing to swear under oath the same as they are saying to Keirnses face," replied Jimmy.

The sergeant came back on the phone speaking quietly for a change, "ya forgot something else, my stupid young fool, you assaulted John Jack Keirns at his residence, knocking him down twice and incidentally, I got that from the old man that lives directly across the road from John Jack Keirns and he told me his wife also witnessed it and that furthermore, he never talked to Keirns about the fact that he witnessed it. That my boy is aggravated assault as it occurred on his property and it is good to give you two years in jail for a start."

Jimmy was silenced. His mother came on the phone now begging him to have common sense and to stay away. He could barely talk, he knew the sergeant had him and that he was going to have to stay away for good. They made an arrangement to talk again in a fortnight's time and in the meantime, if Jimmy could afford to send home some money it would be great.

The sergeant joined in by saying it was the least he could do, to cover the cost to his family of his own stupidity. That was it, on a wet Canning Town street, on an evening in late August, Jimmy knew that Ireland was finished for him. He got a job with a slightly bigger better established dog subbie and managed to get a small pay rise, he now got one hundred and fifty pounds a week for six days and could manage to send the odd hundred home, so there was some small advance there.

The crowd he was now working with were all heavy drinking and they all acted though and were very clannish and they would barely speak to Jimmy because he was not from a Donegal. Jimmy was a good worker and eventually, he became tolerated, if not accepted. This particular dog subbie and his crew were somewhere between the usual dog subbie and their crew, which were mainly composed of men beyond regular work whether through age or drink or more usually a combination of the two and the regular subbie with his crew of reasonably able workmen.

They were about as good as you got on the street pickup scene. There were the usual attempts to control men using coercion and belittlement. From the start Jimmy was upbraided for not going to the pub with them, this despite the fact they were so clannish that they barely spoke to him. When he was four weeks with them and managed to send the second hundred home, he thought it better to attend the odd night, as he was getting enough to keep going from them and he knew of nothing better in prospect.

He attended one night and all seemed to be alright, though he got a few strange looks from another young man who worked for the dog subbie. He was smallish and thick set with a scarred face that looked like he was afflicted by more than acne and he had heard that he had a reputation as a bit of a hard man. Jimmy knew of no reason that he should dislike him, but he knew that reason was not a major attribute with this particular crew or indeed many others. He sought to ignore him.

The odd comment came his way during the following week, "aren't you a lazy bastard too," "is that all ye've done," "I don't know how they keep a wanker like you" and so forth, as Jimmy had more trouble than he ever wished for of late, he ignored him.

The weekend came and they all invited Jimmy to the pub to 'have the crack'; Jimmy was reluctant but they were very insistent, sure he wasn't one of the gang at all, "why would he not come out for a drink Friday night with his workmates" and finally from the dog subbie himself, "come to the pub, there's one or two things I want to speak to you about."

Finally, Jimmy conceded and went to the pub, the principal reason was that with this man he was managing to send a few pounds home and he simply didn't have any better option in view. He hadn't a clue what was in store for him, when he went into the pub, he bought a pint and drank it very slowly as was his usual habit and joined in a desultory conversation, everything seemed to be dull and ordinary despite the claims of the great crack there was going to occur.

The first hint that Jimmy had that anything was awry was when the dog subbie came up to him and looking at him in a furtive sideways manner he said, "well, I suppose that if ye're going to go fighting, there's nothing that I can do about it."

Jimmy looked at him not knowing what to think, when he was struck a hard blow in the face by the individual that was getting on to his case last week, he backed up in a state of utter shock and he received another blow to the face, his opponent tried a third blow, but this one was parried. He then briefly noticed that an excited crowd had gathered around him, it was clear that this event had been anticipated. The most excited was an old man who was nearly salivating with excitement at the violence.

Similarly to Liam Mac Faul, Jimmy had taken up doing exercises and bought some books on self-defence and boxing, these he had followed up to some degree, if not to the same extreme degree as Liam Mac Faul. He struck the individual that had struck him and this appeared to enrage him and he came on in a flurry of fists most of which Jimmy either blocked or evaded. Too late Jimmy realised exactly what the 'crack' for tonight was.

Jimmy threw two overhand punches and they connected well and had the effect of stopping him; he came on again but this time, Jimmy was prepared for him, he drove through his defences and hit him three hard blows to the face which knocked him backwards, by this time Jimmy had lost his temper, the events of the last few weeks, the sensation of being made a fool of, all on the basis of the events on John Cormac's site was too much for him.

He kicked him in the balls as hard as he could, he then kicked him in the face when he straightened up clutching his balls, he repeated this double again and then repeated it a third time harder each time, at this stage the sort of foreman the dog subbie had on the site tried to intervene and Jimmy hit him, levelling him, he then kicked the man who attacked him again in the balls and this time he didn't straighten up, he kicked him in the balls again as hard as he could, at this stage a couple of men assisted by a barman got a hold of Jimmy and with no small amount of effort threw him outside the door.

It was fortunate that it was raining very heavily outside, which distracted Jimmy and assisted him in regaining his reason and balance. He went home and more and more he was comprehending how far from normal his behaviour really was, would he have killed that man if he had been allowed to continue? What in hells name had happened to him? What really was the effect of the events on John Cormac's site on him?

He went home and stayed at home Saturday and Sunday, trying to figure out how to get out of the predicament he was in. He had another arranged phone call with his mother on Sunday night; he was told that they had confirmation that John Jack Keirns had made a formal complaint to the guards about Jimmy several weeks ago and was following it up since, his father was very unsure about his job, could Jimmy make sure the payments he was sending home continued and if possible increased, they were existing on a knife edge.

Try as he might, he could find no alternative to lining out on Monday morning for the dog subbie's van. He knew enough about the building game in general to know that it was unlikely that he would face any sort of sanction or adverse consequences, as he had won the fight, toughness was a valued attribute in men. In fact, everybody was more friendly than usual and his opponent wasn't in work. Even the old dog subbie sort of congratulated him.

"Ya fairly sorted that bollix out the other night, there might be the making of a man in ye yet."

His opponent returned on Thursday, he was clearly marked and walked with his legs apart obviously sparing the family jewels. He said nothing, so neither did Jimmy, but the rest of the crew make him the constant subject of a low level of abuse and derision.

"I thought ye were a hard man, so what's hard about ye today, except of course ye're balls, heh, heh, heh."

Jimmy neither asked for nor wanted this, but he found it hard to feel sorry for his opponent, who now went about the place with a face purple with temper; Jimmy simply done his best to avoid him.

The next day the man spoke to him, utterly without any reason, "you be careful big man, there could be a second round to this."

"What is your problem, what did I do to you anyways," asked Jimmy.

"Fuck you anyways, you wanker," was his answer.

Jimmy challenged him to a round right there and then, but he only muttered something incomprehensible and walked away with his new gait. Jimmy left it at that, though he was strongly tempted to do otherwise. The rest of the crew, however, were not satisfied.

The following Friday night in the pub, the oldest man, the one who had been the most visibly excited the night of the fight and had to be nearing sixty at least, came up to him and told him, that he wasn't safe until he finished that man for good. It was apparent to Jimmy that the boys were anxious to get another night's entertainment out of him.

Jimmy in an impulse normally or at least formally alien to him hit the old man a back hander in the mouth and sat him down on his arse on the floor. This entailed a quiet night in the pub, but his situation was still fraught, he was the butt of the joke at work, with worthless troublesome workmates, living in a dump and having to send his family money and his family in return blaming him for the loss of that money in the first place.

He didn't go to the pub after that. The individual that troubled him, bothered him once more, he simply hit him as hard as he could, levelling him and walked away.

The dog subbie came up to him afterwards and said, "there might be the making of a gangerman in you yet, my boy."

This particular predicament didn't last long, however in late October he was outside his digs in the morning, going to the pickup point, when a small man with the cap pulled down over his face, walked up and almost into Jimmy; indeed, Jimmy barely managed to avoid walking in to him but in that instant he perceived something familiar about the man, this feeling of familiarity proved all too justified a moment later, when the small man pulled the cap back on his head and smiled at Jimmy, his twisted mouth giving him a dry sneering appearance.

"Hi," he shouted at Jimmy, "may I introduce myself. I'm the biggest idiot in all of London, ya can murder a man on one of my sites or at least allow him to be murdered in front of your eyes, while you wank yourself in pleasure at the sight and despite the fact that you're a big strong man that could have easily have broken up the fight and saved a life and guess what?

Are there any consequences for this act, not at all, indeed far from it, a pub where you can partake of your recreation and pleasure in safety from any accidental slip of the tongue that might be made, is set up for you, sure why should your freedom to socialise be compromised, just by you being an accessory to murder.

With another man you'd be doing serious jail time and getting it up the arse every night, but working for this bollix you're in your own specially set up safe pub, so your ability to relax and get drunk is in no way compromised," roared John Cormac O'Mahony at him.

Behind him stood the creeping Jesus, legs apart and bent at the knee, his cap pulled on his head and his mouth alternatively wide open with the lips curled back like a dog or pursed into an 'O' shape, astounded at the dire sight in front of him.

"Well, in all me days and in all I've ever seen, what sort of bollix are you Mac Goldrick," he said.

Mac Bearta was also there, saying nothing but staring harshly at him.

To complete the posse Pete Mac Namee was also there, "what do you think murder is, Mac Goldrick. Do you not realise how serious it is," he asked.

"What would it take to please you," asked John Cormac, "would I need to follow you into the jacks when you're having a shite and wipe your arse for you, exactly what level of service do you require?"

Jimmy was shocked speechless by this turn of events, finally he stammered, "I don't have to work for you forever mister O'Mahony."

"Forever, perhaps not, mister Mac Goldrick," answered John Cormac, "but at least until all trace of this has died down, until the building in Moorgate is occupied and when someone does make a slip of the tongue, as they no doubt will, at least with drink, it's safe to do so, as nobody is going to tear down a completed building to investigate the piles, as they might well with an uncompleted building.

Let me remind you of the events of that day, mister Mac Goldrick. I was up on the London Wall site with plenty of witnesses present, when all six feet of you, allowed a man to be murdered, as you got an orgasm from the spectacle.

At worst, I will go down today as an accessory after the fact but with the excuse of coercion from so many men and the damage to my business, I will probably get off with a suspended sentence; you, however, will get at least ten years in prison, with big strong English thugs raping you every night and to complete matters the boys here waiting for you when you get out.

So, mister Mac Goldrick, make up your own mind, the boys or the law, but stay here you are and someone will get you and get you good."

Jimmy was told not to go to the pickup point that morning and to forget about all the wages he was owed, he was told to get in the van there and then and go to John Cormac's new site on commercial road on the outskirts of the city, Jimmy got in the van. It was the same crew with the addition of two men who had worked on the London Wall site.

Jimmy was put working out of sight and sound of the two new men and everyman with the exception of John Devine and Liam Mac Faul and the two new men, came by to castigate him in turn and when they lapsed, John Cormac himself would come round and say how sad and sorry he was that didn't ring the police that day, seeing how he was thanked for his efforts.

John Cormac now had the crew he wanted to have, with the core captive and under excellent control, things could only get better.

Chapter 10

Liam Mac Faul set out for home, shortly after obtaining permission from John Cormac. He didn't tell anyone he was going, but he did give the landlord an extra week's rent, saying he was working extra-long hours and might not be available to pay him at the usual time.

He had over a thousand pounds saved up and with that he hoped to be able to stay at home long enough to get a job and stay there for good, just like Jimmy Mac Goldrick he wanted no more of John Cormac. He knew that the circumstances at home were not very good, but where else could he go.

Liam was the oldest of seven that lived on a farm of just fifty acres, where there was little enough to go around at any time but he was in a near blind panic to get away, from the whole damn business, any which way that he could. As he approached the family home, he nearly broke down in a similar manner to Jimmy Mac Goldrick did and like him, it was only now, that he began to consider the effects that the event on John Cormac's site had on him in full.

He pulled himself together and entered his home. Greeted not with open arms, but open mouths amazed at his premature return, the first question he was asked was, 'how come he was back so soon' and the second question was 'when would he be going back'. He perceived at once that his return was not akin to that of the prodigal son and that a celebration to commemorate his homecoming was just not to be expected.

His father was an ill made man, of medium height, about six inches shorter than Liam. He was a man about whom it could be said if one was charitable, that he was traditional in attitude; for instance, he had difficulty in seeing the use of an education. A man in many ways challenged by the world, he was not one to hide or diminish his accomplishments or appreciate any form of belittlement and he strongly liked to have his way, especially in what he considered his sphere of influence, which pretty much in total, was his farm and family.

His wife was a large heavy woman, who was from a very poor background and was barely literate and she also could see little value in education, as she had got on without it. Liam barely got a secondary school education and that was at the local technical school and only after the school master had to argue hard with his parents to ensure Liam got even this level of education, as they thought that a strong lad of twelve would be better off on the place, where he would be a big help to his father.

It was now the events that occurred when he left primary school came to mind.

"'Twat would he need to go to secondary school for master," said his father addressing the school master of the primary school.

"Well, if wants to do more in life than the most mundane of tasks, he'll need more than a primary education, at the minimum an intercert, Shamus," the teacher answered his father.

"But twat t'ill he does anyways, other than farm land or go off and be a navy in England like I did myself," came back his father.

"Well, he might like some job above labouring and as to the farm, well, there's six behind him, so he can hardly take over the farm for a while yet, can he," answered the teacher.

Liam's father ran his tongue back and forth between his lips that were turned back and started winking to himself as though he was planning something sly, as was his want when he thought that he was being bested in an argument.

"I might go along a small bit with you about the family, but sure he could be going to England and bringing back the price of more land, like I what done myself in my day and sure, I never went to any secondary school, indeed 'nd I didn't even finish this one here and didn't I get on; didn't I add near ten acres of good land to the old farm and buy a tractor and milking machine with money I made in England as a labourer in only a few years," went his father with a wide sick looking smile on his face.

This was his father's great boast and something he referred to every chance he got, that he had gone to England and brought back the price of nearly ten acres of land beside their farm, which his own father and mother had their eyes on for years, this gave his parents a farm of over fifty acres which was the fulfilment of a lifelong ambition and in thanks, they gave the place to Shamus.

The expected heir and Shamuses older brother Tim returned to England when he heard this and hadn't returned or been in contact for over thirty years, not even attending the funerals of his parents. Rarely did Shamus let a week go by without a blow-by-blow recitation of the great events of that time.

"Maybe Shamus but times change and a man needs an education even on a farm of land"

"'Twhat," interrupted his father.

"Do you want Liam to be going to the postmaster to get any documents about the farm sorted out for him like you do," said the teacher.

Liam's father was stumped at that.

"And 'twhat anyways great job is he going to get out of the secondary," came back Liam's father getting a bit thick at this stage.

"He has a decent average intelligence and could easily enough get a trade like an electrician or mechanic or even a clerks job like in a bank or post office," answered the teacher.

"'Twhat, thaa sure that's not right work like a man I'd do," replied his father heatedly.

"He could even if he went on further and got a leaving cert go on and become a teacher like me, is that a man's job," replied the teacher getting a little heated himself at this vain argument which was solely for the benefit of his opponents' son.

"One of the Mac Fauls a teacher, thwa, thwa, thwa, ya must be joking," replied his father laughing.

This fruitless argument went on for some time, until eventually the teacher pointed out that it was illegal for him to leave school until he was fifteen, so he got to go to the technical school after all. More out of spite of his father than any intellectual yearning. Liam studied fairly hard when he got the chance in between the many chores he had to do around the farm.

The time of the intercert arrived and he did relatively well, he was eighth out of twenty-three. This time, however, his father was not going to be denied in his quest of removing Liam from education.

The headteacher did try, "mister Mac Faul, your son got a decent result in his intercert exam, he was eight out of twenty three. This would strongly suggest that he would be able to get a leaving cert. This, in turn, would open up many opportunities for him, he might even at a push go to university and become a teacher; but for certain many jobs beneath that would be open to him, for instance the guards or the civil service."

"The guards, the civil service, 'twhat sort of jobs are them, sure; one ye're everyman's enemy; the other, sure 'twouldn't be a right job for a man, something for a jackeen or a stuck-up girl," replied his father.

"Well, a teacher is a professional job with relatively short hours, if you wanted to you could farm land as well," replied the teacher trying to get on his good side, it had the opposite effect.

"'Twhat, eh, 'twhat is it that easy to farm land, 'tis that 'twhat ye think, 'tis just as ye'ed expect from a smartarsed townie; 'tis a poor education ya got here, come away now boy, ye have wasted enough time here," was his father's response.

That was the end of his education and for the following two years, Shamus Mac Faul had an easy time about the place, as he thought his son the art of farming, by getting him to do all the work. He also got some small money working for neighbouring farmers.

However over time, it became apparent that he couldn't spend his life on the farm; by the time the last one of the family had grown and left he'd be in his mid-thirties. He simply had to do something else and England was the only viable option.

Shamus agreed to this and went into even more detail in describing his own great triumph when and how he made the farm a proper one, to show Liam what was expected of him. The truth behind the matter was that though Shamus was enjoying the easier times; the place, enhanced by Shamus though it may have been, was simply not capable of keeping a family of seven, even with the bit of money that Liam was contributing.

The only option was to make the family smaller and hopefully get a contribution from England. It times the possibility of an extension on the farm, might be in the offing, indeed should it be that he was like his father, then there was a farm of thirty acres bordering his land, which would if added to his own give him a farm of eighty acres, that would be a farm that would fit to support a few kids on and Shamus Mac Faul would be a man to be reckoned with.

Now all of a sudden, the young lad that should be bringing about this transformation, was at home when he should be working hard in England earning money, Shamus was not impressed and neither was his wife.

"'T'when are ye going back, boy."

"Well, I don't know about going back at all, its mighty rough over there," Liam answered.

"'Twhat are ye on about boy, 'twhat are ye going to do here," responded his father.

His mother was staring at Liam with her lips rounded with shock, though very basically educated she understood well enough the value and sources of money.

"I thought I'd try round here for a while," answered Liam.

"And 'twhat thud be round here now, no more than 'twhen ye left eighteen months ago," almost screeched his mother.

"I have a fair bit of experience of the building trade you know and," started Liam.

"The building trade, what buildings are going on here," interrupted his father his voice now raised.

"There's some shocking rough things that go on over there, ya wouldn't believe it," said Liam.

"'Twhat are ye on about boy, 'twas always a bit rough in England," said his father.

"Yes, well, I assure you it got worse," replied Liam.

"How does everybody else stick it," said his mother in a high excited voice.

"'Twhat are ye saying, boy, here, here stand up straight there beside me," said Shamus.

Liam stood towering over him, "there ye are, look at that, he's bigger than me now, he's bigger than me now, he is," insisted Shamus to his wife and a daughter that sat there silently but curious.

He had as much need of persuasion as to Liam's superior height, as he would have if he was insisting to his wife and daughter, that the sun really did set in the west.

His wife and daughter agreed, "'tisn't he an all, there's no doubt about it."

"Now, me boy, if a smaller man like me can go over there and bring home the price of land and a tractor and milking machine and all home, in only a few years, how come a bigger man like you cannot stick any old job at all," went on his father.

His mother was now sitting down and leaning back in an armchair, her mouth alternatively forming an 'oh' of shock or widening in horror at what she beheld.

"'Tis he a bad rearing de ye think, Shamus," she asked her husband.

"Bedad woman and I don't know, but I'm beginning to doubt it," he answered running his tongue back and forth between his lips and sort of winking to himself as was his wont when he thought someone was besting him, which is what he thought, when any threat to his control over his domain, which is what he considered his family to be.

"'Twhat are we going to do, Shamus," asked his wife still in a high excited voice.

"'Tis a bad one. So, me boy, there's no work around here and there's a big family in this house or have you forgot that; there's plenty of work and money in London and plenty of men even small ones fit to stick it and yet, yet you want to go in the opposite way to the right way, it's fierce hard to make anything out of that, isn't, me boy," said his father.

"Is there something wrong with me trying around here, at least," he asked.

"There's a big crowd in this house already," screeched his mother.

"I actually thought that I was one of this family," answered Liam.

"Me boy, 'tis time ya made yer own living because there's a big crowd here and the farm is too small," began his father.

"I thought you made it big enough," interrupted Liam.

"Sure, I did in the day but times have changed; indeed, when I brought the money home and expanded and modernised the farm it was enough and more and I honestly don't know how any family would be reared on the farm as 't'was but what was fine in the sixties is not good enough any longer. If I was a bit younger I'd give England another go myself but of course, I'm not young enough any longer, but you are and now, it's your turn to go," said his father.

"I don't know what it was like in fifty something but today, it's a dangerous place and I want to at least try something else," answered Liam.

"Ahaa aheick," cried his mother, "there's a big crowd in this house," she went starring at him her mouth opens aghast, showing her broken discoloured teeth.

His father came back, "I was over there from fifty-seven to sixty-three and it could be rough at times too, but I was fit to stick it and so should you."

His mother was lying back in her chair starring at him with a horrified expression, letting out odd cries, as though in great distress; his sister was beside her holding her hand. He knew he wouldn't be over welcome but he hadn't expected this.

His mother was now blubbering while still staring at him in the most aghast manner, his sister beside her also had tears in her eyes. If he had arrived in the door, saying he was going to murder them, he could have hardly expected a worse reaction.

"There's a big crowd here," cried his mother now sobbing.

"'Twhat and I don't know 'twhat to think, tend't but I'm beginning to think yer right and he is a bad rearing," said his father.

"Aheick, aheick," howled his mother.

Liam felt like hitting her.

"Did ye manage to bring a few pounds over with ye?" asked his father winking slyly at his wife and daughter.

His mother stopped her caterwauling and looked at him expectantly.

"Some," replied Liam.

"How much is some?" asked his father.

Liam had been thinking of leaving a hundred pounds with them, which should have defrayed most of the costs of his stay; he thought hard and thought he might be able to afford four hundred pounds, but he did need some money particularly as he was planning to travel round, especially to Dublin to look for work.

"Maybe four hundred," he said.

"That's not good enough. I was hoping for a thousand from you; indeed I was only saying to the woman here last week, that it'd be very handy if that young lad brought home fifteen or sixteen hundred at Christmas, it'd be very handy because the old tractor needs replacing, but then again last week I thought there might be some good to ya," replied his father.

His mother resumed her caterwauling.

"Well, maybe five, possibly a little more," began Liam.

"Give it to me," said his father.

"I'd like to know I'm welcome here first," said Liam, this elicited a loud wail from his mother.

"Can we cut the banshee act out," said Liam, getting angry at his mother's theatrics.

"Aye abuse yer mother and leave yer family destitute, yer a good one surely, yer right woman, he is a bad rearing," went his father.

"There's a big crowd here," gasped his mother.

"Shut up," he roared at her, "I'm staying to give it another try whether ye like it or not."

"Aheik, aheik, 'twhat sort of useless rearing is he," shrieked his mother.

143

"Now look what ye've done," shrieked his sister at him.

"Ye blackguard to treat yer old mother like that," shouted his father at him.

Liam threw his rucksack on the table and took the money out of it and put it in his pocket and then threw the rucksack in the corner.

"I'm for the pub and I'm staying here for a few weeks to try this, my own country, whether ye like it or not," Liam roared at them.

"Akheeik, akheeik, a drunkard and all," screeched his mother.

"Yes, just like your father," Liam roared at her breaking the long-held family taboo of not mentioning the family disgrace of Liam's grandfather drunkenness.

He headed for the door, his mother now silent and starring at him vindictively.

"Are ye going to give me the money as ye said," asked his father.

"No," roared Liam going out the door and slamming it behind him.

He wondered about the place, he had almost never gone to a pub before he left Ireland, as it been banned due to the family experience of his grandfather's drunkenness. In England, his main experience of drinking was in John Cormac's pub and that certainly didn't promote a liking of drink.

He just wandered around the local village which was deserted at this hour. He met no one that he knew well; the first person he met, whom he barely knew, he didn't speak to, but corrected that with the next person he met, as people regularly spoke to everyone else in Ireland whether they knew them or not.

He simply didn't know what to do, go back to London, too well he knew the possibility of danger there; here he had no contacts and knew it was difficult to get anywhere without them in Ireland. He had hoped to get some basic job in Ireland, where it was at least safe and try to progress from that.

He knew the value that was placed on any man in England only too well and simply didn't want to live like that. He tried to think of some way he could get some job here without relying on his family, no aunt or uncle would help him without his family's consent and they weren't fit to be much help at any rate; any friends he had were school friends and they were not fit to help either.

His family's attitude bugged him, he knew that things were tight, but he'd be prepared to pay basic costs to see they weren't put out or put out very little. The main objection of his family was that if he got a job in Ireland he would only be able to give them a limited amount of help, the odd few tenners probably, but thirty acres of land would not be bought or new tractors and this is what his family seemed to expect of him; also the usual avenue for advancement of people in the area was through money from England, this was how one got a bigger farm and got one up on the neighbours.

He had to go back to people who murdered each other and covered it up the same as they would dispose of, well a dead rat, a real one; to accomplish this, all for a family that didn't welcome him and who would offer him no refuge. His mother's pussing and hysterics were venomous and embittering.

Eventually, people started coming out of the pubs and he headed for home. He had reached one decision, if his family succeeded in forcing him back to England without having a decent search for a job here, he'd do just like his uncle Tim and never return, he'd see how much land they'd buy then.

Only his father was up when he entered the house and he didn't speak to him. He had normally slept in a boarded off part of the kitchen, but his younger brother had graduated to that berth and he had to sleep on the sofa in the living room, with an old curtain as a cover. Some homecoming he thought, not a bite to eat, not even a cup of tea, caterwauling and hysterics as a welcome, then silence and he had to sleep near enough rough.

The next morning there was still silence, he was served no breakfast but when he got some bread and poured some tea for himself, nobody said anything but his mother gave him a resentful look. He asked his father if he could borrow the car to speed up his job search and so relieve them of his presence.

His father replied, "no doubt, you got a license in England, knowing well, it was most unlikely but have you get insurance for that car."

He had let Liam drive the car before when it had suited him but was determined not to allow this now.

"What around the local area, the quicker I get a job the quicker I'm off your hands."

"If ye crash, they could follow me and the place could end up having to be sold," replied his father.

"Oh shite, the useless bastard will ruin us yet, what sort of useless rearing is he," lamented his mother.

Liam couldn't take the car which upon reflection was probably just as well, it was a heavily battered mini estate with the number plates held on by twine, it could not do otherwise than make a bad impression. He set off to the local town to try the factory there for a start. He did expect to fit in, despite the lack of welcome from his family.

At first all seemed well, he thumbed a lift into the town and got a lift from a neighbour who seemed welcoming enough.

"Well, if it isn't young Mac Faul, ye're a fine big man now, England seems to be suiting ya."

"Well, it's a bit different sometimes too different," answered Liam.

"They say, the money is great over there."

"Well, fifty a day is easy to come by," answered Liam, making that old mistake of the Irish at home from abroad, of exaggerating at least somewhat the benefits of being abroad.

"Indeed is that so I suppose if any of us were doing the right thing, we'd be over there ourselves," this particular neighbour had one of the best farms in the area over three times the size of Mac Faul's place.

"There's a rough side to it to, there can be little value left on a man by times," answered Liam to try to restore some reality to the conversation.

"Ah aye, for sure the town is always a rough place, but would ye be much safer in Dublin and for sure, you would not be on fifty pounds a day. Ya did the right thing, me lad, there's too many of them round here doing nothing as there is, if there are not careful they'll end up good for nothing, not like yerself," Liam realised that now would not be a good time to bring up his plans.

He started his job search, first he went into the factory. The first person was a neighbour from near him at home, he was a friendly cheerful man if a bit over the top and Liam felt easy talking to him.

"Well, well, Liam Mac Faul, is it you that's in it, you've grown into a powerful man, heh, them is some muscles you have there," he said as he felt Liam's arm through the shirt he wore on this warm day with one hand as he shook hands with the other. "I wouldn't like to go fighting with ye at this stage, this London seems to be doing you good. Ye're back for a bit of a break and some good porter I suppose"

"Heh, heh we might try a pint," said Liam.

"The money is probably a bit better over there than it was with your old man," he went on.

Liam had his first genuine laugh in a long time at this obvious truism. "Well, that's true and it would not have to be very high to accomplish that," laughed Liam.

"Do you know what, young Liam, if I was half way to being right in the head meself, isn't it over there with ye I'd be, instead of here; one hundred and three pounds a week and me going home to two kids and a wife in the family way again if you get my meaning," he went on.

"Well, the money might be a bit better alright but it can be one dodgy town at times. Indeed, that's why I'm here. I just wonder if anything is going here because I'd like to give old Ireland another go before I give in completely to England," said Liam.

The man's smile disappeared to be replaced by an offended look, "young Mac Faul, I don't know about that at all. We're struggling around here and as for outsiders coming in to take the bit, well."

"Since when did I become an outsider," asked Liam getting offended in turn.

"Well, you're in England, aren't you and if you're set up there and sound what business have you coming back here taking from us that haven't enough," he responded.

"What I've no right to look for a job in my own country?"

"Well, as you must know, there's not enough to go around on ourselves without accommodating others."

"Who are these 'others' you're on about."

"People that have been away have options that we don't and let me start off by saying there's nothing going around here for anyone."

This sudden change of tone, with no doubt the influence of the events of the previous few months caused Liam to act aggressively, drawing himself up to his full height, he shouted at his old neighbour, "why am I an outsider, did I become an Englishman when I went to England or what and who the hell are you to define me your near neighbour as foreign."

Taking into account the increased size and bulk and the different mien of a lad he had thought of as a quiet easy-going youngster, the neighbour moderated his tone and stance.

"Now, hold on a minute, young Mac Faul, I'm on your side. I'm only saying what people around here think, if you're gone it's assumed you're provided for and that the few bits and pieces that are round here, should go to someone from around here and anyways, would you be content working for eighty pounds a week, which is all you'd get if you started here; I'm only telling you what people around here think, to stop you expecting what cannot be given."

"I know what the wages are here and I wouldn't be looking for a job here if they weren't good enough for me, also I never said money was my objective.

England can be a dangerous and evil place for a Paddy, I know I was there and I'm not content to live my life in such an environment."

"There's plenty of them that's smaller and weaker than you that's fit to stick it out and thrive."

"If it's such a good place why do you not go."

"What with two stroke three kids."

"Well, if it's such a great place surely you'd be doing them a favour."

"This country is known to be a better place to rear kids in, but if I wasn't married I'd be off."

Liam just walked away. He had known the neighbour as a friendly and popular man, now he wasn't sure he knew him at all.

There was a building site in town and some groundworks were taking place; Liam decided to ask there. He was told there was nothing going there. He turned to leave when a workman on site came up and greeted him, it was another neighbour.

"Sure you're Shamus Mac Faul's son. What brings you round here."

"I was asking for work but I've been told there's nothing going."

"Well, there isn't, I suppose, its tight these times. But wait," he said frowning, "aren't you in England."

"I was thinking of giving this place a go, as I don't want to commit myself to England completely as yet," replied Liam.

"I don't know about that, there's barely enough around here for ourselves."

"Whose these 'ourselves' you're on about."

"People from around here that don't have good jobs in England to go to."

"I don't remember saying what job in England I have to go to."

"It's generally considered to be good in England, the same cannot be said for around here."

"There's more than just money involved, it's one rough and dangerous place at times."

"Well, others can stick it out no problem, young Mac Faul, a big strong man like you should have no problem."

"A point I'd like to make is that I'm from here just as much as you with the same rights as you."

"Young Mac Faul, you don't seem to realise that people around here consider that when you're gone to England and you're getting on, it's expected you'll stay and leave what's here for the people that's here, which isn't enough to begin with."

"So, I'm barred from my own country, is that it."

"Well, no there's holidays and if you were going to set up a business."

"I have to pay my ways back a bribe is that it," interrupted Liam and for the second time that day turned his back on someone he had thought of as a neighbour.

He went to the other factory in town, a small specialised plastic factory that was German owned and ran, "nein is no zobs zere," was the response he got; at least, that refusal had the merit of being honest, he thought and not connected to the fact that he was now considered a foreigner.

Thinking about it, he noticed that nobody reacted against genuine foreigners who were working in the country and it struck a strange note. It was a confusing and most disappointing day. He came home or to what he formally thought of as home, he didn't really know what it was now. He saw through the kitchen window his mother in conversation with his aunt Fanny, they both seemed very content, but Liam knew that this could change fast.

His aunt Fanny was the oldest of his mother's family and a deeply ignorant and excitable woman given to hysterics. His mother was the forth child in a family of eight. This was not a very unusual sized family for the period, but it they were all born in a period of nine-years on a farm of thirty-two acres. If things were well running and more to the point soberly ran, it would be tight going to rear such a family on such a place in that period. This was not the case, however, as the father was a complete drunkard.

The family lurched from crisis to crisis; the father would run out of money and then he would do some work and run the farm in a reasonable manner, but eventually he would get some money and the drink would start and the work would fail and things would go down, his usually pregnant wife would try to cope but would fail and things would fall apart.

The only port of call in those days and in that area was the church, a small amount of charity and a strong lecture to the father from the canon, was all they received from that quarter and that was quite simply inadequate. Fanny the oldest left school at nine, she was barely fit to read or write but with seven younger siblings including a new born baby, her help was needed at home. She could dress and feed herself and clean and carry things so she was needed, she was supposed to return to school the following year but it never happened.

The next two siblings were boys who left school at eleven, initially glad to leave school as is the want of young boys, they grew to regret it as they matured; their lot was to run the farm, which increasingly they did with more competence, which gave the family a few easier years.

As time passed the two brothers grew dissatisfied with their lot and initially, the older one followed a cousin to London at the age of fifteen; no more was ever heard of him, but for a few rumours that he had gone on the drink; two years later the younger one followed and he did pay the occasional visit home and gave some small help, to the family, he'd buy some clothes or shoes for the kids and such like.

Myra who was Liam's mother was next, she left school at eleven, poorly literate and with very limited horizons. For a while her older brothers made an effort around the farm and they had a viable if very sparse livelihood but when her brothers departed to England, things just went to hell; cattle died on the land, animal fodder wasn't saved, nor peat the only fuel they could get; in an era and area, that mechanisation was sparse, some input from a man was necessary to keep a farm on track and viable and with Myra's father this was just not forthcoming.

Her father's effort was to sell a field and say nothing to his wife; when she found out and confronted him, he beat her up in front of the children. She went to the guards and the sergeant's response was to give her father a few hard blows in the face and tell him he'd get twice as much, if he beat up his wife again.

The next to Myra was unlike any of his older siblings and wanted to stay on at school until he was thirteen and got the national leaving cert as it was called, which would help him to get working in a shop or get an apprenticeship or be something above a common labourer. His father would have none of it, he wanted him to do as his brothers had done and make some attempt to run the place, when his son defied him he battered him up, when his wife intervened, he battered her up.

She got the guards, the sergeant gave Myra's father twice as good as beating as before just as promised and Myra's brother who was eleven months younger than her became the first to finish the primary or as it was called national school. Finally, the canon got Myra to scrub the church floor every week and for this she got two shillings, which he thought was adequate as the church floor was usually scrubbed once a month which was seen as adequate, so it was a sort of charity, this brought in enough flour for the week.

The family lurched from crisis to failure. When Myra's younger brother left school the canon was influential in getting him a position as an apprentice shop boy, the canon also had to pay ten pounds towards his food and board for the first year, something he hinted very strongly that he wanted back eventually. It was at least one less mouth in the house.

The next, a sister left school at eleven but she didn't get good results and she joined her two older sisters about the house. Myra got some other heavy cleaning jobs and even got odd bits of work for her sisters. The situation in the house wasn't quite as dire as before but it was still poor. Fanny was an ill looking misshapen girl and any attempt to marry her off failed. The younger sister Agnes was reasonably good looking and at seventeen, she married a local farmer in his mid-thirties; it was another mouth less in the house.

The last two sisters had left the school at this time, the second youngest got a place in the local convent for three years so she could do the intercert, this was designed to prepare Irish girls to go to England nursing. The youngest of the family also got in on this but she was reasonably good at school, so when she did the intercert, her sister who was married to the farmer got him to pay for her to do a leaving cert. She did this and got good results and got a job in the civil service in Dublin.

The first weekend that she returned from Dublin, her father told her that he was proud of the good job he had done on her and asked her for money; if she did come home after that it was on a Saturday evening and sometimes she did give some money to her mother. Finally, Myra was getting ready to go to England at the age of twenty-three, when she struck up with a man from about five miles away who was returning from England having done well at least according to his own accounts.

He was a badly built ill looking man and his farm was not very big for all his talk, but he didn't drink. He didn't drink and for Myra and her mother, this was a cardinal attribute. What knowledge did Myra have of England, indeed what knowledge had she of anything outside the local area, a non-drinking farmer who seemed to some degree successful, she stuck for it. Fanny was left with her broken mother and her worthless father on the farm.

Her father died when he fell into a ditch while drunk and drowned, a fate that surprised no one. Her mother was in the county home with dementia. She still lived in the old house and she rented the land at low money to her brother-in-law and on that and a bit of social she existed.

Liam knew his mother's and aunt's background and to some degree sympathised, but their longing for an easy life, however understandable, was going to force him back into the company of murderers and those who left no value whatsoever on human life. Well, he was not going to have it; if they could not listen and to some degree try and to understand him through either ignorance or obstinacy, then though, he was going to defy them.

He had to go away and work for scum like John Cormac O'Mahony and bring back the price of thirty acres and the money to upgrade the machinery and the rest, they were asking altogether too much, for one thing how would such money be got on the rates that John Cormac paid. He did feel some empathy for them and more so, for his younger brother and sisters and he would be willing to give some help, as long as he was at least safe and to some degree content in his work.

He entered the house expecting opposition and ignorance as the medium to express that opposition and he in turn was determined to resist it. They were chatting quietly but the moment he entered the room his mother let out a wail.

"Uuhaal aafaa, here's the useless rearing."

"Arra and shite upon ye, anyways," went his aunt Fanny in greeting.

"Uhaa, ahaa, ahaa 'twhat am I to do," his mother screeched grabbing her sister's arm, "look at the size of him and he won't do any work or anything."

"Arra and shite upon you anyways," responded Fanny.

"'Twhad and six children in the house already, to be fed and everything and he comes back to add to the lot, ahaa, ahaa ahiek," went on his mother, "sure there's them that's half his size beyond, sending money home to their poor old whammy, to ease her in her old age and look what I have to put up with, aheik, aheik, aheik," now almost shrieked his mother.

"Arra and shite upon ya anyways," went aunt Fanny.

Liam went to the fridge and made himself a sandwich with plenty of ham in it and he poured the last of the tea from the pot his aunt and mother had been sharing into a mug for himself.

"Is there any food at all, left in the house after ye," said his mother in an angry but normal voice. "'Tisn't this it too, he eats enough for two, akiek, ahiek," went his mother returning to her caterwauling mode, "'twhat are we going to do at all, it isn't as though we haven't enough of problems already, a big crowd and now, this useless bustard on top of it," she continued.

"Arra and shite upon you anyways," came back aunt Fanny in chorus.

"And on top of that, isn't he on the drink as well," went on his mother.

"Isn't that in the family tradition," said Liam lying back on the settee affecting detachment from their theatrics.

"Aheik, aheik what am I to do with a useless rearing like that," went on his mother.

"Arra and shite upon you anyways," came back fanny in what was now a continual chorus.

Several more versus went by as Liam finished his sandwich.

His father came in and asked, "are ye still causing upset."

"No, I'm eating a sandwich."

"Did ye pay for it?"

"No and I don't intend to," this gave rise to a wail from his mother and from aunt Fanny.

"Arra and shite upon ya anyways."

"And what are we supposed to do, ya can't be round here at this stage, ye were reared and given a good education, three years in the teck and all, ya can't expect more from us," said his father.

"Ahaa, ahaa, he's a useless rearing," went his mother.

"Arra and shite upon you anyways," said aunt fanny.

"What I want is a chance to get a job in this country, the same as plenty of others, Am I welcome to try that," replied Liam.

"But sure there's nothing round here," answered his father his mouth pulled into an incredulous smile and winking to himself as always when he was under pressure.

"Other people get work, why should I not, is there something different about me," Liam said.

His mother let out another caterwaul.

"Silence or I'll do ya," said Liam his patience spent.

"Ahaa, aheik, aheik, sure isn't he threatening me now, 'twhere did I get him from ahaa," went his mother.

"Arra and shite be upon ya anyways," went aunt Fanny.

Liam got up and went out the door for fear of his own reaction. Though he could to some degree understand his mother's hysterics, her background, her near non-education which limited the way she could communicate, the poor income and large family, still the rejection of the mother stung. Even if he got work in another town and lived away which seemed the only option, he be happy to do so much; but they wanted the big bucks and that only came from England in their experience.

Basically put, he was supposed to work in a business where a man's life was worth nothing, to satisfy their greed and to somehow make their hard unsuccessful lives easy and successful, it couldn't be done. It was a dank, dark, dreary night which suited his mood. What was he to do? He was qualified for nothing but the buildings and hc couldn't even enhance that by doing a trade any longer, if he did have the co-operation of his parents it was probably not too late, but he could sing for that.

It all came down to the time he left school if, but if, he had done the leaving cert as the head teacher said he was well fit to do, instead of giving his father two easy years around the farm, then what could he not do, certainly a trade, even something like an office job, what of the civil service, even at a push, the teacher had said he might be fit to do a teaching job; teaching children, a professional man.

What would the difference be; if one teacher stabbed another to death, something he had never heard tell of, would the other teachers and the head teacher and the school inspector band together to cover up the murder and dispose of the body, the thought was farcical, utterly ridiculous, you'd not see it on something like spitting images the farfetched satirical television program. Just how far from what could be consider civilised and proper was he.

He might get a poor job here and alienate all his family, he could go back to John Cormac and his murderous crew and that was more or less it, at the age of two months shy of twenty-one years. The drizzle fell but he didn't notice it, in the throes of dawning realisation, that at short of twenty-one years of age he was in many ways finished, his prospects were poor, his future in general was daunting and dangerous to say nothing of being unproductive, in pretty much any which way that you looked at it.

The night and his mood matched, a darkness without the slightest spark of light. Finally the fact that he was sopping wet, came to his notice and he returned to the house. His aunt had left and his mother was in an upper room with the children, his father was there but he didn't speak. He towelled his head and hands dry and made himself another ham sandwich and tea.

His mother entered, "aheik, there'll be nothing left for the children," she wailed.

"Am I welcome to nothing," he shouted.

"Yes, in your day but them days are gone," said his father.

"I told ye I only intend to stay here until I get a job," he said.

"Sure, there's nothing round here," said his father with his thin incredulous smile.

"Well, I intend to try and try hard and ye'll have to put up with it," Liam answered to exasperated clicks of the tongue from his father and a shriek from his mother.

He went into the living room and lay down on the sofa with the old curtain as a cover, just as he did the night before, only tonight he was damper. He went to the nearest big town the day after, where there was a variety of factories and warehouses and garages where work might be going, there might even be some building work going on.

He entered a building site and was asked a few questions about the work which he answered well, he was asked where he obtained such knowledge and he answered England, with that the interview was abruptly terminated and he was told to go back there. He followed the foreman into the site and asked him what he meant by that, he was told that if there were any jobs going there, they were going to a local that needed it and if he was used to England, to go back there.

Liam left for fear of his own reaction. He spent an exhaustive day trying everyplace he could, in most places he was informed straight off there was no work; in a couple there seemed some interest but when he mentioned his English work experience, interest disappeared at once. He thumbed a lift home and was picked up by a neighbour he had always considered a bit unfriendly but now he seemed friendly enough, but the reason for it was that this neighbour had spent a good part of his life in England and viewed Liam as a fellow traveller.

He'd been in England twelve years but had to come home as his father had a stroke and his two brothers that were also in England were married, he'd added a bit of land to the farm and done his best with it, but he never seen right money again. His lot had been simply to subsist on small money and to cater for parents until they died. He got some very intermittent help from his two sisters who were married in Dublin and an odd few pounds from his brothers while his parents had been alive.

He told Liam he was sorry he ever left England. Liam thought that this might be someone they could talk to. Did he ever feel that people were unfriendly when he came back? He did, it was the dint of jealousy and nothing else, they wanted

155

you to spend your money, but were resentful you had it in the first place. They wanted you to come back for a good holiday and to spend plenty of money and leave what was here for them, but whatever ya do don't expect something from them and don't do something like buy land. What they want is their cake and to eat it.

He then enquired about the dangers of England, the answer, ya just had to get as rough and though as the rest of them, behind it all a lot of them weren't up to much when it was put up to them, was his experience. The advice was in some ways a relief to Liam, it did show that he was not alone, but he was determined not to go back while any possible option existed.

"Ahaa, ahaa, are ye still here," his mother greeted him when he came in the door.

He ignored her, made himself a sandwich, lay down on the sofa and ate the sandwich and read the local paper. Caterwauls, attempts to start arguments, even attempts to start an ordinary conversation were all ignored. After three hours of hisses and wails and laments he got fed up and stood up and said it was time for the pub and went for a walk out the fields where he could think.

One point that did strike him from the day, was the fact that there were people in a similar situation to him, so to some degree at least he was not alone. The other point that was to some degree salient, was that they were not that though if it was put up to them. He was a big man and if necessary, he could hit hard; he didn't want that sort of life but if necessary he could live such a life.

The next day he went to Dublin on the train. The first things he noticed was that there were far fewer tower cranes over Dublin than you would get over London. Another difference was that he was told on the bigger sites that they were closed shop and that meant that he had to be a member of a union to even apply for a job there. On the smaller sites where he could apply for a job, the reaction was the same as down the country, what experience you have, where did you get it, England, go back there.

Warehouses, factories full up, no jobs, we're leaving people off, we're closing down soon, fuck off, in one or two places, shops, you don't look like a shop worker; in more than one place, he was told quietly a good strong young man like himself should be heading for Don Laoghaire the usual port of departure for England.

He returned to the now usual wails and theatrics and ignored them. He returned to Dublin the next day and resumed his search. He didn't mention his

English experience to anyone, but it didn't seem to make any difference, there were no jobs. Chance England was the advice he got in many places.

The unwelcome return, the caterwauls and hysterics all the same and as was becoming routine, he ignored it all. As it was a Friday night he did venture into one of the local pubs. He was apparently made welcome, even by people he had little to do with in the past.

At this stage he was somewhat wiser about what their real feelings were likely to be, so wishing for a break he kept the subject to the affairs of the locality, the neighbours, their health and what they were at, even questions about England he answered as briefly and blandly as possible, even to the couple of people who expressed an interest in going there.

He was careful and diplomatic but realised that night was a luxury, that reality was different. Behind it all perhaps was the hope that he was still part of the gang, one of the neighbours, of the clan and that they would accept him back. He returned to the pub, the following night prepared to explore to some degree, the prospects of getting a job here; the plan was to say he missed the neighbours and the neighbourliness and the bit of crack too much, to come at the subject from the soft side so to speak.

He was careful as his recent experiences conditioned him to be, "eh, em, well, you know that England is all right for the money, but there's very poor nature to the people, l mean like you couldn't come in to English company and have the crack like this you know and I miss that, I'd just like to give here another try first."

He was quickly corrected, "Can you eat the 'crack', will it put a roof over your head or a car under you, stay where you are, you young idiot ya," "stay where ya are ya fool," "aye sure we should be over there with ye, if we were doing the right thing at all," "if it wasn't for the wife and kids I be along with ya on the boat back," "that's right, the way things arc in this country right now, tis a country for no-one."

"Yes, England can be alright for money, but it's a right rough place at times, there's simply no value left on a man there." "there's plenty of smaller ones seem to be able to stick it out," "ya can be as big and strong as you like, but if they come for your back what can you do and over there they'd not think twice about it," "sure what different boat is any other man in, no young man you'd be a fool to think about here again" and so on.

The sentiment was strongly against his return and the worst of it was that most of them seemed to be genuinely giving him what they thought was good advice; they probably thought they were giving him the right advice and doing him a favour. He moved on to another pub that was open late.

There the theme of the advice was the same, not to return, but put blunter, "Are ye sure the problem isn't the work that ye don't like," "no I'm sure the problem isn't the work, I'd hardly get easy work around here."

"Sure, if you come home, it means some other man will have to go, someone who won't be used to the pitfalls like you and they will be in more danger at least according to what you say; you're at least aware of the dangers so the risk for you is less." "How come no one else that's in London is on about these dangers," "who did you ask, someone who's been there for a three-week holiday or maybe has never been there."

The conversation continued on this theme and got more heated, "so you would expect one of us to give up our jobs to facilitate you," "no, I wouldn't," "well that's pretty much what would have to happen, isn't it," "well I suppose it would give you the chance to go over to London and make this big money ye're always claiming that can be made over there."

They were joined by a man called Jerry Lynch, who was the son of the head teacher of the local secondary school, he was a few years older than Liam and had gone to university and was now working as an assistant county engineer. He showed none of this intelligence while going to school and it was generally considered that he got both his university placement and job due to his father's contacts which included a cousin that was a TD.

"I thought there was a bit of cutting to you, young Mac Faul, at least you went off and got a job, unlike a number of fellows from round that could be mentioned and here you are backtracking," he said to Liam.

"I just consider that I have as much right to you as a job around here as you or anyone else around here. I am actually from around here," replied Liam.

"What job is that; does that mean some man with a family will have to give up his job and country to make place for you," said Lynch.

"I asking nobody to sacrifice their job for me, but I do say that I should have as much right to look for a job around here as anyone else round here," came back Liam.

"You have options that others don't, so you should let people here have what little is going," replied Lynch.

158

"What particular options are you talking about, is England barred to these people, am I not from here," answered Liam.

"You know England they don't, you've been there and you know the territory, you know the pitfalls, the ups and downs, the dangers and the opportunities. I don't think it's too much to ask you to return there and leave the bit that's here, for the people that's here and don't have that experience and knowledge," replied Lynch.

"Well, you never had to worry about England, mister Lynch, did you, tanks to your cousin Ger Lynch TD," answered Liam getting a little heated.

"Ya cheeky little bastard ya, I'm trying to stop you making a bollix out of yourself and this is your response abuse and lies," responded Lynch.

"What lies?" asked Liam, "and who's the little bastard," standing up straight and showing that he was at least half a foot taller than him.

The rest started laughing and Lynch marched off fuming but afraid to do anything. After that, however, the rest of the company wouldn't engage him in conversation about jobs and Ireland, so yet another night was ending in rejection and frustration. The next day was a Sunday and he intended to go to mass to try to meet some of the neighbours, but when morning came he found he just not up to it, his humour was just not right for socialising. This failure to attend mass brought further condemnation from his family especially from his mother.

"Aheik, aheik worse and worse it gets, one thing after another and now, no religion, 'twhat and 'twhere did we get him out of."

Liam was getting fed up with this and he said to his father if there was more shrieking he'd give her a reason for it.

"Ya'd strick yer old mother by Christ, yer right woman, he is gone to hell."

Another row broke and even the righteous were late for mass. He went to the pub that evening and found he was being avoided, those he talked to were polite but they wouldn't be drawn on the subject of work and money, only to say things were very poor and there was barely enough for who was there, word spreads fast in a small village, everyone knew his business and none were supportive.

The next day Monday, he went back to the big town to check places he hadn't been before but with fast vanishing hope. The results and advice were the same. On Tuesday, he hit for a smaller town some miles away, that had the reputation of doing a bit better than its neighbours. He was told to keep in touch in a couple of places, but in another word had reached them that he had been in England, no doubt from some neighbour, he got the now familiar exhortation to return there.

There were changes at home that evening, there was no food in the fridge or indeed anyplace in the house, Liam couldn't make his usual sandwich, but there seemed to be nothing for anyone else either. He sat down to see what the plan was, just before the normal time, for tea his mother and sister went off to the local shop and bought just enough to feed everyone but him, they then cooked it and ate it in front of him.

"Am I going to get nothing," he questioned them.

"Ya have been told time and again, there's no money in this house to feed ya, if ye want to pay for it, it a different thing," answered his father.

"Aheik, aheik he'll take the bit from the children's mouth," went on his mother.

Liam left for fear of his own reaction. He went to the pub and feasted on four bags of crisps; he was being openly avoided in the pub now; well, at least one good thing about this, he thought; at least now, he knew who his friends were. He went to another town in the area the next day, it had a factory in it and a cattle mart. He looked in both places without success and to be thorough he looked in a hotel which had a night club attached, to see if there was anything going there, he was asked if he would he consider a bouncer's job and that was it, the only near positive of the entire quest, but his overall quest was to avoid violence and hassle, not put himself in the way of it.

The reception was the same that evening and once again he existed on a few bags of crisps in the pub. The following day it just got too much, the caterwauls, the hisses, the silences, the sheer sense of rejection; he had hardly even spoken to his sisters or brother. He packed up that afternoon, getting ready for the afternoon train to Dublin so he could get the night sailing to Holyhead.

"Are ye off?" asked his father.

"Yes."

"Oh, thank God, at last," said his mother.

"Well, that's the right thing to do," said his father, "ye wouldn't leave us the few pounds like ye said ye would."

"No," roared Liam in response.

"What's your brother's name, Tim isn't it," he asked his father, "and yours, isn't it Padraig," he said to his mother, referring to their brothers that had gone to England and never made contact again, "I'm going to join them."

"There's a big crowd in this house," screeched his mother, looking at him with her mouth open as though aghast at his ignorance and failure to understand her problems, "sure what can we do, we can hardly manage as it is," she went on probably realising now that she had overplayed her hand.

"I asked for not one thing from this house, but to provide a base for me to look for a job in this country. I was willing even to pay for the bit I ate while I was here, which would not happen in any other household, all I wanted was a chance to look for a job and if after a proper search I didn't get one then good and well, I'd go back to England, but ye wouldn't let me, all I wanted was a chance."

"But sure, there's nothing here," said his father with his mouth pulled into an incredulous smile and winking at himself as was his wont when under pressure.

"There's jobs for many here, but as I have said if I tried and got a proper chance to try and failed, then I'd go back to England, but ye denied me the chance, I was even willing to pay for the bit I ate which no one on a break does, well right I know when I'm not welcomed," said Liam.

"There's a big crowd in this house, aheik, aheik," wailed his mother.

"Caterwaul at me like that again and I'll wallop ye, mother or not," roared Liam on the brink of losing it.

"Jesus. Mary and Joseph he threatening to hit his old whammy," she screeched.

"Enough," he roared and he grabbed his bag and left the house with the fervent desire never to return again.

He caught the train and the boat and was back in North Acton nine days after he left it resolving never to see it again. While he had been away, his housemates had reported his behaviour in full to his landlord, the excessive exercising, the brooding silences, even not answering sometimes when spoken to, general unsociability and being withdrawn constantly; both landlord and housemates hoped that he would not return. But he did and wrapped up in further miseries, he barely acknowledged them, a nod a grunt.

He went to the landlord and paid the rent a day early, a gruff, "hello, here's the rent."

His size and mien stopped the landlord from throwing him out there and then. He did fifty press ups that night and more exercises, the next morning he ran two miles and did near an hour exercise and after that he went looking for work. The one thing he could do to improve his lot was to work for someone else besides

John Cormac O'Mahony, he had worked for 'boy' O'Malley and knew him to be a mate of John Cormac's so he couldn't go near him, he had to go elsewhere.

He spent that day looking at sites on the docklands and got several offers, apparently work was more plentiful than he thought. After some consideration he picked a subbie from Wexford, as that part of Ireland was as far away as possible, from where John Cormac came from, thus he would be somewhat less likely to have any contact or influence with that subbie.

He was due to start the following Monday on fifty pounds a day with a promise of a rise if it was deserved. He realised now that while he was captured in John Cormac's web, both work and in turn wages had gone up without his knowledge. He stuck into the work manfully and that and his size and strength muted the normal resentment there was to a new man entering a crew, especially a man from another part of Ireland.

The next week he got a rise to sixty pounds a day. He then set about the business of getting someplace to stay, to complete the break between John Cormac and himself. What was an advantage in one way was a disadvantage in others, the size and muscularity that recommended him to an employer, put prospective landlords off. The fact he was Irish was also no advantage. The upshot of it was, that he had to remain in North Acton.

Now, detained where he was, he continued with his exercising and training to an even greater degree. He set up a sort of punchbag in the shed and often spent an hour pounding it and increased all other exercises. The people in the house were near petrified of him, but he said nothing or done nothing to them and was co-operative indeed helpful in any joint undertakings like cleaning, so they could make no complaint against him.

Someone finally asked him what he was training for and caught in the spur of the moment, the only response he could think was that it was out of fear of ill health that had afflicted a mate of his and he didn't want to suffer the same fate. The question made him reflect for the first time that he might be causing concern by his activities to his housemates, but all he could think to do was to invite his questioner to use the punchbag if he wanted to get fit, one way or another, he was afraid to stop his exercising.

The job was OK, at least in comparison to John Cormac's job, for instance the boss did have some notion of ground works and did do so much to allow his workers to develop; for instance, he put Liam working with a highly experienced pipe lawyer so he could lay learn to lay pipes properly. This continued for over

162

a month and Liam was beginning to feel relaxed and he was even saving some money; thoughts were beginning to come into his head about working elsewhere, for instance in Birmingham.

But on one fine day in late September, a brilliant day for work with a slight wind and warm but not hot weather, he was down in a trench learning to lay pipes and making progress, when he was summoned by the subbie and directed to the little hut the subbie used on the site, as someone wanted to see him. He went into the hut and saw a small man sitting behind the desk with his cap pulled down low over his face. Fear rose in Liam and was rapidly justified when the small man straightened up and pulled the cap back, it was John Cormac.

"Hi, hello there, how are you, are you not the man that I covered up a murder for," he said.

"I never murdered anyone."

"Was I there to see what you or anyone else done."

"I don't have to work for you forever, mister subcontractor O'Mahony," answered Liam, he now noticed Mac Bearta and the creeping Jesus standing at the back of the hut in the shadows.

"Mister navy Mac Faul, you have to work for me until at least the dangers of discovery are past and that is well after the building in Moorgate is completed and occupied. You see how it goes is this, if I pay you money to work for me, you work for me until one of us gets dissatisfied with the other. If I go totally and completely out of my way for you by protecting you against a conviction for being an accessory to murder and do it against my own will."

Here John Cormac stopped and shook his head sorrowfully, "then mister navy Mac Faul, you owe me, if instead you were in jail and all the hard English boys were testing themselves against the big paddy, then I safely say that your attitude would be quite different."

"Ya ungrateful little bastard ye and as well as that what about all the dangers that ye're putting the rest of us in, into the pub, a couple extra and out with the whole fucking thing," said the creeping Jesus.

"I'm very careful with beer, my gr," at this stage Liam stopped himself, for such was his wariness of this crew that he would not give them such a weak lead on him, of knowledge of his long dead grandfather's drunkenness and this despite his estrangement from his family.

163

"Nobody, not me," said Mac Bearta pointing to himself, "not you, not him, not anybody is safe with drink on them and that is why a safe house was arranged for us all."

"What sort of fool was it, that just didn't lift up the phone and call the police and himself perfectly safe with plenty of witnesses to say where I was," said John Cormac shaking his head.

"'Tis too good ya were boss," said the creeping Jesus, "remember the boys I'll get you if no others," he continued.

"You're going to get me," said Liam standing over the creeping Jesus.

"It's not just me, it's all of us and who we know, that you have to look out for. It's as simple as this much my lad, I'm not going to go to jail because you let the side down and I'm sorry if you don't like it, but that's it and if it comes down to it someone or two or three will deal with you, as big and hard as you are," said the creeping Jesus, his head moving up and down emphatically.

Liam looked as though he would hit him, but Mac Bearta intervened, "remember boy, you had a free vote and you voted not to call the authorities and you were free to speak and you remained silent."

"That's right, mister navy Mac Faul and if you will remember that I alone voted to call the authorities and argued against the rest of you to do that, but ye all opposed me and reluctantly I acceded to yer wishes, so now I don't think it's too much to ask ye to stick by the choice that ye, but not me, made," said John Cormac.

Liam started to vacillate, "yes but I work for another man now, I can hardly leave him in the lurch."

"You don't need to worry about him," replied John Cormac and told Liam the van was outside.

"I can hardly leave in the middle of the day," protested Liam.

"Oh but you can," replied John Cormac.

They left the hut and the subbie that Liam was working for came up and paid him his wages in full up the end of the week, this was two days more than he strictly owed, which was most unusual as this subbie, as similar to all other subbies, he was usually late and if anything short with wages.

"I can send ye another man now, Pat, if ye want," said John Cormac to him.

"No," was the answer and the man turned his back and walked off, he obviously didn't like what happened but didn't seem able or willing to do anything about it.

Liam was like a man that was indentured as of old, he could only walk where his master John Cormac said he could.

Chapter 11

Liam Mac Faul was learning the hard and fast way, that prisons are not just composed of concrete and steel bars, that someone else built a long time ago; we build them ourselves, those that oppress us and are oppressed with us build them. These walls are composed of ever reduced and constrained circumstances, ever narrowed horizons and ever lesser prospects, that entailed our ambitions are lessened and thus hope.

He could only be a building labourer, semi-skilled at best a pipe layer or the like and now he could only work for someone who covered up a murder to save themselves some money. It was only days ago that he had lamented the fact that he could no longer get himself a trade and was it not the case that once upon a time somebody claimed he could be a teacher. It was so far away from what was real that sometimes he wondered if he dreamt it, not remembered it.

He started at John Cormac's new site on Commercial Road, beside Aldgate on the outskirts of the city. The old crew were all there with the exception of Mac Goldrick and there were two new men who were kept working in an area as far apart from where the rest were working as possible. Liam got bulls looks from all the men with the exception of John Devine who had visibly aged and had lost weight.

He started work that very afternoon and he was put with his old mate John Devine. It could be said to be against his nature to slack off, but every shovelful was like he was shovelling lead; the conditions and sheer domination that he worked under was discouraging in the extreme. He was still fit to keep up with Pakie Mac Grath who was working nearby, but he was no place near the Mac Faul of old.

It was not long before it was noticed, "ahhah me boy, ye're intending to swing the lead I see," said John Cormac, "well, me boy, ye should have learned your lesson at this stage, but if not, that's OK, I'll just pay ye twenty pounds a day or even less and when ye come that cheap, ye'll have to stay even longer as well."

Mac Bearta came over, "what in the name of the living fuck are ye at? Dossing isn't going to get ye anyplace, ye're going to have stay the distance and do the work whether ye like it or not. Ye're fucking all of us up because remember this is more for the boys' benefit than him, he wasn't around when that thing happened, but you were."

"I was down in the big trench I didn't see anything."

"How do I know where you were, I wasn't there either," answered Mac Bearta and walked off without permitting any answer from Liam.

The next to come was the creeping Jesus, "in the name of fuck, Mac Faul, what are ye at slacking like that for."

"I'm still doing more than you anyways, not that that's hard," replied Liam getting heated at all the abuse.

"Ye're acting the bollix, don't ya realise that, that man can just lift the phone if he thinks he's been pissed on and that's exactly what he'll do. He has proof he was elsewhere and he can make the reasonable excuse that he was coerced into it for fear of losing his business and fear of the men. Have ye ever thought, ye little bastard, of that man there," he said pointing at John Devine.

"He's trying to rear a family on this job, what if he gets taken up by the cops and it's alright saying ye were down in the big trench at the time, but how can you prove it, other than the testimonies of the boys, which 'ill hardly be forthcoming if ye leave them in the shit," he then quickly left denying Liam any chance of a response.

The day ended and Liam ended up in the same tube carriage as Pakie Mac Grath, who tried to speak to him several times, Liam avoided him; at Shepherds Bush station, he said to Liam that he'd stay on as far as North Acton as he wanted to have a word with him; Liam caught him and threw him with all the force he could out of the carriage, where he hit one of the columns dividing the platforms at that end of the platforms, otherwise he would have been likely to carry on across both platforms and onto the opposite tracks of the railway for one evening; Liam had had enough.

After a sleepless night of solid despair and frantic thinking as to how to evade John Cormac, all Liam could do was to go back to John Cormac, for at least the time being he was defeated. John Cormac told him that he was going to be lenient with him for one last time and that he would forgive the dossing yesterday, as it

167

must have come as a shock to him to be caught out but today, he'd have to produce the goodies.

To spare his head by preventing comment and hassle, he did try to move faster and was faster than Pete Mac Namee who was working nearby, but Liam was still not up to his old level.

The comments arrived rapidly, "I'll just pay ya less," from John Cormac.

"Yer here and yer going to have stay here and acting the bollix will only make things worse for everyone," from Mac Bearta.

"Ya'd piss on yer mates, yer some prick, aren't ye Mac Faul," from the creeping Jesus and on and on.

All these barbs were delivered in low voices and with bulls looks carefully directed at him to hide this activity from the two new workers, who were not 'au fait' with the great skeleton in the closet, otherwise they would have been unbearable. After a while John Devine suggested to him that it would probably be better to speed up a bit just to save one's ears, which he did, but the episodes of abuse still came only spaced further apart.

Finally when Pakie Mac Grath came up for his turn, John Devine told him to fuck off or he'd make him fuck off and that enough was enough, this did quiet things down a bit, but it was a long, long day. He was walking up Hounditch on his was to Liverpool Street station, when Pakie Mac Grath tried to talk to him.

"I wonder, young Mac Faul, if you're up with the crack at all."

Liam came for him and he had to retreat by running in and out between the traffic to cross the road to get away from Liam and it was just as well as Liam had enough for that day. Three times that evening he did fifty press ups and a serious session on the punchbag and the other people in the house began to make plans to leave.

The pub was schedule for the weekend and Liam tried to beg off, his excuse being that he had no money; that was no problem John Cormac told him as he paid all wages in the pub now, so if he got there, he'd get money, John Cormac paid him forty pounds for two days and told him the wages would go up to thirty pounds a day next week, if and only if he pulled his socks up; this was just half what he was getting from the other subbie.

The only bright point in the entire firmament was that Jimmy Mac Goldrick seemed to have evaded the round up and Liam envied him. The next week there was the same miserable old routine. Liam upped the rate of his work, just not to be listening to abuse and this took an amount of effort that surprised him, his will to work was defiantly being sapped.

This still did not please John Cormac, "a bit more would do no harm, no harm at all."

Unless it involved work, no other man on site spoke to him but John Devine. On Thursday afternoon John Cormac told him to increase the rate of work, particularly that afternoon if he wanted thirty pounds a day that week. Figuring that there was no other option, he upped the work rate. He then noticed that John Cormac was bringing men he had recently started and showing them Liam at work as an example of what was required.

"Stand there now and take it easy, now look carefully at that man there and what he's doing and how fast he's doing it. Take your time now and take it all in; you see that's what expected of you around here, is that clear now, right now you know what you have to do to hang on to your job."

Later that day they found out that these new men were paid forty-five pounds a day, once and a half what the rest of the lads were. Futilely this was mentioned in the pub, "and exactly what murder did I cover up for them lads," was the predictable response.

Wages were rising and even at forty-five pounds a shift, men of any quality weren't staying with John Cormac. This fact more and more reinforced the necessity of having a captive core of cheap and capable labour. The new men joined them in the pub and didn't like it and had to be persuaded to stay using it by John Cormac.

"This is where all business is conducted, this is where I pay the wages, otherwise I have to give you a check, which you can only cash in this pub."

The landlord lost out on cashing cheques but he had more customers; John Cormac now employed seventeen men on four different sites, he was indeed a proud man. The shift in the pub was probably the most painful of all, conventionally the pub was a release from the pressure and hassle of work but here, it did the opposite, it increased the pressure; certainly Liam Mac Faul hated it more than work.

He truly envied Jimmy Mac Goldrick who had got away from this trap. This continued for another two weeks, then Jimmy Mac Goldrick was recaptured. The crew were all back on ship, they were paid little more than half what the others were and they had to work hard to set an example for other men to follow and on a day-to-day basis they would have to set up a fast rate for the other men to keep up with, which was used, all too often for correcting the errors of John Cormac and even occasionally Mac Bearta.

In general, they created a situation where the many deficits of knowledge of John Cormac and to a lesser degree Mac Bearta had, about the work could be afforded and made good within the price, a mistake or blunder could be cheaply corrected, John Cormac was a made man. Complaints from all quarters finally forced John Cormac to raise the wages by a fiver a shift.

Pressure was applied to Mac Faul and Mac Goldrick to produce more and they were held up to the new men as examples of what was expected from them and this put such men under pressure and in turn weighted against them forming any friendship or camaraderie with Mac Faul or Mac Goldrick, thus keeping them isolated, usually after the first few days, the new men only spoke to them, when it was absolutely necessary.

This state of affairs continued in the pub, except for sleep and travelling on the tube, one lived the entire time in an atmosphere of hostility and isolation from others; it would be considered most unusual by virtually all other inhabitants of London, but the tube appeared a relatively friendly place compared to all the other environments, that the workforce of John Cormac O'Mahony were forced to inhabit.

One day during a brief lull caused by Mac Bearta failing to order some pipes, John Devine and Liam Mac Faul fell into conversation with an old labourer for the main contractors, like many of his sort he was embittered with his lot and the lot of the Irish in general. He was talking about the ill effect of the subbies on the Irish and the power they had.

"They have ye by the bollix, there's no place or nobody ye can turn to, if anything wrong is done to ya."

"True, true," replied Devine and Mac Faul with certainty to their answers.

"Ya see ya can't turn to the authorities, even if they were to help ya and that's unlikely in the first place, most men are compromised someplace along the line, like they've been working cash in hand or drawing and working or the tax hasn't been paid either by them or more likely the so and so's they've been working for and that's what the authorities are after."

"Ya can hardly expect the kid's to eat grass," said John Devine, "if there's work going cash in hand, ya more or less have to take it."

"The hands of the man with responsibilities are tied, he has to get money how he can and yet he's the man a more honest and right-minded environment would suit, but with a family he's tied in further with the subbies and their crooked goings on than ever."

"If a man got a skelping in a pub and he went to the police, sure he'd probably be lynched by his own people," said John Devine.

"That's right and that attitude only supports the subbie," replied the man.

"Is there no such thing as the subbies doing the right thing and playing a fair game," said Liam Mac Faul.

"No because they are not fit to do their job in the first place, the wild west, where no rules apply, favour the cowboy," the man replied, "ya could kill a man, kill a man I say on site and you'd get away with it if it suited the subbie," he said in conclusion.

Though they couldn't and didn't agree publicly, but both John Devine and Liam Mac Faul could absolutely believe that statement. Liam Mac Faul was realising that the answer to the question of what exactly he was; was that he was littler and lesser than he had ever imagined. Another aspect of these narrowed horizons came that weekend, while they were doing what they were becoming to think off more and more as the pub shift.

They were in the usual group with Jimmy Mac Goldrick standing on one side of them and Liam Mac Faul sitting on a stool on the other side of the group, both silent amid the loud conversation of little substance and forced laughter that emitted from the group. Unusually for this pub, a few girls entered and ordered drinks, they were already a bit tipsy and in a flirty mood.

The boldest of their number was eyeing up the 'talent' and she spotted Liam Mac Faul; he was clearly a large powerful and muscular man and she decided to explore a bit further so she went up and stood beside him, which made her even more appreciative of his size and sheer masculinity.

"You come here often," she remarked to him, this barely elicited a response.

"Uh uh," he said.

She didn't know what to make out of this, but Liam Mac Faul was a fine specimen. She decided to try further.

"You know, you should offer your stool to a lady," she said.

"Uh oh, er, sorry," went Liam and he stood up and gave her the stool and walked over behind the group to stand still and unspeaking beside Jimmy Mac Goldrick, totally unresponsive to her overtures.

Her overtures were not totally without response, John Cormac was always the boy for the women or at least in his own estimation he was and he did spot her overture. He went up to where she was perched on her stool at the end of a line of men.

"How are ye, I've not seen you here before," he said.

Somewhat peeved in the first place at Liam's total non-response to her charms, she was not impressed by the forward intrusion of this far inferior specimen and she looked at him as though he was a piece of dog shite and John Cormac noticed this, so he decided to state his position in the hope of making the right impression and perhaps putting her in her place.

"I'm the main man round here, all these men work for me," said John Cormac.

"Who gives a fuck," she replied.

John Cormac was undeterred, as he had an ever-high opinion of himself and only understood his own point of view.

"Ya look like ye're on the outlook of a man, well I'm the main man around here, so why don't we get to know each a bit better."

Angry at being rejected and leaving herself open to any little pervert of an opportunist by her actions she didn't spare John Cormac.

"A man but not a little pervert shite, which is all you fucking are," she replied, jumping down from her stool and going over to join her companions whom she enjoined to leave as "there was only seedy little creeps in here."

Jerry Cawley and Martin Mac Donogh were sitting next to the woman and witnessed the encounter with John Cormac in full, they immediately got involved in the most intense discussion which bordered on the argumentative, this drew the attention of Pete Mac Namee and Mac Bearta who were further up the bar and were shielded from the encounter between the woman and John Cormac by Cawley and Mac Donogh. The more they listened to this argument the more puzzled they became, as it seemed to be without a subject.

"No, I'm telling ye, ye put it up."

"No round."

"No, how would ya do that."

"Sure, don't I know."

"It's round, er, up I mean."

"Ah ah, sure, that wouldn't work at all."

"It would, I'm telling ya."

"Round is the only ways."

"No, up."

"no round."

At this stage John Cormac interrupted them and both Cawley and Mac Donogh seemed startled.

"The problem with this pub is that the women that come in here are only trash," he said.

"Ah right, OK," they said distantly as though not really comprehending what he was talking about.

Liam Mac Faul on the other side of the group was totally oblivious to the entire episode, for women didn't really figure in his world. In early November, an old acquaintance of Jimmy Mac Goldrick reappeared by pure chance, it was the fellow he had fought when he had worked for the dog subbie. He was returning to the site with Liam Mac Faul after they had a cup of tea, when his old adversary appeared.

"Are ye still around, ya wanker ya," he said shoving aggressively into him. Jimmy backed away not knowing what to do, Liam Mac Faul told him to fuck off.

"Who's the freak," he asked Jimmy and Liam hit him a perfect uppercut that actually lifted him off his feet with the force of the belt, he fell backwards into the recessed doorway of a shop clearly out for the count.

This was witnessed by two of his workmates who came to his aid, as Liam and Jimmy walked away; it took several glasses of water poured over him and the full of twenty minutes before he was able to get to his feet again and he was still unsteady.

John Cormac also witnessed this and always the boy to see the potential in a situation, he began to visualise Liam Mac Faul as an enforcer or ganger.

Chapter 12

One perfect day, just a perfect day goes the song and sometimes such days do occur. It was a Monday the day of the subbies golf match and the day itself was a perfect example of 'old maids' summer, sparkling sunshine, a soft breeze, but with just a touch of a bite to it to remind people that it was November, truly a day to lift the spirits.

Most unusually on this day all the big boys were present, 'boy' O'Malley, Uncle 'tot' O'Mahony and that great man Paddy O'Riordan and of course, John Cormac, himself. There started a round of golf as a foursome, with 'boy' and John Cormac versus 'tot' and Paddy O'Riordan.

For once and when it was the last thing he wanted, his game was excellent, indeed he almost sunk a hole in one at the first, it ended up only four inches from the hole and he didn't know what to do, to get out of it, but at the last minute inspiration came to him and he hit it straight and hard over the hole and twenty feet away and from there he could mess around and allow the rest to catch up and it would look legitimate.

It was the same on the second hole, despite the fact he aimed well wide, it dropped about five feet from the hole. John Cormac hit it well wide. But not wide enough to make it look as though he wasn't trying, it nearly went in but luckily he hit it hard enough so it continued on, almost into the rough, where he could muck around and let the others get ahead of him; shaking his head at his bad fortune he went after it.

John Cormac and 'boy' finished the third hole and Paddy O'Riordan and 'tot' were about halfway through it, when Paddy looked up at the cloudless sky and decided it was going to rain and suggested moving to the nineteenth hole, they all agreed with this and John Cormac and 'boy' paid over the hundred pound stake to Paddy and 'tot' as they were the winners having taken less strokes and therefore, having a lower par; the fact that they did not finish the hole was, of course, not considered.

They adjourned to the bar and settled in one corner away from the others, so they could speak privately. John Cormac ordered and after a bit of small talk, Paddy O'Riordan looked over at John Cormac with a though looking smile on his face and a glint in his eye; more than ever his face looked like a tube train coming out of a tunnel, low bald forehead, eyes slanting down at the side, though pronounced jaw.

"I heard ya had a, em, sticky sort of problem earlier in the year, but handled it well," he said to John Cormac.

"Well, we managed," replied John Cormac, 'boy' and 'tot' were smiling at him now with the same tough smiles as Paddy had.

"That's the mark of the right man, he can handle things when they get tough or as I should say 'sticky'," said 'boy', to a burst of laughter at his witty usage of the word sticky.

"Well, in all honesty, Mac Bearta was a fair good help to me," answered John Cormac.

"What the fuck else would he be for, but you're still the boss, the top boy; so top credit goes to you," answered 'boy'.

John Cormac recognised this for what it was, it was a coronation, it was full entry into the big boys' club, he was one of the right boys now.

"When the going gets tough, the tough get going," chimed in uncle 'tot'.

"Ye're a right one of the O'Mahonys and no doubt about it."

"Heh, heh heh," went Paddy O'Riordan, "I always knew that we had a right one in ya; aye, I could see ya had it in ya, it's the man that can handle the thought ones that ya need as boss; the rest simply can't cut it and therefore they cannot be the boss."

"Truer words were never said," came in 'boy'.

"They go on about brains and knowing this and that," went on Paddy, "but in the end of the day it's the balls not the brains that count, the balls."

Approbation from 'tot' and 'boy', "the balls, the balls, the balls," they coursed with John Cormac joining in.

Though looking smiles from a group across the bar that had overheard this, they knew what they on about as they were the right sort of boys too. John Cormac was made. The day went on and the drink went in, and 'tot' in particular was in seventh heaven.

"'Twas always in the O'Mahonys to be the big boys to be the boss; me father, his grandfather was a cattle jobber and publican and later on an auctioneer, he was a powerful boy he was and his father before that was a jobber and it has been said, a great fighting man, so it goes back that far and here is another."

"If ye're able to handle the likes of that then ye're fit for more or less anything and that's what it takes to be the main boy," said 'boy'.

"It a great test the likes of that and in its way its lucky that it came yer way early because then, it's clear what ye're up to or not, as the case may be," said Paddy.

A man like Paddy O'Riordan actually praising him, it was almost beyond belief and what did lie ahead, could he ever be a man like Paddy O Riordan someday. The day passed and there were some mighty stories, Boy told one.

"I had a few skins working for me, just on a day to day basis and I used to pay them fifteen pounds a day, but there was this day anyways and I took a sort of dislike to the attitude, the work was done, but they just threw the shovels there when they were finished and I thought that a bit of a lesson was in order.

So, I told them at the drop off point that the rate for that day was ten; there was a big burst of bullshit at this, and what were they not going to do; right says I and I sent the gangerman, Brenden Chambers, do ye remember the Chambers brothers."

"Aye."

"Rings a bell."

"Up ahead. I said to the pub to get money to pay them, but he got his brother Frankie and Jim and Pat Joyce who were his cousins and right hard men and another mate of theirs and I said to the skins 'now boys the next time I offer ye a tenner, ye'll find ye'll take it and I'm going to show ye why' and the boys hammered straight into them and thrashed fuck out of them;

There was one, one of the mouthiest, lying on the ground sort of whinging like some woman; ' now boys do ye understand why ye should take a tenner when its proffered."

"Heh, heh, heh."

"Ha, ha, ha, ha," the laughter rose the roof.

"Ye able to handle the dogs alright O'Malley."

"The right ganger man is the answer."

"Ya have to pick ones that like the aggro," said 'tot'.

"Ahaa, ahaa, O'Mahony ye have it off to a tee surely," replied Paddy O'Riordan to this remark.

The day passed quickly like all good days do; beer to brandy and the crack was mighty. John Cormac was initially cautious least the great secret leaked out, but the boys advised him that in time it would be no harm if it got known, it would show what sort of man he was and that there was no fooling about with him.

The secret was when to let it be known, like among the subbies, the right boys early on, this would garner him respect there and then and a couple of years down the road among the men. John Cormac was reluctant to let things be known to the men; for instance, what about a report to the authorities.

'Boy' answered him, "in three years' time, I'll only be a rumour and who the hell is going to tear down a twelve story commercial grade building in the city of London on the basis of a rumour and the rumour about a dead Paddy at that."

"Aye that's right, a bit of time and it can be known but won't matter, except to those that are considering acting the bollix with ye," from Paddy O'Riordan; truly Paddy was one smart man, "when ye're capable of handling that, ye're capable of anything and then ye have them by the balls and when ye have them by the balls, ye have a solid grip, they'll not defy you," went on Paddy.

"The balls, the balls, the balls," coursed the boys, a small bit out of context perhaps but appreciated and understood all around the bar, there were though smiles and nods and winks all around, truly they were the right boys.

Even before the end of that day it became known that John Cormac was as much one of the right boys as anyone else there. He had had to rely on 'boy' O'Malley for help locating Mac Faul and Mac Goldrick but in future, his own sway would be good enough, when he put the 'word' out that someone was wanted, then other men would co-operate automatically.

'T'was a powerful evening and men of note, O'Brien, Mac Carthy, O'Neill, Lee, O'Flattley, Reynolds, Mac Ginley, Corcoron and more, were all greeting John Cormac as equals, proposing meeting up to discuss business, going for a drink, meetings with others, it couldn't be any better. The drink began to add up and the boys were getting a bit boisterous.

Paddy O'Riordan was telling a story about a great ganger man he had once and how he used to, handle the men, "and that he'd kick them up in the arse and if, if they turned round to face him didn't he, didn't he kick them up in the balls."

"The balls, the balls, the balls," the boys coursed and a cheer arose from the house.

However, 'boy' fell off his stool and when he got up he was going to fight with someone, so John Cormac and the club steward led him out, as this house had the wrong clientele to go fighting with. He pissed himself in the cab and the cab driver threw him out of the cab and was making a fuss about the smell.

The steward of the golf club hit the cab driver levelling him in response to his complaint saying, "'tisn't what he deserves, him complaining about the smell and him a frigging paki, what sort of smell is there off him," there was a powerful laugh from all and sundry at this comment.

A special cab that catered for these sorts of cases was called and John Cormac paid him, as 'boy' in the humour that he was in might be difficult and John Cormac didn't want 'boy' upset. That great man Paddy O'Riordan was next to leave and John Cormac escorted him out in case that anyone would take advantage of the state he was in and try to get information out of him or such like, if something like this did happen, then when Paddy came to realise it there could be adverse consequences for all.

Paddy stood up to have a piss on the stairs and it mainly went down his trousers; this was a sort of problem with Paddy after drink, but hadn't he a wife to take care of it and he mainly kept to company, where most knew him and who and what he was, so there were no consequences or indeed comment about the matter.

The club steward was there looking at Paddy and going red in the face, but he didn't dare do or say anything, when you were the top boy you did as you liked. John Cormac and uncle 'tot' were left, one advantage to being a publican's son was that you were good at handling drink. They discussed his plans; was John Cormac still going for the kill or was he going to try regular subbying.

He thought about this and said both, he may as well knock a bit of extra money out of it for a while and this would also help him to maximise the amount he would get when he went for the kill; 'tot' agreed this was good thinking. More men came up and made themselves known to John Cormac, a lot of the men there already knew 'tot' and used him to get acquainted with John Cormac.

John Cormac overheard them being called the O'Mahony subbies and this was as much confirmation as he would need that he had gained entrée into the big boys' league, he was definitely a made man. He wasn't all that sure how he got home that night, but it was 2 o'clock the next afternoon before he could get up and he had a headache like someone was operating a jackhammer in there, but the remembrance of the great day that went before soothed it.

He decided he was a bit too reserved in his actions. More boldness and aggression should be the order of the day, there was still a number of people that looked down on him; well, maybe he'd show them, in the end of the day he wanted John Cormac O'Mahony to be a name to be reckoned with; he had a fair feather in his cap already, only he had to keep it hidden for the moment.

What about big Mac Faul, could he ever be got to give a slap or two to certain individuals at John Cormac's behest, from what he had seen, he was well fit to. It was Wednesday before John Cormac was fit to face the sites, but he made it his mission to awaken those that were there. He had a total of four sites under his dominion now; there was still four men on the St Swithuns Lane site, the men had been hired after the main contract was finished and didn't know the rest of the gang, they were even excused attendance at the pub, he wanted no slip ups or at least not yet he didn't.

He reared upon every man in the gang and even got a bit scratchy with John Devine who was indeed failing; John Devine went to the pub that lunch time and didn't return to the site, a first ever for John Devine. At the end of the day he thought progress was up and he felt better about himself than ever. He even got an order for two more men from the London wall site and was asked to look over a new site, everything was on the up and up.

He visited aunt Myra that evening and got a glass of whiskey from her for the first time ever. He was one powerful bit of a man even if he only said so himself. On that Thursday, he wanted a jackhammer and he went over with Mac Bearta to a neighbouring site where he knew that an Irish subby was operating, intending to borrow a jackhammer, but didn't see anyone about they could talk to, it was lunchtime and they were likely to be in the pub; they saw an unused jackhammer and took it away.

Two hours later, the foreman from that site and a large workman, probably the chargehand, arrived on John Cormac's site and took the jackhammer back, the foreman challenged John Cormac to come off site with him and he'd sort him out. John Cormac baulked at this and lost face, to the regulars he mentioned that he was wary of any hassle still because of 'the affair in the city' as the murder of the 'rat' was now known as.

However, a plan formed in his mind, Mac Faul was looking more and more like the incredible hulk and was very powerful, if he could be got to strike the foreman on the other site and level him, honour would be restored to John

Cormac as he was one of John Cormac's men and a healthy fear would put into the men on the other site.

He planned a way to go about it that would still leave Mac Faul subservient to him. If he ordered him to do it, he could and probably would consider this act as extra to his debt and this would loosen his grip upon him, maybe break it and Mac Faul was the best worker he had since John Devine started failing.

John Cormac consulted Mac Bearta and a plan was formulated, the creeping Jesus would put Mac Faul up to asking for a pay rise and John Cormac would agree it was deserved, but demand as a gesture of loyalty, after all his disloyalty, that he hit the foreman from the other site. On Friday, Martin Mac Donogh was put working with Liam Mac Faul, who clearly outworked him, unusually instead of finding fault with his work and trying to draw level in 'production terms' from that angle, he complimented him and encouraged him to ask for a pay rise.

"Ye know, young Mac Faul, ye're a solid worker, 'tis a pity ye're not reliable, ye deserve a pay rise."

"It appears that I must work for thirty-five pounds a day whether I like it or not," he answered.

"It's not right that; ye should work here surely, for nothing else is safe, for all out sakes, but ye deserve more money."

"How is that got?"

"I'll tell ya what, I'll go with ye to the boss in the pub Saturday night and we'll ask for more money."

"How come you have my good in mind all of a sudden."

"Well, I don't like ye running away and betraying the boys, young Mac Faul, as you should know well one slip could destroy all of us, but for all that ye're still a good worker and ye do deserve more money, so I'm prepared to ye're request for more pay if ye make it Saturday night," went the creeping Jesus.

Liam Mac Faul could see nothing wrong with this on the surface, but was still suspicious of this sudden change of heart by a known John Cormac creature. When Saturday night came, he thought why not? He may as well get more money out of it. They were in the pub Saturday night as ordered, trying to pass the time and making some sort of pretence of enjoying themselves as would be expected from one in a pub.

Martin Mac Donogh brought Liam over to John Cormac where he was standing by the bar most unusually on his own and away from anyone else in the bar. They or rather the creeping Jesus made the pitch.

"In all fairness this man is a good worker and while no one can approve of his letting us all down, he should get more than thirty-five pounds a day; ya should see all he does in a day compared with many of the others, 'tis only fair play."

"Those that do less than me get paid more than me, it is not fair," said Liam trying in some way to back up his own claim.

John Cormac shook his head.

The creeping Jesus tried again, "there's more than one man saying it's unfair, boss, he's clearly a good worker, even Devine is hardly as good today."

"Ya know, what I got elsewhere," said Liam in support of his claim.

"Aye that's the problem, ye can't be trusted elsewhere," said John Cormac, "so moving isn't an option."

"That's accepted, he can't work elsewhere, but he should get paid more for what he does," said the creeping Jesus.

"It's unfair," added Liam.

"Alright, alright, alright," went John Cormac his hands up defensively as though warding off a torrent of abusive argument, though the creeping Jesus and Liam were barely speaking above a whisper, "I suppose, there's a point there, alright, ye're a fair good worker. I've seen better but also a fair few worse, it's not that, that's the problem, the problem is that I can't trust you, you let me down."

John Cormac paused and Liam looked at the ground and showed signs of yielding, so John Cormac went on, "but I'm a very fair man, too fair for me own good to be honest," here John Cormac paused and shook his head looking at the ground and then he went on, "I'll tell you what I'll do if you prove to me that I can rely on you, then I'll raise your wages by a tenner a day."

"What do ye want me to do," asked Liam.

John Cormac didn't reply and appeared to be musing over the matter. Liam had in mind a display of a very fast work rate as an example for new men.

"Alright, do ye remember that thick bollix of a foreman from the site across the road that reared up on me the other day and because I didn't want to take any chance of the authorities getting involved, to ensure you lot were safe, I could do nothing," asked John Cormac.

Liam answered in the affirmative.

"Well, I want you to strike that man one blow, one right blow, but only one and say that this is from John Cormac O'Mahony. If you do that for me then I will know that I can trust you and then I'll raise your wages by a tenner a day," went on John Cormac.

"I don't want anything to do with such carry on," answered Liam, "and will it not possibly involve the authorities."

"I know well you don't want anything to do with the likes of this, that is why I am asking you to do it, to know that you are willing to do something against your will to please me, if you arc, then I know that I can trust you, if not why should I not cut your wages, instead of raising them.

The boys will sort you out if you leave; they have no choice but to, so that they can protect themselves. As for the authorities we'll pick a spot off site, so if he does go to the authorities he'll have trouble proving it, as we'll all say you were on site at the time."

Martin Mac Donogh nodded at this, "and he'll lose face so I think you're fairly safe. But the main fact is, that you'll take such a risk for me, so it'll prove I can trust you," finished up John Cormac with what he thought was a stroke of genius, changing an argument 'against the action, into one for the action'.

Liam first thought was to go to the police, anti-Irish bigots or not and tell all and hope for the best, for just how deep anyways was this hole that John Cormac was digging for him, what else would he be asked to do? But all council from everyone was against such an act and as for dealing with the boys; well, he was afraid of none of them on their own, but men that could act as they had acted and dispose of one of their own workmates in a piling hole, were capable of coming at him from any angle, with any instrument and in any numbers.

Martin Mac Donogh drew him away from John Cormac and spoke privately with him, "it's only one slap and that foreman was one thick bastard and again it'd reassure the boys that you were reliable and you'd stand up with the gang if necessary, go for it I say."

"And spend the rest of my life doing the same for that little piece of shite," replied Liam.

"No one said that and if such a thing comes up, we'll deal with it then, but I do think this once would be a good idea," answered Martin.

Liam and the creeping Jesus returned to John Cormac, "just this once," said Liam.

"I don't remember saying anything else," answered John Cormac, not entirely pleased with the answer, but content that he would get his claws a bit further into Liam Mac Faul and if he done the dirty for him once, it wouldn't be such a big deal the next time.

He nodded to the creeping Jesus and this signified that his wages would be going up to fifty-five pounds a shift. They re-joined the rest of the group, where Martin joined with the humourless near mindless chitchat and Liam to stand like a gatepost and as silent as a gatepost at the end of the group. Honour was indeed dead.

Martin Mac Donogh kept an eye out for the foreman and quickly ascertained that he went to the pub each day about midday and returned about an hour later, his only companion was a smallish older man who Martin correctly surmised was his own alternative, 'the creeping Jesus' on that site.

He told John Cormac who planned for Liam to meet the foreman one day coming back from the pub and hit the foreman just one blow, one hard blow and say this is from John Cormac O'Mahony. The first day Liam baulked and John Cormac informed him his wages would be cut to twenty-five pounds a day.

The next day he agreed and it was only when he was walking down the street to the rendezvous with the foreman, did it occur to him that he should have. mentioned it to John Devine to see if there was anything he could have done, but it was too late for that as the creeping Jesus was shadowing him to see that he done the deed.

He hit the foreman as hard as he could and laid him out and he said to him 'that's from John Cormac O'Mahony', but only the foreman's companion heard it, as the foreman himself though a big strong man was unconscious. John Cormac witnessed this and when Liam returned to site, he informed that his wages would be rose to forty-five pounds a day backdated to the day before as a bonus.

Liam told him that it was a one off, John Cormac replied, "we'll deal with that when it comes up, but that's all I require for the moment," which was an answer that portended all the wrong things.

Things simply could not be going better; he, John Cormac O'Mahony, was a legend. Martin Mac Donogh didn't get thanked, he got a tenner a day rise from the end of the month with the stipulation that he'd have to up production to hang on to it.

He went up to Liam Mac Faul in the pub and said to him, "now remember, I'm always behind the boy's and ye've got yer pay rise to prove it."

"I'll hit you a lot harder than I ever hit that foreman, if you don't fuck off out of my presence right now," replied Liam, he knew he was hooked but simply didn't know what to do about it.

He told everything to John Devine in the desperate hope of some help, but John Devine's response was to hit the top shelf; Liam Mac Faul and Jimmy Mac Goldrick had to carry him to a cab and out of the cab and up to his front door, this was another lifetime's first for John Devine. The main job was ahead of schedule and this was something that just didn't happen on John Cormac's jobs before the 'affair in the city'.

John Cormac had ten men on the main site on Commercial Road and a machine, that he got cheap from a mate of 'boy' O'Malley and he had nine other men on four other sites including the St Swithuns Lane site doing bits of snagging and accommodating changed plans.

He got an early payment of the Commercial Road job in early December, for once he didn't need it but thought it good practice to demand it anyways and he was even able to give back a bit to good old aunt Myra, about a tenth of what he owed her, but a lot more than she had expected this early, he got a double whiskey from her the next time he visited her, which was approval indeed.

It was nearing Christmas and as was his custom and indeed the usual custom with a lot of the subbies, he was going to let a few men go, this would discipline the rest and when the men he had let go came back in January begging for work as expected, he would do the great favour of allowing them back but at a lower rate.

However, this particular year there was a lot of work on and if he let men go he might not get them back, so he contented himself with letting go the 'bolowan' O'Meara and a notorious drunkard from the London wall site, nobody would be likely to take them on and it would be some lesson for the rest of the men. The core crew who wished to be let go, as they wished for nothing else was not, of course, considered for such discipline.

Things were only getting better and better. It was looking like being a very merry Christmas this year. Uncle 'tot' was thinking of heading back this year and so was 'boy' O'Malley, so if they could meet up there would be great crack. His father would be proud and the misadventures of yesteryear would be as nothing; yes, the future was indeed bright.

Chapter 13

Christmas was coming and was being looked forward to in a dramatically different manner, depending on whether you were John Cormac or his crew. John Cormac would return home for the break, able to report triumph; there was now, what could be called a sizeable operation underway and things were only looking better.

A meet up with the right boys, 'boy' and 'tot' was a possibility and if such should occur and with his father contacts, then plans could be developed for his eventual return with the 'mullah', truly the times were only getting better. Mac Bearta would go back and see his family and he would try to work on a few contacts and also try and get out of this backwater he was in with John Cormac but for all that, he would still be available to John Cormac throughout the holiday if he was needed.

Martin Mac Donogh was facing an even more miserable Christmas than was expected and his expectations were low. One of the nearest neighbours of his brother and sister-in-law had seen him making a piss along the side of the road after coming from the pub. She made a voluble and forceful complaint to his sister-in-law across the garden fence, at the nearest point to the garden shed where Martin resided, just after he entered the shed, so that he was sure to hear, she threatened to call the police if that 'down and out' that they were allowing to shelter in their garden shed ever acted like that again.

"Charity was all well and good, but you had a right to expect some sort of reasonable behaviour in return."

Unnecessarily, this was repeated to Martin with even more force and it was the first time that Martin realised what his declared status in the house was; he had often wondered at the standoffishness of the neighbours when he had ventured to speak to them. His brother wouldn't even as much as answer him, when he complained to him about this.

This Christmas was going to be colder than ever no matter what the weather was going to be like. He couldn't even indulge in drink or at least to the level, that he would like to. Jerry Cawley was going back for Christmas, his wife or was it girlfriend, only he knew for certain which and her status changed depending on the conversation, was staying behind with the two kids, glad of the break from Jerry.

He wasn't as bad as usual with the drink for a while back, but he was bringing in less money and was ever critical of everything she done, this she knew was because there was some sort of bee in his bonnet and he was letting it out on her.

He was going back because he was royally fed up of John Cormac's pub and there were reports, the dog subbie that he had fucked up was in town and that could well mean danger to him; the reason he gave for spending that Christmas at home was that his family at home were getting older and he wanted to spend some time with them "while they were in it'.

He came from an area not that far from where the 'rat' came from in Ireland. When John Cormac realised this, he gave him instructions to keep his ear to the ground, if he happened to be in that area, he wasn't to suggest or mention anything, but he was to see if there was any talk going around and he was to be careful with drink while doing it.

Pete Mac Namee lived about twenty miles from Cawley at home and again not that far from where the 'rat' came from and he was also going home on his own; what his wife was doing was not known, indeed no mention of this woman was made since the day of the 'rat's' murder, where her existence apparently slipped out of Pete when he under pressure from the threat of involvement of the authorities.

Pete was also prepped to keep an ear to the ground around that area to see if he picked up any talk going about. Mac Bearta upon hearing of John Cormac's half-baked plan initially objected to it, as an unnecessary risk, the 'rat' had been a young man with a family so he would be missed at some level, so why take the risk of pointing in any direction; but realising that it was going ahead despite what he thought, he then decided if such a thing was going ahead, then a proper effort, with better scrutiny should be made.

Jerry Cawley and Pete Mac Namee would meet up and go to the town that the 'rat' came from, they would go into the local pubs and interact with the locals, they would under no circumstances mention the 'rat's' name or make any mention of any knowledge of such a man.

They would merely state who they were working for and possibly give a rough location of the work if they were talking to people with knowledge of London, as was likely in the west of Ireland and see if it elicited any response, if nothing was mentioned then good and well, if something was mentioned they were to be very cautious in their response.

They would not respond to a name, but if shown a photograph, then one of the two might vaguely recognise it as a man he might have worked with at the beginning of the year, the other would not recognise it at all and this should pass given that no one had seen the 'rat' since at least last April and of that fact they were most sure.

This should allow then to gauge how much of a fuss the 'rat's' disappearance was causing; if heavy pressure came on and say the family got involved, they were to remain vague and unsure in their identification, but they would proffer to contact the boss for them and leave it at that; then Mac Bearta would take things in hand and as an extreme he would arrange for the family to meet John Cormac, which he would direct and this should deflect any attention from John Cormac's set up.

They were warned strongly about drink, a pint or at very most two taken slowly in each pub, if they wanted an excuse it was that a relative of theirs in the guards warned them strongly about drink driving and that there was a clampdown in progress this year.

John Cormac was initially not in favour of the plan as he didn't want any face-to-face meeting with any relatives of the 'rat', it was bringing matters too close to home, but Mac Bearta insisted if any sort of suspicion was going around then it was better to meet it head on, as evasion could only fuel suspicion; and another reason that occurred to John Cormac is that it was a test of the sort of balls he had, if he could stand that sort of test, then what could he not front up to.

It was, therefore, arranged for Jerry Cawley and Pete Mac Namee to spend one night in the 'rat's' town over Christmas, seeking any trace of activity over the 'rat's' disappearance.

Jimmy Mac Goldrick sent home every penny he thought he reasonably could about two weeks before Christmas, some three hundred pounds, the response to this was to ask if he could send more and the news that his father was put on a three-day week, four other workers at the factory were also put on short time, but they were the most junior workers all with less than two years' experience, unlike his father who had put in twenty-eight years there.

The shop steward said there was nothing he could do, the most he could do was to see he kept the job, this just showed the pressure that was being applied to get Jimmy's father, the sack. Jimmy now considered going home and doing John Jack Keirns. He sent another hundred home which would mean, he would barely eat over the Christmas, never mind celebrate.

He sat on the smelly mattress in the dump he lived in, in Canning Town and cried despite his size and strength and age with pure misery. The bolowan O'Meara borrowed or more truthfully, received the charitable donation of two hundred pounds from his aunt Nelly to keep him going over the Christmas.

It was not the first time that this happened, but Nelly was old and she had few relatives who bothered with her and she hated to see him going without at Christmas, so at no small expense to herself she gave him money for yet another year, despite the knowledge that she was highly unlikely to see any of it back, maybe twenty or forty at best.

The bolowan then went to all his old haunts excoriating John Cormac O'Mahony and then he would hint darkly that he could destroy the said John Cormac and finally, at the end of the night letting the big dark 'secret' out, to universal disbelief and disdain, considering the source, a well-known liar and bolowan.

If he had chanced into a strange pub he might have had some effect but the bolowan never chanced into a pub outside his own acquaintance, with the exception of John Cormac's pub. All in all, a bitter frugal Christmas was spent and it wasn't the first one.

John Devine came home the day they broke up, he dumped his tools, barely washed his face and changed only his jacket and went to rush off to the pub, avoiding the outstretched arms of his little daughter, as she tried to get him to pick her up. His wife who was now severely disturbed by his behaviour ran out after him into the street, asking him what was the matter, in response he asked her if she needed any money and she said a hundred would be handy, this he gave her and another twenty and turned and nearly ran to the pub.

His wife was now nearing despair, she had known the perils of marrying a man in the building trade, unreliability of work thus income, a work hard, play hard mentality, a crude and rough mode of living and bad company from any sort of background which could not but intrude to some degree into home life, but she did think that in John Devine she had a better than average man, who would be able to resist these perils to a major degree, in short a strong man and indeed up to some point earlier this year.

She couldn't exactly say when, he had displayed such resistance; sure he had his few pints when he met his mates and he was a bit rough and ready, but in general herself and the kids were his priorities, but something had changed or gone awry, something drastic and she didn't know what it was and it frightened her more and more as time went by.

He stayed in the pub over the Christmas during the day and the night. She made a number of enquiries which were in the main shrugged off or answered by some comment like ''tis Christmas' or suchlike, but finally he did volunteer that he had a hard and disappointing year and was just letting off steam over Christmas. This she had to accept.

He gave money to her regularly, but on Monday the forth of January the last night of the holidays, he asked her for money back that night, no such thing had ever happened before and shocked, she refused, he said it was alright, that the publican would have to sub him for once, he'd already had enough of his money.

It was minor in the particular but vast overall, John Devine was just not a man to put drink before his wife and kids to any extent or at least, the old model of John Devine was not. She didn't know what to do, or who to turn to.

Her education was poor, she had done the intercert and hadn't done that well, but she was going to do the leaving cert, when an older sister returned from London with talk of plenty of jobs and money and as she wasn't that good at school, a fair bit below the halfway mark in the class rankings, she thought, why not try it, where was she going anyways, her family agreed, with both her and her sister gone, there would be only five of the original seven mouths to feed and cater for.

She got a job in a warehouse, followed by a job on a checkout in the Brent Cross shopping centre and made a passable living and after a few mundane and quite boring years, she had met John Devine and eventually cast her lot in with him.

All had gone all right until recent times but now, things were going south fast and she simply didn't know what to do, or where to turn to, she hadn't the resources or education or experience to get assistance and for the Irish in England, self-help groups and assistance for any form of behavioural or social problem simply did not exist. A pall was cast over the future.

Liam Mac Faul had no thought of the pub. Three times a day he worked out, he even bought magazines on the subject of boxing and martial arts and this training now even included some consideration of diet.

The other people in the house were now preparing to move out and this was despite the fact, that Liam sensed how they felt to some degree and tried to be friendly and helpful; if someone was cleaning the house, he'd help even if it wasn't his turn; if something heavy needed to be lifted, he volunteered, but his obsessive and prolonged secessions of working out, his silent grim mien, even if friendly when spoken to, still frightened them.

This changed over Christmas, one of his housemates came home obviously hurt and marked, he was a small quiet lad and unlikely to cause trouble as far as Liam could see. Liam asked him what happened and he told him that he was leaving a pub in Shepherds Bush called the Wellsey when two bouncers from the pub turned on him and beat him up, for no reason.

Liam had heard of this pub and of the two bouncers who were from Dublin and noted bullies; well, thought Liam if he could hit someone, for one as unworthy as John Cormac, then he could hit someone for one who deserved help and cement his place in this house, where for all his power, he was afraid to leave, being afraid of London in general, the 'rat's' demise still rattled him.

He told the lad to go down with him to Shepherds Bush and together they would ask the bouncers what the problem was. Liam approached the door of the pub and asked the two bouncers why they had hit his mate.

"We'll do youse too," was his answer, he invited them to do so.

Firstly as they stepped down into the street they realised that the size advantage was on the other side, but cocky as anything they came on and that was a mistake. Liam hit the first one a haymaker in the mouth and knocked him out cold; the other he hit with his left hand and he bounced off the wall. Liam then hit him with his right hand, he went down; the first was out for the count, the second still stirred, so Liam kicked him on the side of the jaw and he stirred no more.

From that onwards his popularity did a U-turn in that house, he became perceived to be a very valuable and useful man indeed, especially in the violence prone world of the Irish in London. He didn't perceive the difference with the old Liam, but it was there. He didn't contact home that Christmas and no contact was made with him.

Pete Mac Namee and Jerry Cawley set off on their mission to the 'rat's' town on the evening of Sunday the twenty-seventh of December. They had been tutored four times over the phone that day by Mac Bearta who very thoroughly make them repeat back all the instructions word for word.

Mac Bearta was in fact getting more and more dubious over the entire affair, never all that much in favour of it, he now considered that if nothing had surfaced so far, then it was better to let sleeping dogs lie, but John Cormac disagreed, he wanted the entire affair tidied up and done with, if there any loose ends, he wanted them taken care of.

Pete and Jerry were also against the idea at this stage but on account of the amount of tutorage they had to undergo and the fact it would entail a sober or near sober night over Christmas, they had been most specifically warned about drink and to refuse to have more than one or two on the grounds they were warned by Jerry's cousin in the guards, not to take any chances with drink driving this Christmas.

There were four pubs in the town, one was a backward-looking bit of a shebeen, so they ruled that one out. The method approved beforehand by Mac Bearta was simple they would enter the pub and then they would locate the biggest group and sit next to them and engage them in conversation, they would say that they were a group that were home from London for the Christmas and they were going to Cawley's town for a party and they took the notion when they were passing through this town to stop and have a pint.

In the first pub some of the locals had been in England, as was to be expected and they got chatting to them, they mentioned who they were working for but apparently got no bites. They moved on refusing to join the company, as they had been warned the cops were out for drink drivers that Christmas and saying they would like to look into the other pubs when they got then chance, as they were going back to England after the holidays and mightn't be around this way for while again.

They went to the second pub which was a little busier, they made the same play again, they got talking to some of the locals and mentioned that they worked in England, again as expected some of the locals also had worked in England and they got into conversation with them. They mentioned who they were working for and roughly where, but once again as in the first pub, they got no bites and therefore, they moved on to the last pub, with their excuse of wariness of the guards as they had been warned against drink driving.

The third pub was not as busy but was smaller and therefore, appeared more crowded. They took the same course of action, sitting down adjacent to the biggest group and engaging them in conversation, they once again mentioned that they worked in London and found a few people who worked there in the past and as the conversation developed, they mentioned who they were working for.

Once again they failed to get any bites and were thinking of calling it a night and were feeling somewhat relieved, when a new individual joined the group; he asked who they were working for and when they answered, he asked them if they happened to know a cousin of his, who had not been in contact with home in a long time, a James Patrick Kilfeather.

They both said 'no' as they were told not to react to a name, only to a photograph and then only one of them, to leave the recognition as vague as possible. The new individual who did resemble the 'rat' somewhat, kept going on.

His cousin had been working for some O'Mahony and John Cormac sounded right, a Sligoman he believed; last April he abruptly stopped all contact with his family, which was not like him at all, he rang home nearly every week since they got the phone in and indeed it was he who had paid to have the phone put in about last christmas and even before that he always wrote; his mother was beside herself with worry.

They enquired for the name again, "Kilfeather," "no," they didn't recognise it. They now recognised the new individual from the last pub they went into. Did he know what site his cousin was on. He wasn't sure but he thought it was in the city, which was the commercial area he believed.

Well, that was where nearly all O'Mahony's work was, could he be more specific. The man then produced a small photograph, it was of the 'rat'. Pete Mac Namee looked at it and shook his head, he looked at it again holding it up to the light and looking more closely, "no definitely not someone that he knew," he passed the photograph to Cawley.

Jerry Cawley took the photograph and looked at it long and hard, he rubbed his chin contemplatively and looked at it again held up to the light.

"It's not a great photograph, but maybe I did see such a man on one of O'Mahony's sites; this would not be a big man and thin."

"Yes, that's right about your size," replied the cousin.

"He'd be a bit smaller than me," replied Cawley quickly, always resenting any belittlement.

"Maybe but not much," replied the cousin, "so you do know him."

"Now hold on, I said I might know a man like him. The man that I'm thinking of I only seen briefly and I never spoke to him; this could be the man but I'm not one hundred per cent certain, like I said, I only seen this man briefly once or twice and it's some time ago."

"Since last April," enquired the cousin.

"Oh no definitely before that, February perhaps," replied Cawley.

The man appeared to be getting a bit agitated and insisted that he wanted certainty. Cawley said he could not give it to him. Pete Mac Namee looked at the photograph again and asked Jerry Cawley what site it was on.

"Down from Bank station," replied Cawley which was as about as generic a reply as could be given to locate an address in the city of London.

"No I was only on that site briefly and well later than February," replied Mac Namee.

Jerry took the photograph and looked carefully at it again and replied, "the story in full is this, I think but am not one hundred per cent sure that I saw this man briefly once or twice on one of O'Mahony's sites in the city of London.

I never worked with man or spoke to this man or for that matter had anything to do with him. I didn't spend much time on that site anyways and I cannot help you any further than that."

He then handed the photograph back to the 'rat's' cousin who seemed to be getting more and more agitated, "the family is getting very worried at this stage, he hasn't even been in contact even over Christmas, which just isn't his style."

"My man, I've told you what I can," replied Cawley spreading his hands in a helpless manner, "now, we're expected at a party in Ballathone and we have to head there."

"Stay and have another drink," said the 'rat's' cousin in anything but an inviting manner.

"No, we've been warned by my own cousin, who's a sergeant in the guards in Athlone, that the guards are hitting down hard on the drinking driving this year and I depend on the car when I'm at home, especially as the family aren't getting any younger and I do a bit of running around for them while I'm here," replied Cawley.

"I've never heard that," said the 'rat's' cousin in a belligerent manner, but other people around him disagreed, saying they had heard there was a crackdown.

Cawley shook his head and at other times there would have been an argument, but the intense tutelage of Mac Bearta paid off.

"I assure you, my man that I'm not making it up," he replied.

"Alright, alright, but we're desperate and this is the only thing any of us have heard since he went missing."

Jerry stood up and drained his pint and went to leave, "fellow, I've told everything that I can think of, now I must be on my way," he said.

"Is there anything else you could think of, anyone else we could contact," the 'rat's' cousin asked.

Pete Mac Namee said just audibly to Cawley, "you could contact O'Mahony himself."

Cawley frowned and said, "I suppose," he turned to the 'rat's' cousin and said, "I tell you what I'll do now, give me your phone number and I'll call O'Mahony himself and see if there's something he can do for you, beyond that I cannot think of anything I can do for you."

"I don't have a phone," the cousin replied.

"What I thought you said you got phone calls from the, r, lad," replied Cawley nearly slipping.

"Ah hold on my aunt's number," he said and got a piece of paper from the barman and wrote down a number and gave it to Jerry Cawley.

"Right I'll ring O'Mahony and I'll ring this number tomorrow that's Monday evening between 4 or 5 o'clock or if not then Tuesday evening about the same time and tell you if he'll see you but I have to say this to you, men come and go in the building game, so he might not be able to be of much help to you, there's no point in getting your hopes up too high," said Cawley.

"Well, at least, it's something, my aunt will answer the phone but I will have her fully briefed beforehand, so she'll be expecting the call and be able to deal with it, er, em, thanks for that," said the 'rat's' cousin.

"Just don't get your hopes up too high, for instance, I never heard O'Mahony mention the man's name," said Cawley as they left the pub.

They thought they had obeyed the instructions to the letter and all in all pulled it off well. They rang Mac Bearta later that evening to report the results of their visit to the 'rat's' town and later on made a report to John Cormac himself.

John Cormac was very full of himself, "ha ha so Mac Bearta is the clever man, leave sleeping dogs lie," he said. "Well, how heavily were those dogs sleeping hah, it goes to show who has the real brain in the end of the day, doesn't it."

Three times he went over the brief exchange with the 'rat's' cousin and then he consulted Mac Bearta. There were lengthy discussions and arguments about what to do; initially John Cormac held to his position, that Mac Bearta was wrong and that obviously there was a stink to be smothered, but Mac Bearta pointed out that no word had reached England in near eight months, so how big was the stink.

They went back and forth but eventually Mac Bearta had to concede that even if it had not reached England, there was no guarantee that it would not, so to quash it here or at least, direct it away from them was probably the best job overall; left unsaid by Mac Bearta was his real objection and that was that John Cormac was not the right man for the job.

Making the best of things, Mac Bearta did his best to tutor John Cormac and plan the whole thing as well as possible; when progress was poor due in large part to John Cormac assumption of near infallibility due to the fact he was right about checking to see if there was any 'talk' going about in the 'rat's' hometown. He eventually drove down from the top of Donegal to Sligo to meet up with John Cormac to sort out things properly, he even had to sleep in his car, as John Cormac's hospitability was poor, but as John Cormac said, he hadn't ordered Mac Bearta down south to Sligo.

A plan was formulated and debated and eventually practiced to perfection. Cawley rang the number he had been given on Tuesday evening and was answered by the 'rat's' mother, he repeated to her what he had told the cousin and said that he contacted John Cormac O'Mahony and John Cormac had said that he remembered very little of James Patrick Kilfeather, he said he'd ring England and get them to check the records in the office and that he'd try and do what he could for them, but he stressed that he could make no promises of definite help.

He would be available on new year's day in O'Mahony's pub between 7 and 8 o'clock in the evening to anybody that wanted to see him and he'd see what he could do for them. The 'rat's' mother said, she go herself with her daughter, who had a car as Pat, who was apparently the cousin, wasn't very good at talking to people.

The die was cast then; John Cormac partook in more discussion which turned into instruction and argument with Mac Bearta. He was psyched up for this meeting which he considered would qualify him as having the balls for anything, just about anything.

Chapter 14

O'Mahony's pub on the square, as it was known as, was not really a pub that one went to for the quality of beer or for socialising or as would be said 'to have the crack', it was more a pub where business was transacted and to be seen in, if one wanted to show that they were in with the right boys.

It was the watering hole of a 'man of affairs'. John Cormac was dressed in an expensive tweed suit and had both lifts and high heels on his shoes to give him more height. He knew enough to make the right impression and even where to make it, in his father's pub no one would comment either on his increase in height or his dear suit. Though he was in his father's pub, he was fully sober as he waited in an upstairs room facing the street and he thought about the past.

It hadn't always been that good, the past had it. It was that stupid little bitch, Marie Cassidy that had been the cause of all the trouble. He was nineteen, well nearly twenty and he had never got the ride and well naturally he had wanted to find out what it was all about, just like any other red-blooded man.

The problem was he couldn't get it from anyone and every other lad seemed to be able to get it. On top of that was the consciousness of the fact that he was the son of John D O'Mahony one of the big men of the town, which did nothing to dampen his sense of competition with every other lad. All this added up to danger. Of course, he realised later on that there was probably a lot more talk, than action from his mates but not at the time.

Well, he got wound up and finally frustrated and then one night at a 'teenies disco' he seemed to score. He was admittedly in a pretty desperate state, that he went in there in the first place, but he was up for all options at that stage. His height and the fact that he was about five years older than anyone else in there and therefore, not recognisable from school or underage sporting activities or suchlike as he had been finished with such activities before anybody at the disco started them, which meant that he did not stand out in any way.

197

He got into the action and had a few dances with this particular one and in fairness she was big, bigger than him and well developed. He began to fancy his chances and they had a mineral together, as it was all there was available. He told her that he thought she was beautiful and she told him she though that he was sexy and they began to kiss. They talked for a while and he told her he had a car, which he had.

He was doing a private bookkeeping course in Dublin at that time not having got good enough of results in his leaving cert to get into a polytechnic and certainly not a university and he needed a car so his father had bought him one. She told him she didn't believe him, as how could he have a licence. He said he hadn't but he still drove the car, this was the truth.

She wanted to see it, John Cormac considered himself elected. They went out and got into the car. It was a snazzy red ford escort and she was entranced. He started the car and drove up the road from the old hall the disco was being held in and back again. She opened her mouth wide with the pleasure and novelty of being in a car with a possible boyfriend.

John Cormac drove back into the same place and parked up. He tried a kiss and she responded; he went further, a kiss on the mouth and again she responded. He started feeling her up and at first she let this go, but then she started squirming and saying 'no'; however, it was too late, for John Cormac was beyond turning back.

He let the seat back, shoved her back and got on top of her. He tore off her clothes beneath the waist, he was going for it big time. She was screeching now, but he put his hand over her mouth and carried on. Finally, he sort of got inside her but came too soon and the job was only half done but John Cormac considered himself a man at last.

He relaxed back and the shrieking resumed, he put his hand over her mouth and tried to calm her, "ssh, hsh, yer a proper woman now, did ye not know that ye're not a proper one, 'til ye do that." "sure everybody does that," "I'll give ye a good few pounds if ye shut up. I honestly thought ye were up for it sorry if ye weren't", reality now returning fast.

She tried to struggle and get out the door and he had to hit her. "I'll get ye a good few pounds two or three hundred, maybe even more, my father 'ill help your father, he's John D O'Mahony, the auctioneer," he said now in desperation, but it was useless.

Dark desperate thoughts entered his head. Then someone knocked on the window of the car, rapidly he snapped the locks on the front doors. Then someone opened the back door on her side, it was some woman, with that distraction and the help of the woman and above all the fact that the fecking seat was still down, she managed to get out, with her clothes mainly pulled off.

John Cormac didn't know what to do, firstly he thought of getting out and claiming it was just something that went too far, then he remembered that it was a teeny disco. The only thing he could do was rev up the car and go, but he forgot to close the door and it swung out hitting another car making it easily identifiable. If he had headed to Dublin there and then he might just have been alright, but he headed home thinking that nobody would touch the home of John D O'Mahony.

He cleaned up the car and went to bed nervous because he realised that he had made a big mistake, as she might have been only fourteen but there was also a certain feeling of satisfaction, as he had done the job, he was a man now, even if things could have been handled an awful lot better.

He thought about what he should have done for a while; he should have drove away and done her someplace else, he should have drove somewhere else straight afterwards and let her cool down but with that thought came the alternative thought what if she didn't cool down, then just how much could he have got away with; among these thoughts came sleep. He was awakened the next morning with the news the guards were looking for him at the front door.

He went down and found out that it was two new guards to the area, and for the first time, trepidation arose in him; behind it all he had always thought that if the worst came to the worst then his father would sort it out. If the sergeant, who was a mate of his fathers, was there it would have been different. He was arrested and taken to the garda barracks. There he found out he was been accused of the rape of a minor, this was serious.

However, from the beginning he was able enough for them, for a start he claimed to be seventeen and that meant they couldn't question him, without his father or a lawyer being present. His father's lawyer old Seamus O'Dea came to the station, he didn't bat an eyelid at the charges, he just lit his cigar and started asking the guards questions, "was the girls examined by a doctor; presumably if she was fourteen then she must still be a virgin, so the hymen must be torn if she was raped, was this checked"

"Er, I don't know," replied the guard.

"Were the clothes examined for signs of violence or sexual activity?"

"Er, um I don't know," again replied the guard.

"Has the name, age, school status, reputation, any mental health problems or indeed any physical health problems being independently verified?"

"Er, um I don't know," yet again replied the guard.

"There's a lot a lot you don't seem to know about this case for which you are hoping to prosecute my client, isn't there guard. You are not certain of the identity of the alleged victim, to a proper legal standard, if an actual crime had been committed or anything much else about the alleged victim, are you guard. I would like to apply for his immediate release."

The guard refused, but by this time the sergeant who was a mate of his fathers was on hand. He took the guard into the next room where a heated discussion took place, which they could just overhear.

"This is a disgusting crime, sergeant."

"We have to go by the law and at this time we cannot hold him."

"Ye're hardly going to, release the bastard."

"If we hold him without due process and taking the proper steps, we will weaken our eventual case against him, we have to be seen as fair and impartial."

John Cormac was released. His father was angry at him and cursed him for being a fool.

"How could he have fucked a bloody fourteen-year-old and got caught, what class of bollix was he anyways."

But the real shock was his mother's reaction; an automaton who cooked and cleaned and worked in the pub and the shop and had no input into any of the decisions about family affairs, beyond what she or her two daughters wore; she was known to take the odd nip of gin, but beyond that she appeared to have no feelings or indeed thoughts.

She belted him in the mouth four times, drawing blood and shrieking, "ya dirty piece of filth where did I get ye from."

He did not expect this and in many ways it was the worst part of the whole affair. He asked his father how he would get out of it when he recovered. His father said he didn't deserve to get out of it, but he'd manage it. His mother returned to her normal state of an automaton.

The girl's father was a Jim Cassidy who worked as a storeman for the local agricultural co-operative and John D was on the committee that oversaw the running of the co-operative, so there some sort of hold on the situation for a start. It was not as easy as all that, however, he was locked up the next day in the main garda barracks in another town, where his father's influence was not as strong and he was kept there overnight.

The next day, however, brought Seamus O'Dea to the scene. He asked John Cormac what happened and he gave the lawyer a well-watered version of what had occurred; unfortunately, he was drunk and he followed company into the disco, where upon they had deserted him, he hadn't realised what sort of disco it was.

Well, the next thing was this girl came on to him really strong and unfortunately, with the drink and everything else he bit, eventually they went out to his car at her invitation; of course, he could now see, that someone with a car, was exciting to one of her age; one thing led to another and there was some bungled attempt at sex led on totally by her.

Was it full sexual intercourse the lawyer asked.

"No," replied John Cormac remembering that he hadn't done the job properly and now maybe it was just as well.

The lawyer told him that the hymen was not broken; thus, she was still a virgin, rape was off the table. He was released on bail the next day. The proposed charges were now either attempted rape or sexual assault.

Seamus O'Dea told him that the first charge of attempted rape was very unlikely to be pressed, but the second of sexual assault could well be and would entail a sentence of about twelve months in jail or possibly more.

"Time for your old man to pull some strings," he said to John Cormac with a wink.

He was confined to the house, the course in Dublin was abandoned; firstly his mother wouldn't cook for him, but his father intervened.

"It's hard to say he's worth it, but nothing will come of not feeding him."

The house was like a prison, there was toing and froing, sometimes his parents talked of it, sometimes they whined at him for the trouble he caused them, his mother constantly declaring herself mortified, sometimes they left him in dead silence. There were meetings with the lawyer, with the local sergeant of the guards and even the local superintendent of the guards, with local councillors and members of the co-op committee.

One day his father was in a savage mood, he said to him it was better if he had never been born and that he could prepare to depart to England that very day, he had to see Roger Mac Sherry of the government party and Ned Tealon of the other party to try and get this shit sorted out, there was no doubt it would cost tens of thousands of pounds. He would pay it alright, but only to preserve the good name of the family and not to preserve John Cormac's skin.

About a week later, roughly a month after the incident, there was a meeting in the house; his father told him to wait at the top of the stairs and listen to the effort and trouble that was going into getting him off and after that he could prepare for England. Present at the meeting was Tom Glavin the local councillor who was the chairman of the council for that year; the sergeant and Seamus O'Dea the lawyer and finally Conor O'Rourke chairman of the board of the agricultural co-op that Jim Cassidy the girl's father worked for.

His mother served brandy and biscuits to begin with and cigarettes, cigars and pipes were lit and they got down to business.

"Where do we stand?" asked his father.

"Well, the charge is sexual assault and unfortunately, there's good evidence behind it, a witness and finger prints and torn clothes; luckily the rape charge is off the table and they're still accepting that he is seventeen, so things are a lot better than they could be at this stage. However, if things progress forwards they cannot but get his right age and that and the fact that he gave a false age in the first place, could mean things could get serious enough yet," answered the sergeant.

"The bloody idiot," said his father, "what are the chances in court."

"Well, it can be pleaded down and made to look like youthful idiocy, the fact he didn't do the job in full is greatly to his benefit. If it was a case of a nineteen-year-old adult raping a fourteen-year-old child then it would be very bad, possibly fifteen years with the wrong sign on your back in jail, but he still has to be looking at about a year in jail or at least eight months," answered the lawyer.

"That and the disgrace," said his father, "how was it clear he didn't do the job right."

"Well, the hymen was not broken and the girl was examined by her own doctor, that old doctor Flynn who's a bit of a feminist I'd say," said the sergeant.

"I had to straighten out her thinking a bit, she originally answered me, that the hymen was not broken but bruised. I asked her straight up if rape took place or not, she answered me, no but something happened.

I said, doctor I asked you if rape took place or not, if it did not you must say so, if I go into court and I say rape took place and the hymen is still intact, the case will be thrown out and I will be in trouble myself, now which was it rape or no rape. She replied no and I told her to make sure to say the same thing to the parents."

"Good man," responded his father, "I was in touch with Mac Sherry and he says he will leave word down the line that the case is to be treated easy, something like attempted sexual assault with provocation on her side and too much drink on his. I was also in touch with your man Tealon and he won't pursue things if approached," said his father addressing Tom Glavin.

"If I'm approached as expected, I'll insist that I can't interfere with a court action," added Tom Glavin.

"This is very good and could mean a suspended sentence," said the lawyer.

"The best thing of all would be to quash it completely at this stage," replied his father.

There was silence, finally the sergeant spoke, "if things are handled rightly, we might try a deal with the father, but it has to be said, that he is greatly vexed at the moment. Myself and Seamus will go to him, as soon as the new recommendations for charges come down the line and with them in hand, I'll put the case to him that the young fellow is looking at twelve months suspended and the girl will be disgraced in court.

I have two young fellows that are prepared to testify that they saw her lead him out of the hall; now I'll say to him, that I'm happy to go along with the idea that she just wanted to look at the car but what will be thought of it in court or what interpretation is likely to be put on her actions, it cannot but look very bad indeed for her; oh incidentally, they don't actually have any car of their own, so I don't think the schillings are likely to be too heavy."

"An interesting point, how much would he be paid," his father asked the chairman of the co-op.

"About eighty or a little short of it, but he has four kids so he's likely to be tight enough with money," answered Connor O Rourke.

The sergeant resumed the conversation, "I'll say the alternative is far better, even if he does get convicted and nothing is certain, then he'll be prancing around the streets talking about what he done and what will that do to his daughter and to himself and that should certainly give him food for thought.

I'll then say that the family is totally embarrassed at his role in it and they have made an alternative offer, which I can only strongly recommend from his point of view. Five grand down and a grand a year for five years and the young fellow goes to England and stays there for donkey years and none of ye ever have to see him. Can I say that?" the sergeant asked his father.

"Yes," answered his father. "Also he works eight miles away from where he lives, despite there being a co-op store beside him and I notice that he cycles, so a change cannot but be welcome and if he gets promotion as well, he could hardly refuse," said the sergeant.

"What do ye say, Conor," asked his father.

"Well there's an assistant managers job going beside him, that'd be a rise of over forty pounds a week for him; plus, it'd be handier by far for him, but there's a strong candidate there already," answered Connor O Rourke.

"Can you do it for me, Connor," interrupted his father.

"Yes," replied Connor after a pause which was to emphasise that it would be difficult for him and that he would need to be taken care of, for doing it.

"Alright sergeant, tell him that also but emphasise the other side as well, that if he doesn't agree, then he'll lose the job he has and that he'll get no other one around here and there will be other costs, emphasise that sergeant," said his father.

"I'll tell him, you're in with everyone around here that means anything," said the sergeant.

"Basically it's all win one way, all lose the other. He might well not agree at once, give him twenty-four hours and tell him that charges will have to be proffered at that stage and the deal goes out the window and emphasise to him he'll pay and believe you me he will. Tom, he may well come to you for advice and assistance, if he does ask him what options have been offered to him and when he tells you, advise him strongly to take the deal," went on his father.

"Right, I'll put him straight," answered Tom Glavin.

His father continued on, "sergeant, you and Seamus go to him today and if it takes it, tomorrow as well; you go into the house to him sergeant and talk to him, as soon as he agrees, you go into him, Seamus and get him to sign to a withdrawal of charges there and then and give him a cheque for five thousand pounds, warn him the deal is made and he has to abide by it.

If the sergeant fails, then you will have to try Seamus, emphasise that he will be a lot better off leaving town, if he doesn't agree to the deal, if in turn that fails, then the young lad will have to skip it to England and I shall harshly with mister Cassidy. Remember any and all payments depends on your success."

After another round of brandies, the meeting broke up. There was silence for a week, his father only remarking that it would cost him an arm and a leg and that the first round of talks had failed. But the following week John Cormac was informed that agreement had been reached and shortly afterwards they received official notification that all proceedings against John Cormac were being dropped.

The week after that, he was off to England. Much later on he asked his father how much the whole thing had cost, he was told it cost over forty-five thousand.

The specific costs were, five thousand straight up for Cassidy and five further annual payments of one thousand pounds, there was five thousand for the sergeant and five thousand for Seamus O'Dea, there was seven thousand for Roger Mac Sherry and three thousand for Ned Tealon, Tom Glavin got five thousand, as did Conner O'Rourke.

Despite the fact that Jim Cassidy did not get the job in the co-op store beside him, but Connor O'Rourke was further up the feeding chain than John D O'Mahony, thus had to be compensated despite lack of action and then there were two payments of five hundred pounds each to two lads or rather their fathers, so they would say they seen the girl lead John Cormac out of the disco and finally, there were two special payments of two thousand pounds to two men, who raided the isolated farmhouse where Jim Cassidy's elderly parents lived and then they beat them and tied them up, and then finally they informed Jim Cassidy of the plight of his parents, by throwing a concrete block through his window in the middle of the night, to gain his attention and shouting at him to check on his parents.

It was this that finally convinced Jim Cassidy to follow the more sensible course, there was another few bits and pieces, so the total came to over forty-five thousand pounds; a certain amount of money was saved by not getting Jim Cassidy the job beside him, this was to teach him the value of co-operation, especially with the right people. It was a most valuable and insightful in power and the privileges that it brought.

It wasn't much over twelve years since that had occurred and there had been some changes since, but what would have happened if his father had not been able to sort it out. The majority or indeed all of those years, might have spent in prison, for the rape of a child, where he would be at the bottom of the pecking order, would he even have survived it and what sort of state would he be in now.

Power and privilege must be protected and that was what he was going to do tonight. His mother came to the top of the stairs where he was now standing, he had done little but scoff at her since the incident years ago.

"You're done up well tonight, are ye going out," she asked him.

"Do ye not know yet woman, that I'm a businessman in my own right as big or bigger than Dad and have to dress appropriately," he answered her.

"I suppose," she mumbled and continued on with her work of carrying drinks down to the bar.

It was coming up to a quarter to seven, so he went down to the bar. He straightened his waistcoat and entered the bar and got himself a pint just to be at something and nodded at some of the people there. One of them, a sycophant of his fathers remarked that he must be on the pull tonight, he replied 'business' and the conversation halted.

Shortly afterwards, two women entered the bar; one woman was older and she grasped the two lapels of the top she was wearing in one hand nervously and she clasped her handbag in the other hand, and she looked briefly from side, clearly ill at ease in this environment.

The other woman was much younger and also seemed a bit nervous but not as intimidated by her surroundings as the older woman. They ordered a drink and when the barman returned with it, the younger woman spoke to him and the barman came down to John Cormac and told him that a Mrs Kilfeather wanted to see him. John Cormac straightened himself up and walked around the bar towards her.

"Mrs Kilfeather," she nodded, "good night to ye, ma'am, John Cormac O'Mahony, good night, miss," he said to the younger woman.

The older woman looked in some awe at John Cormac, "ah, er, Mr O'Mahony, it's, er, it's very good of you to see us, this is my daughter, Mareaid. I'm sure you're a busy man."

"That's all-right, ma'am. I always try to do my best for my own people," replied John Cormac.

"And God bless you," she replied, "will ye 'er' have a drink."

"No ma'am, I'm fine, the only problem now is that I don't know that I can be of any help to ye. Ye're enquiring about your son, James Patrick Kilfeather, er, he hasn't been in contact of late or something."

"That's right Mr O'Mahony, James Patrick was always a great one for ringing up, but last April he stopped ringing for some reason and we've had no contact since, which just isn't like him, even before we had the phone he always wrote every two weeks or so and suddenly, a blank and we're getting very worried."

"It sounds strange," agreed John Cormac, "but all I could do for ya was to check the records and with the people that were working with him and this, I did since that fellow that works for me, rang me from Longford the other night.

Ye see, I have a number of jobs on and a fair bit to look after, so my own memory of him is very limited. I think he was known as being handy and able to turn his hand to a variety of jobs and generally, well thought of indeed, but beyond that I cannot remember anything."

"I know, no doubt someone in a big way like yourself would find it hard to remember just one man," she replied.

"He was definitely handy, he could fix anything around the house," spoke up the sister for the first time.

"I spoke to the foreman and he remembers that he left without giving any notice but then again, that is not all that unusual in the building game. He also said that he was a decent worker and as you say handy, but its awhile back and he doesn't remember much about him.

I've got the dates that he started and finished from the office; the office is open even though I'm not there and they have the records. He started during the third week of January, the nineteenth, I see and he left on the Eight of April, a Wednesday I see," said John Cormac looking at a piece of paper that he took out of his pocket with these dates wrote on it.

It reduced the actual time that the 'rat' had worked for him by four weeks, two on either side, this was Mac Bearta's recommendation, so as to make him less easy to remember, yet to admit the truth that he had worked for John Cormac.

"And I see actually that he was owed a couple of days. I wasn't around the site much that week as we were opening up on another site. and it was the next week until I noticed he or rather a man was missing and I was told it was him and that he just didn't turn up and that he hadn't said anything to anybody," said John Cormac, "and beyond that I cannot say much else."

"Is there anything else ye can think of," said the mother looking desperate.

"Well, when I talked to the foreman, he did say he thought that someone said that he wasn't that happy about the place where he was staying, but the foreman wasn't very sure about this," said John Cormac.

"Yes, he didn't like the place he was living in," said the sister, "and when he didn't ring up as expected for the first few times, we thought that he was just moving and couldn't get things sorted out."

"Well, I suppose that could be it, if he got a place far from where he had been living, he might get a job there as well, as it would be handier for him and I suppose that could also explain why he jacked," said John Cormac.

"Yes, but it was eight months ago and he'd have called back since," came in the sister.

"Well, it could be just that things didn't work out and maybe with one thing and another going wrong, he never got round to ringing," said John Cormac.

Both women shook their heads.

"That's just not him," said the sister, the mother agreeing, "no, not him."

"Well, I'm just trying to think of something that might be a problem. Did he have any close friends or relatives over there to turn to if anything did happen," asked John Cormac.

"No, my own people are in Manchester and he left on the spur of the moment, when a job he was counting on in Carrick on Shannon, didn't come up," answered the mother.

"Well, there must be some neighbours or something," asked John Cormac in a concerned manner.

"There were some neighbours, but he settled into work and seemed to concentrate on that. I think he met up with some of them, but just casually, but he didn't have much got to with them," he was answered.

The news was getting better and better.

"But surely there was someone he could turn to, if something bad happened. London can be a strange old place at times, it's not like round here, you don't know anyone really," said John Cormac now frowning with concern.

"He wanted to get, some money together and to come back; he didn't really want a social life at the moment. That was why he lived where he did, it was cheap," answered the sister.

"Yes, he loved Ireland, but he couldn't get any job there or at least any proper job, bits and pieces, people more or less using him when they got stuck," added the mother.

"I know as much as you do at this stage and I've given you all the knowledge I have of him, even the foreman that was over him didn't pay much attention to him, as he got on with his work; it was the others that weren't getting on with their work, he was watching as I'm sure you can imagine. The only thing I can do now is make a couple of suggestions on the basis of my knowledge of the place," said John Cormac.

"And God bless you," said the mother, "are you sure ya won't have a drink, a drop of whiskey or something."

"No, no thanks, ma'am. It's hard for me to ask this and indeed nothing I have heard of him would suggest this, but could he have, through bad company for instance, have got into trouble of any sort," asked John Cormac.

"No, he was just not the type, if there was trouble somewhere, he got out of there," answered the sister, the mother nodding in agreement.

"Yes, but I know the case of a lad, just holding a package for another lad from the same house, just as a favour like ya would here at home and thinking no more of it no doubt; and the police raided the house and found drugs in the package and indeed 'twas the lad that kept the package that got blamed and ended up in jail.

Now, the reason I'm telling ye this is that he spent a year and a half in prison and was too ashamed to contact his family and they were giving up on him, but some neighbour from at home came across him on a site, after he got out of prison, you see so much time had passed and so many things had happened that he couldn't bring himself to contact home. That sort of thing can happen in London," said John Cormac.

Both women shook their heads.

"Ye know ye can be as peaceful as you wish and indeed anything that I have heard about James Patrick would point to that, but you can meet the wrong type, as you can anyplace; for instance you say the place he was staying in wasn't that good, could he have met the wrong sort there," said John Cormac. "Ya see, if he did come across the wrong sort or something happened or he was trying to avoid someone, he could have got on a train in the morning and being in Edinburgh in the afternoon. Lads do come and go in the buildings."

"No he'd have made some contact," said the mother, the sister nodding in agreement.

"Was there nothing anybody noticed out of the ordinary," asked the sister.

"No, as I said he was one of the ones that just got on with his work and didn't draw any attention to himself, if there was one thing out of the ordinary it was the fact he jacked abruptly without saying anything; when I rang round I asked the same question and that is the response that I got," answered John Cormac, "there is nothing ye can think of yerselves that struck a strange note," he added.

Both women shook their heads.

"I don't like to mention this in front of ye now, ma'am, but to cover every possibility could he have any dealings with a woman, it's not only the wrong sort of men ye can meet over there, but ye can also meet the wrong sort of woman," he asked.

"No, if anything, he was too reserved in that line," answered his sister.

"He always planned to settle at home," added his mother.

John Cormac looked down at the floor in a state of deep contemplation, "I can't think off the top of my head anything else obvious that would go wrong. He'd never go on the drink; it can happen to people who you'd never suspect it would happen to."

"No, there were neighbours next door to us and three down the other side that utterly destroyed themselves and their families with drink, so that's one lesson he definitely should have off," answered the mother.

John Cormac looked at the floor and the bar and the ceiling and shook his head, "if it was an accident, like a traffic accident, the police would contact ye," he said, "and I suppose you could try the police," he added in a dubious tone.

"Everybody says it'd be a waste of time, that they won't try for a paddy," said the sister.

"Well, there's no doubt that's true," said John Cormac shaking his head, "but I'm out of suggestions."

"Is there nothing you can think of Mr O'Mahony," asked the mother.

"No, ma'am, 'tis like I feared, I can be of no help to ye," shaking his head and looking at the ground despondently.

The 'rat's' mother looked close to tears and John Cormac wanted no scenes in his father's pub.

"I tell you what now just occurs to me and I doubt if it can help, but it's all that I can do. My work is generally centred in the commercial area of London, it's called the city," the sister nodded signifying that she knew this, "and I have contact with most of the other subbies that do the same sort of work in that area, now I could get them to have a look out for him and to report to me if he is working or had been working for them.

I'll take your phone number and if I hear anything I'll ring you from England. If he is working for any of them, then I'll go myself personally to him and report this visit and your concerns about him and tell him to contact you at once," said John Cormac.

"And God bless you," said the mother, "sure aren't ya great. Sure, ye'll have a drop of whiskey or brandy or something."

"No thanks, ma'am, as I say I try my best for my own people and I don't want you to get your hopes up, if he was working in the city, then I doubt some of the boys would have spotted him since last April, it's not that big of an area. Now beyond that I cannot think of anything that I can do to help you," said John Cormac.

"Well, it's so much anyways," said the mother, writing down her phone number on a piece of paper she had in her handbag and giving it too John Cormac and God bless you are ye sure ye won't have something to drink; I feel bad not getting you a drink and all yer doing for us."

"No thanks, ma'am. I've a business meeting later on and I don't want much drink and besides I haven't done anything for you yet and I cannot but repeat that asking the other subbies is a very, long shot indeed," replied John Cormac taking the piece of paper from her and folding it carefully and putting it into his wallet.

They left soon afterwards. John Cormac O'Mahony was taking a piss on the side of the drive leading up to his father's house and was indulging in pleasant contemplation, by any set of standards he was an operator, he had the balls for anything, to have faced the 'rat's' mother and end up having her eating out of his hand; what limits were there to his capabilities. It was new year's day 1988 and 1988 was looking like it was going to be a very good year indeed.